At the Clamina... ...be, his expression serious. As the band hammered its way to a big finish with the "The Stars and Stripes Forever," Bunnie climbed the single step to the stage and stood behind the podium. I scanned the crowd for Stevie, but didn't see him. Evidently, Bunnie was done waiting.

From my perch on the curb, I glanced over at the Claminator. Sonny and Cabe's conversation grew more intense. Even from thirty feet away, I could tell Sonny was unhappy about the fire. Livvie scooted over to speak to him, then walked away, looking concerned. Sonny lifted the mesh skirting of the Claminator and aimed the hose he'd been using to spray the canvas at the fire to dampen it. He jumped back as the flames surged outward, like a grease fire. But there was no grease in a clambake meal that could drip into the fire. I'd worked at the clambake for years and had never seen anything like it. But then we'd never cooked on the pier before. This was the maiden voyage of the Claminator.

Sonny said something urgently to Cabe, who jogged toward the fire truck parked on the street beside the pier. Sonny bent down and lifted the metal skirting again, a poker in hand. The crowd surged around him, blocking my view. Sonny swore loudly.

I shoved forward. "Please! Let me through!"

The crowd parted just in time for me to see something that looked like a charred human foot fall out of the fire onto the pier . . .

Books by Barbara Ross

CLAMMED UP

BOILED OVER

Published by Kensington Publishing Corporation

BOILED OVER

Barbara Ross

KENSINGTON BOOKS
http://www.kensingtonbooks.com

KENSINGTON BOOKS are published by

Kensington Publishing Corp.
119 West 40th Street
New York, NY 10018

All Kensington titles, imprints and distributed lines are available at special quantity discounts for bulk purchases for sales promotion, premiums, fund-raising, educational or institutional use. Special book excerpts or customized printings can also be created to fit specific needs. For details, write or phone the office of the Kensington Special Sales Manager: Kensington Publishing Corp., 119 West 40th Street, New York, NY, 10018. Attn. Special Sales Department. Phone: 1-800-221-2647.

Kensington and the K logo Reg. U.S. Pat. & TM Off.

ISBN-13: 978-0-7582-8687-1
ISBN-10: 0-7582-8687-2
First Kensington Mass Market Edition: May 2014

eISBN-13: 978-0-7582-8688-8
eISBN-10: 0-7582-8688-0
First Kensington Electronic Edition: May 2014

10 9 8 7 6 5 4 3

Printed in the United States of America

*This book is dedicated to my son Robert Carito,
the funny, caring, searingly honest old soul who,
as my first-born, taught me more than anyone
about what it means to love.*

Chapter 1

"Excuse me! Sorry. Coming through."

I elbowed my way through the crowd on the town pier, barely taking in the sights, sounds, and smells of Founder's Weekend in Busman's Harbor. Mother Nature had smiled on us, providing a sunny, dry morning fanned by a comforting sea breeze—the kind of weather that convinced tourists there was nowhere better to spend an August Saturday than on the coast of Maine.

"Coming through." My dual roles as a member of the Founder's Weekend committee and manager of the Snowden Family Clambake had conflicted. I was late.

In a semicircle around the pier, four food vendors prepared for the lunch rush, set to commence immediately after the opening ceremonies. In the Snowden Family Clambake area, my sister Livvie stirred a vat of her amazing clam chowder. Her husband Sonny and Cabe Stone, his young helper, sprayed saltwater onto the untreated canvas draped over the seaweed covering the lobsters, clams, corn, potatoes, onions, and eggs we would soon serve to the first three hundred people who came through our buffet line.

Normally, we ran our clambakes on Morrow Island, the private island my mother owned two miles southeast along the coast. On the island, we cooked everything in a big hole in the ground on rocks heated by a hardwood fire. When I'd first proposed to my brother-in-law that we provide food for Founder's Weekend, he'd reacted with the same stubborn negativity with which he greeted all new ideas—particularly mine. He reddened from the base of his wide neck to the top of his red-haired, buzz-cut scalp.

But my sister Livvie had backed me up. She had to. She was the whole reason I was on the stupid Founder's Weekend committee in the first place. So, Sonny did a one-eighty and spent hours with Cabe figuring out how to cook safely on the pier.

The result was an oddly beautiful contraption Sonny had proudly dubbed, "The Claminator." Twenty feet long and four feet wide, it looked like a cross between an enormous steam table from a high school cafeteria and a gurney for Frankenstein's monster. Raised edges around its table-height top held perforated metal baskets containing the mounds of food. A dense mesh curtain designed to contain the blazing wood fire underneath surrounded the lower part of the Claminator. Thank goodness the pier was concrete, or we'd have burned down the town.

A thin cloud of smoke hung over the pier and I wondered if the Claminator fire was burning too hot. But Sonny was watching it and he was the expert. The smoke must be coming from Weezer's Barbecue located next to us. I wasn't sure what barbecue had to do with Maine cuisine, but the sweet, smoky smell of Weezer's sizzling pork ribs made me think traitorous thoughts about heading through his line when it came time to eat.

"The Claminator is gorgeous," I said when I finally reached Sonny. I had to give him his due.

"Works great, too!" he shouted in the direction of Weezer's barbecue. "At least, I'm not cooking on something that looks like a tanning bed for pig parts!"

Weezer grilled his meat on a weird rig that looked like a hot-water heater sawed in half.

"At least I'm not cooking bugs wrapped in seaweed!" Weezer shot back.

"We'll see who gets the longer lines!"

I had a feeling they'd been going at it all morning.

The other businesses in the semicircle were the town ice cream parlor and the Busman's Harbor bakery, which at this time of year was selling pretty much anything on earth that could be made with blueberries. The owners went quietly about their business, ignoring Sonny and Weezer.

"What a glorious morning." Richelle Rose touched my arm to get my attention. She was a tour guide, a decade or so older than my thirty years. Tall and Amazon-glamorous, she had breathtaking, dark blue eyes and the kind of white-blond hair most people lost after childhood.

Everything seemed under control in the clambake area, so we moved away from the noise of the crowd to a spot at the edge of the pier where we could talk. I stood on the cement curb so we'd be face-to-face. "Thanks for being so flexible."

"Glad we could work it out." Normally, Richelle would have brought her busload of tourists out to our island, providing them with a scenic harbor cruise as well as a meal. To accommodate Founder's Weekend, she'd agreed we could feed her clients on the pier. Though they'd miss the cruise and seeing the island, they'd get the benefit of all the Founder's Weekend activities—the windjammer parade and lobster boat races, the art show and concert, and finally, a gigantic fireworks display—before they were loaded onto their bus and driven on to their next hotel up the coast in Camden.

"How is this group?" I asked.

She rolled her eyes. "Shopaholics." She'd shepherded her charges through the outlet stores in Freeport before they'd even arrived in Busman's Harbor that morning. Richelle had an expansive knowledge of all things Maine—history, geography, flora and fauna on land and at sea. Though she kept a smile on her face, I knew it drove her crazy when she had a group who only wanted to see the inside of a mall.

As we chatted, I gazed at the ring of buildings that backed onto the pier. With all the people milling around, I couldn't see much, but I could look up.

Sometimes being short gave me an interesting perspective. Up on a top floor balcony at the Lighthouse Inn, a broad-shouldered man shot photos through a lens as long as a spyglass. Another camera with a shorter, but still impressive, lens sat on a tripod next to him. Most of the balconies were occupied by folks enjoying the festivities on the pier. Well, maybe not so much *enjoying* as *recording*. Every person up there observed the pier through some sort of device—phone, camera, tablet computer—as if documenting the scene was more important than being part of it.

"Who's that working the clambake with Sonny and Livvie?" Richelle asked.

"Cabe Stone. He's new. I hired him at the end of June."

"Seems like a good worker."

"He's terrific," I assured her. "Don't worry, your customers are going to be thrilled with their meals, even though we're cooking them on that thing." I pointed at the Claminator and Richelle laughed.

In front of the makeshift stage, our high school band began an enthusiastic, if only moderately on-key and on-tempo rendition of "You're a Grand Old Flag." Fee Snuggs, my seventy-four-year-old neighbor puffed out her cheeks and blew into her slide trombone. Busman's Harbor High wasn't big, so once you were in its marching band, you didn't get out until you moved away or died.

Across the way, Bunnie Getts, the chair of the Founder's Weekend committee, finished an emphatic conversation and hurried toward me. "Ten minutes, Julia!" Bunnie called over the noise. "As soon as the band stops, I'll give a little history of the town and then I'll introduce the committee. Make sure you're up at the front, so we don't have to wait for you."

I nodded to show I understood, and she went on without taking a breath. "Have you seen Stevie? I've rounded up all the Founder's Weekend committee members except him. And, Bud, of course. But I know better than to expect Bud."

I shook my head. "I'm surprised Stevie isn't here. He's been excited about the opening ceremony since day one." The ebullient owner of the local RV campground, Stevie had been a relentless booster of Founder's Weekend for all the tedious months the committee had labored to pull this first-time event together. I started to tell Bunnie I'd look for him, but she'd already pinged off in another direction.

At the Claminator, Sonny conferred with Cabe, his expression serious. As the band hammered its way to a big finish with the "The Stars and Stripes Forever," Bunnie climbed the single step to the stage and stood behind the podium. I scanned the crowd for Stevie, but didn't see him. Evidently, Bunnie was done waiting.

From my perch on the curb, I glanced over at the Claminator. Sonny and Cabe's conversation grew more intense. Even from thirty feet away, I could tell Sonny was unhappy about the fire. Livvie scooted over to speak to him, then walked away, looking concerned. Sonny lifted the mesh skirting of the Claminator and aimed the hose he'd been using to spray the canvas at the fire to dampen it. He jumped back as the flames surged outward like a grease fire. But there was no grease in a clambake meal that could drip into the fire. I'd worked at the clambake for years and had never seen anything like it. But then we'd never cooked on the pier before. This was the maiden voyage of the Claminator.

Sonny said something urgently to Cabe, who jogged toward the fire truck parked on the street beside the pier. Sonny bent down, lifted the metal skirting again with a poker in his hand, and swore loudly.

The crowd surged around him, blocking my view. I shoved forward. "Please! Let me through!"

The crowd parted just in time for me to see something that looked like a charred human foot and part of a leg fall out of the fire onto the pier.

Sonny jumped back. A woman screamed. I reached his side, "Oh my God, Sonny. Is that—?"

He grabbed my hand and we advanced toward the thing. I looked away. I couldn't stare directly at it. Out of the corner of my eye, I spotted Cabe running, in long, loping strides, not toward us, or toward the fire engine, but off the pier and up the steep street.

As Sonny used his poker to confirm what my mind was denying, there was another terrified scream, this time from behind us. I whirled around. The crowd parted again. Richelle Rose lay on the ground, her head resting awkwardly on the cement curb where we'd just stood.

Chapter 2

I spun back toward the Claminator, then back to Richelle. My brain felt like it would split in two. Richelle was probably alive. There was no hope for the thing that had fallen out of the clambake fire. I ran toward Richelle.

Before I reached her prone body, she was surrounded by firefighters. Three cops materialized out of nowhere. An ambulance pulled up at the entrance to the pier. Seeing she was well taken care of, I headed back toward the Claminator.

Sonny had doused the fire. He stood with the hose in one hand and his other arm was around my sister Livvie, whose auburn head curled into his powerful neck. Her body shook and I could tell she was crying. I put my hand on her back and patted gently, wishing my boyfriend Chris were there to put his arms around me.

"Please tell me that isn't what I think it is," I whispered.

"It's exactly what you think it is," Sonny answered

through clenched teeth. He nodded toward Livvie's shaking back, indicating he didn't want to say more.

A police car and a county sheriff's car blocked the end of the pier, leaving a narrow corridor for people to get out. Two officers stood taking contact information from each person as they left. Several people stopped to tell their stories, gesturing and pointing. I looked up at the balcony of the Lighthouse Inn where the photographer had been. He was gone.

"Julia, are you okay?" Jamie Dawes, my childhood friend, now a rookie on the Busman's Harbor force, appeared beside me. Things had been strained between us since that spring when we'd sort of accidentally, drunkenly kissed. My sister maintained it hadn't been so much of an accident—he wanted more from me than friendship, but I was head-over-heels for Chris Durand.

"How's my friend, Richelle—the woman who fainted?"

"Alive," Jamie said. "Though it looks like she has a serious head injury from falling on the curb."

A siren brup-brup-brupped as the ambulance inched its way through the crowd.

"And the . . . thing?" I couldn't bring myself to say foot . . . or to look. I pointed vaguely in the direction of the charred body part.

"I have to secure the scene," Jamie said almost apologetically.

"Do whatever you have to," I reassured him.

When I stepped back out of his way, I became aware of a voice keening above the hubbub of the crowd. Bunnie Getts stood behind the microphone on the little stage, wailing. Jamie noticed her, too. Gesturing to his partner to stay with the Claminator, Jamie moved toward the stage as quickly as the crowd allowed. I was right behind him.

"It's over, over, over!" Bunnie howled. "All my hard work. Ruined!"

"Ms. Getts, maybe if you could—"

But Bunnie had spotted me coming toward the stage. "You!" she shouted, pointing dramatically. "This is all your fault!"

Heads spun in my direction.

"Ms. Getts," Jamie insisted, using his all business, police officer voice. Most people paid attention when he spoke that way.

But not Bunnie. "You don't *see* dead people," she spat toward me. "You *attract* them!"

She had a point. Only eight weeks earlier, someone had been murdered on our island. And now there was a bare human foot, a shin, and, I shuddered, maybe more in the wood fire under the Claminator.

Jamie finally grabbed the mike and turned it off.

But that didn't slow Bunnie down. "It's ruined," she cried. "Everything I've worked so hard for. Ruined."

I realized she might be right. What was going to happen? The town was filled to bursting with tourists. Would they all check out of their hotels and melt away?

"Founder's Weekend isn't ruined," I said. "Right, Officer Dawes? There are lots of places other than this pier to watch the windjammer parade." The magnificent sailboats were already in place just outside the mouth of the harbor, ready to begin their stately progression. "The art show is set up on the town common. And the concert and fireworks are in Waterfront Park tonight. We don't need to use the pier for any of those activities."

"Julia, we barely had enough officers before this happened." Jamie gestured toward the crowd. "Look at the number of people."

"Can you get more help? The state police will be here soon to investigate the, um, thing. Can you request more backup from the neighboring towns? You know what Founder's Weekend means."

Jamie had lived in Busman's Harbor his whole life and knew everyone in town was in some way dependent on tourism. Founder's Weekend should have been the busiest days of the summer. "All right. I'll talk to the chief. We'll figure it out."

Bunnie wasn't mollified, but at least now she had a mission. She scurried off to tell the other committee members the show might go on, more or less as planned.

Jamie's partner appeared at the edge of the stage. "Lieutenant Binder's on his way."

Lieutenant Binder of the State Police Major Crimes Unit.

"He wants to meet with us as soon as he arrives. You, too, Ms. Snowden. The lieutenant wants to see you right after he's finished with us."

* * *

The first state police officers to arrive at the scene commandeered the pizza joint that backed onto the pier as a makeshift headquarters. I paced under the watchful eyes of a trooper until Lieutenant Binder and Sergeant Flynn arrived from Augusta. While we waited, the Claminator was cordoned off with crime scene tape. The police cars at the end of the pier moved out of the way and the ambulance sped off with Richelle, running its siren full-out as it reached Main Street.

At the entrance to the pier, Bunnie argued with a uniformed officer. I imagined her telling him she was much too important to be stuck there. The cop held up his palm, signaling for her to be patient. I saw my boyfriend Chris on the other side of the barricade. He seemed to insist he had to get onto the pier. It warmed me to see he wanted to be with me. I waved to get his attention, but he didn't see me.

Finally the Major Crimes Unit arrived. I paced some more while they met with the local cops. Then I was called inside.

Lieutenant Jerry Binder and Sergeant Tom Flynn stood in the noisy room, a little apart from the uniformed officers and crime scene techs who bustled in and out. "Ms. Snowden. We meet again," Binder said.

Indeed. When we'd had a murder on our island in the spring, Binder and Flynn had been the principle investigators. For the most part, I liked Binder. He had an even-handed, methodical way about him, which I'd come to appreciate, though it had been more than a little aggravating when my family's property and livelihood had hung in the balance. He had warm brown eyes over a ski-slope nose. What was left of the hair ringing his head was medium brown.

Flynn was more difficult to know. His hard body, bearing, and short hair suggested a military background, but our conversations had been all business, so that was pure speculation on my part. It was obvious from their relationship that Binder had total confidence in Flynn, and that gave me confidence, too, despite Flynn's closed-off manner.

Binder indicated one of the restaurant's tables and we sat down. "How are you?"

"I was better an hour and a half ago."

"I know. It's tough. My understanding is the remains were found in a wood fire you were using for your clambake."

"That's correct. At least I assume it's correct. All I saw was a foot, an ankle, and a bit of calf. Was it a whole body?"

"There was more than what you saw, but we won't know how complete the remains are until the medical examiner finishes," Binder answered.

"Do you know who it is?"

"No," Binder responded. "Do you?"

"I think it's Stevie Noyes." My answer popped out before I could stop it. While I'd waited, I'd wondered who the person attached to that foot might be. It was so odd that Stevie wasn't at the opening ceremonies. He'd been looking forward to Founder's Weekend for months. Somehow, my worries about Stevie's absence had combined with the foot's presence to convince me the foot belonged to him.

Flynn fixed me with a level gaze. "Why Noyes?"

"No reason. Except he wasn't at the opening ceremonies. And he should have been. He was on the committee and loved the idea of our first Founder's Weekend."

"Where does Mr. Noyes live?"

"Just up the peninsula. He owns Camp Glooscap, the RV park, and lives on the property."

Flynn wrote in his notebook.

"Did you build the clambake fire this morning?" Binder asked.

I shook my head. "My brother-in-law Sonny did. Or I assume he did. With his assistant Cabe Stone. I didn't get to the pier until much later. I'm on the Founder's Weekend committee and had other things to take care of."

"When the body was discovered, where were you?" Binder asked.

"About thirty feet away, standing on the curb next to Richelle Rose."

"The woman who was injured? Did you see her go down?"

"No, by then I was running toward the clambake."

"Who else had access to the fire?" Binder asked.

"There were maybe six hundred people on the pier."

"No, I mean earlier. During setup."

"'I'm sorry. Like I said, I wasn't there." I was beginning to feel less than useless.

"What about"—Flynn glanced at his notes though I had a feeling he didn't actually need to—"this Cabe Stone, the person who was assisting your brother-in-law?"

"He's the new guy, so he had to work with Sonny today. Most of our employees have the day off." The town clambake, unlike the sit-down meal we served on the island, was strictly buffet, which meant a rare holiday in the middle of the high season for our employees.

"What did Stone do when the body was discovered?" Again, I felt like Flynn was asking a question he already knew the answer to.

"He left."

"Left the fire?"

"Left the pier."

"Walking? Running?"

"Jogging." In my mind's eye, I saw Cabe loping away, just before the local cops appeared.

"What do you know about Mr. Stone?" Binder asked.

"He's a hard worker. A good person." I wanted to make sure Binder and Flynn understood that.

"Yes. But what do you *know* about him? For example, where does he live?"

I shook my head.

"Where did he work before?"

I shook it again.

"Is he a native of Busman's Harbor? Does he have people in the area? Do you have any idea where he might likely go?"

"No, not that I know of, and no."

"This guy works for you full-time?" Binder's eyebrows rose, indicating either he didn't believe me or I was an absolutely terrible employer.

"Yes, but my brother-in-law supervised him at the fire pit. You'll have to ask Sonny."

"Great." Flynn didn't look like he thought this was so great. Sonny had been less than forthcoming with the cops the last time they'd been in town.

"Do you have anything in your employee records with his address or phone number on it?" Binder asked.

"Maybe his employment application. I'll look." A flush crept up my neck. I was certain Binder and Flynn noticed. I couldn't remember exactly what information I'd collected from Cabe, but I had a terrible feeling it wasn't much. At the time, I was desperate for a warm body. *Ugh. I'll never use that phrase again.*

"Is there anything else you can tell us that might help?" Binder asked.

"Just one thing. It's tiny, really." I wasn't even sure if I should mention it, but I was struggling to find some way to be helpful. Both officers looked interested. More interested than my information warranted. "There was a man on the balcony of the Lighthouse Inn. He was taking photos of the activity on the pier using a big lens. I wonder if he might have captured something."

"Was he out there early this morning?" Flynn moved forward in his seat like it was new information.

"Like I said, I didn't get to the pier until later. Do

you think that's when the . . . body . . . was put in the firewood?"

"We don't know yet. Where was this photographer exactly?"

I squinted to bring back the scene. "Lighthouse Inn, third floor, second balcony from the left."

"Thanks. You'll still have to make a formal witness statement. The officer over there will take it." Binder pointed in the direction of the officer.

"I understand."

"Oh, and Julia, I'd like you to keep your ears open and keep us in the loop. You live in town. You'll pick up things we won't."

So I was *Julia* now, was I? This was apparently as close as Binder was willing to go in acknowledging my help on his last case. The one he wouldn't have solved without me.

"Absolutely," I said. And meant it.

Chapter 3

Binder directed me to a business-like state police detective who methodically took notes while she walked me back over the ground I'd just covered. When we were done, she sent me out the pizza parlor's front door onto Main Street.

Outside, I blinked in the mid-afternoon sunshine. Gangs of tourists laughed and called to one another as they ducked in and out of shops. It seemed so incongruous given the grim scene on the pier behind the buildings.

I wanted to ask Sonny all the questions Binder and Flynn had asked me. When had he and Cabe set up the Claminator, and who'd been around? And find out if he, who worked side by side with Cabe, knew any more about him than I did. But Sonny and Livvie were still on the cordoned-off pier, waiting their turns with the state police. There was no way to get back to them and it wasn't a conversation I wanted to have over our cell phones.

Meanwhile, Founder's Weekend went on around me. My next scheduled committee job was to check on the art show already in progress on the town common. I headed up the hill.

The common was mobbed. A steady breeze billowed the tops of the white tents where the artists displayed their wares. Around me I heard comments— "I love it," "I hate it," "It matches the couch,"—and bargaining, "I'll give you forty dollars for it." The happy sounds of commerce.

"At least something's going right." Bunnie stood on the path, trapping me between two tents.

"Bunnie. They let you off the pier."

"Yes, the police finally took my information and told me I could go. I'm surprised they were done with you so quickly. After all, it was your contraption that cooked that poor soul. And the killer was your employee."

"The killer? I'm not aware anyone has been arrested."

"The young man. What's his name? He hasn't been arrested, yet, but it's just a matter of time, I hear."

"His name is Cabe Stone. Who told you he was going to be arrested?"

Bunnie waved a hand, taking in the entire common. "Everyone. I heard he was a juvenile delinquent with a record as long as your arm. And he ran away from the pier as soon as the body was discovered. I saw it with my own eyes."

"That's ridiculous." *Is it?* "Why would Cabe kill Stevie Noyes?"

The color drained from behind Bunnie's makeup. "Stevie? Who said the victim was Stevie?"

"No one," I admitted. I couldn't believe I'd blurted out Stevie's name again, this time to Bunnie, of all people. "I just find it terribly odd he's not here today."

A bit of pink returned to her cheeks. "Oh, is that all? I don't think it's odd he's not here. People let you down, Julia. They let you down terribly. When you're older, you'll know." She paused. "You shouldn't spread gossip. It can be very hurtful. The last thing we want is Stevie's friends hearing unfounded rumors of his death."

I had to admit she had a point. Her emphatic tone gave me hope Stevie was safe and sound at the RV park.

Bunnie hurried off to boss someone else around. I stood for a moment in the crowd, listening more carefully. Sure enough, below the happy chatter about the watercolors of lobster buoys and the oil paintings of crashing waves, there was a low throb of commentary from the local people on the other side of the tables.

"They say it was the boy, the one who ran away."

"I heard he's wanted by the police up in Washington County."

"I heard he escaped from prison."

"I heard he's a serial killer."

"What was a person like that doing working for the Snowdens?"

And always, the refrain, "If he didn't do anything, why did he run?"

Sometimes I frickin' hated living in a small town.

Chapter 4

From the town common, I walked to Waterfront Park. Busman's Harbor's teens were running relay races passing a ten pound dead cod instead of a baton, cheered on by a mixed crowd of tourists, parents, and classmates. In the chilly water of the harbor, lobstermen ran across the tops of bobbing lobster traps. The person who crossed the most traps before falling in won.

Everything appeared to be running smoothly, so I crossed the footbridge that bisected the inner harbor and headed toward my mother's house at the top of the hill. Painted a deep yellow, with a cupola on top of its mansard roof, the house could be seen for miles around from land or sea.

From our front walk, I watched the parade of windjammers, commanding beauties with three, four, even five tall masts, sails unfurled. They sailed as close to the head of the harbor as they dared and then pivoted, like beautiful models at the end of a runway, and sailed away again. The crowd along the banks roared its appreciation.

I found Sonny and Livvie sitting on our screened-in front porch. Sonny nursed a beer and they both looked exhausted. Through the doorway, I heard my mother and Page, Livvie and Sonny's nine-year-old daughter, chatting away in the kitchen.

"Where'd you go?" Sonny asked.

I flopped into the soft cushions of the wicker love seat. "Binder and Flynn interviewed me at the pizza place and then sent me out the other door. I couldn't get back to the pier." It was true, though I also hadn't tried. "Then I had to check on some events for the committee. What did I miss?"

"They took the Claminator apart—completely destroyed her." Sonny put his freckled face into his big hands so all I could see of his head was his flaming orange buzz cut. It was typical that he'd named, and assigned a gender to, his beloved cooking contraption. It was also typical that on a day when someone had been killed, cooked even, and one of our employees was the rumored suspect, Sonny's main preoccupation was with his invention.

He pulled his face out of his hands. "Binder and Flynn questioned me for *hours*."

From her perch on the porch swing, Livvie nodded confirmation.

"What did they ask?"

"What didn't they ask? Mostly about the Claminator. When did we set it up? Was Cabe alone with it?"

"Was he?"

Sonny spread his great paws on his knees. "Yes."

"How long?"

"All night. Since we built the Claminator originally on Morrow Island, we had to break it down to get it onto the Whaler."

Our Boston Whaler was used for runs back and forth from the island to the harbor.

"We brought the Claminator over last night, after work."

The second seating at the clambake typically ended around nine, but Sonny and Cabe would have been able to leave an hour earlier when their duties at the fire pit were complete.

"We also brought over a load of firewood. Cabe and I reassembled the Claminator. When I left, I asked Cabe to set the logs under it, ready for today, and then to stay and guard it."

"You left Cabe out on the pier all night! Alone? What time did you leave him?"

"I left around one AM. All the other vendors were gone. Someone had to stay. The Claminator's a valuable piece of equipment." Sonny's voice rose, as it always did when he felt defensive. And he always felt defensive when he knew he was in the wrong. "It's no big deal," he insisted. "When I was Cabe's age, we used to do things like sleep on the pier all the time."

I didn't know where to begin. The inappropriateness of asking an employee to sleep in a public place was just for starters. Not to mention to work for thirty-six straight hours. I couldn't argue the Claminator didn't need to be guarded. Obviously, it did. Though not against theft. Against having a human being stuffed among the fire logs.

"This morning, I brought Livvie and Page over from the island," Sonny continued.

My sister and her family were spending the summer in the house my grandfather built next to the dock on Morrow Island. My mother had spent her girl-hood summers there, as had Livvie and I.

"We stopped at the lobster pound and picked up the seafood."

"And when you got to the pier, Cabe was there?"

"Cabe, Weezer, the Smalls, and the public works guys setting up the stage. There were probably twenty people there."

"Who started the clambake fire this morning, you or Cabe?"

Sonny looked at the ceiling. "Me."

"And you didn't notice anything odd?"

He was losing his patience. "No. The police asked me that, too. The fire was laid just like I'd instructed. I remember, I complimented Cabe. The dead guy must have been tucked way inside."

"And you told the police all this?"

"Of course," Sonny said, as if there could be no doubt about it.

"What else did the police ask you?"

"After the where-was-I-every-moment-from-last-night-through-this-morning questions, Binder and Flynn started asking about Cabe's background. Why did I hire him? Where did he come from? Had he ever talked about his family? And so on."

"Had he ever talked about his family?"

"Not that I remember."

Sheesh. Typical man. "What *do* you guys talk about down at the fire pit all day long?"

Sonny rolled his big shoulders. "Baseball, fishing, the usual stuff. You hired him. You checked his references, right?"

My face gave me away.

"Julia!"

"We were so busy trying to reopen the clambake in less than two weeks after the—"

"Murder? Fire? I remember. I was there. But I trusted you to hire a member of my team. Did you at least get his social security number?"

Heat radiated from my face. "I thought I would get to it later. I meant to."

"Are you joking? You told me this kid was okay!"

The tables were turned. Sonny was on offense and I was defending myself.

"You like Cabe," I reminded him. "You told me he was a great fit for the job. You *thanked* me for hiring him."

"That was because I thought you'd done your job."

Sonny hadn't been sure about Cabe when I'd hired him at the end of June. That spring, we'd had a series of tragedies, including a murder on Morrow Island and a fire that destroyed my ancestors' abandoned twenty-seven-room mansion. The Snowden Family Clambake had been in financial trouble even before that, and we were desperate to reopen before Fourth of July weekend. It was late in the season to be hiring. Everyone we reached out to already had a job. So when my restaurant-owner friend Gus recommended Cabe, I hired him on the spot.

At nineteen, he was younger than the other guys, all long-term clambake employees, who worked the fire. He was average height, about five foot ten, but skinny.

Sonny was our bakemaster, in charge of the fire pit. He resisted at first, worried Cabe's lanky frame meant he wouldn't be strong enough for the hot, heavy work. But he soon came around. Cabe was strong, reliable, and hardworking. He had an optimistic, we-can-figure-this-out attitude that made him a perfect partner on the Claminator project.

I'd taken a risk, but it had worked out.

"Sonny, I'm sorry." What else could I say? "You know he's not responsible for whatever was in the fire."

"Yeah," Sonny admitted. "I know it."

"Enough," Livvie said. "It's done."

Sonny was gracious. "He's a good kid, Julia. A really good kid. This will turn out to have nothing to do with him. I'm sure of it."

Chapter 5

I got up off the love seat and went to the kitchen. Mom and Page were packing a cooler with picnic goodies for tonight's concert in the park. The food was spread out on our big kitchen island, and the moment I saw it, my mouth began to water. I hadn't eaten since breakfast. There were plastic containers of Livvie's fabulous lobster salad and potato salad. Page was cutting blueberry lemon squares into two-bite chunks, while Mom put her delicious lobster-filled deviled eggs into a specially designed container.

My mother was a terrible cook. Brought up by a father who saw no value in food beyond sustenance, she'd never developed the knack. But the one thing she could prepare brilliantly was lobster deviled eggs. So she did. She took them to every party, potluck, picnic, or other powwow our family was invited to. Despite that, I never got tired of her eggs. They were that good. The smooth texture and pure taste of the egg white, such a handy container for finger food, contrasted with the sweetness of the lobster and the zesty, full-flavored yolk. Her secret ingredient was horseradish. Mom's deviled eggs were as close to perfect as any food gets.

Mom closed the cooler with a thwamp and slung it to the floor. She was small and blond and deceptively strong, like me. Those were the only ways we were alike.

"Get a sweater," she advised. "We're leaving in ten minutes so we'll be sure to get a prime spot."

Waterfront Park was high on a grassy point across the footbridge on the other side of the inner harbor. My mother, who loved nothing more than a good pyrotechnic display, wanted to make sure the family had a great view of the fireworks.

"I'm not going," I said. Firmly.

"Not going? Don't be ridiculous. You're on the committee."

"I'm exhausted. It's been a long day. Besides the best place in the harbor to watch fireworks is right here on our front porch."

"I bet her *boyfriend's* coming over!" Page sang. She was tall for her nine years and had Livvie's swimmer's body and Sonny's flaming red hair. She was one of my favorite people in the world, and at that moment, I could have cheerfully strangled her.

"Oh," Mom said. It was just one syllable, a sound more than a word, yet my mother could pack it with an astounding level of disapproval.

My entire family had a capital *B*, capital *A*, Bad Attitude about my relationship—which annoyed me to no end. First of all, Chris had done nothing over the course of our brief time together to earn their disrespect. Second, since I'd lived in New York City for the past nine years, it was the only relationship of mine, aside from one very ill-advised boyfriend visit during college, that they'd even been aware of, much less been in a position to have an opinion about. So I thought they should cut me some slack.

My mother's attitude annoyed me most of all. It was so hypocritical. She was the one who'd defied her family to marry the penniless boy who delivered groceries in his skiff to their private island. She, more than anyone, knew what it was like to have disapproval rain down on one's romance. Yet she persisted in throwing cold water on mine.

When they were at the front door, Sonny with the heavy cooler on his shoulder and Livvie carrying an old wool blanket, Mom hesitated. "You're sure you won't come?"

I thought about the delicious food in that cooler and almost changed my mind, but I shook my head.

"C'mon, c'mon, c'mon." Page danced on the sidewalk. She'd been living on Morrow Island for six weeks. I knew she loved it there, just as Livvie and I had when we were girls, but I could tell Page was excited at the prospect of seeing her school friends at the concert.

"Have a great time," I called.

"You, too," Page responded. No one else said a word.

After they left, I locked the screen door behind them. People in the harbor had a funny attitude about locks. They didn't believe in them. "I never lock my house." "I wouldn't think to lock my car." "I don't even own keys to my home."

I thought they were all crazy. Busman's Harbor was a small town, but it was also in the real world. Theft was rare, but it did happen. People had small appliances and jewelry stolen from their houses, purses lifted from their cars. Besides, I'd lived in New York City for nine years. Locking doors was a reflex.

I called the hospital to ask about Richelle Rose. Stable, they told me. Awake and resting, but they had to keep her overnight for observation because she had a head injury.

As soon as I hung up from that call, my cell phone chirped.

"Julia? Lieutenant Binder. I wanted to thank you for the tip on Stephen Noyes."

"Was it him?" I'd given the police Stevie's name, but I hoped I was wrong.

"Unconfirmed. His neighbors at the RV park tell us he hasn't been seen since yesterday and no lights were on in his trailer last night. We've reached his dentist who's bringing his records. We should be able to rule him in or out pretty soon. Potentially, you've saved us a lot of time. Thank you."

"Let me know if it's definite." I hung up, fearful I'd been right. Stevie hardly left Camp Glooscap during the season. He came to town once a day, like clockwork, got his mail, ran a few errands, ate lunch at Gus's to catch the latest news, and headed back to the RV park. Like all of us, he had only a few months to make money, and a lot of work to do. He would never have wandered off at the height of the season.

Pushing my worries about Stevie away, I made a turkey sandwich and ate it on the porch. The sounds of a rousing swing number floated faintly over the water. The summer days were still long. It wouldn't be dark enough for fireworks for a couple hours.

Chris and I had only been going out for a short time, but the truth was, I'd had a crush on him since I was in seventh grade and he was a junior in high school. Not in a psycho-stalker way. I'd gone to prep school in New Hampshire, college in Massachusetts, and business school in New York City. During most of that time, I hadn't thought much about him. I'd had other relationships and Lord knows, he had, too. I was still discovering how many, through a series of awkward encounters with ex-girlfriends and their families around town.

But the moment I'd come back to Busman's Harbor, my crush returned with a vengeance. The surprise was discovering he felt the same way.

I settled into the cushions of the love seat. Aside from the music carried on the breeze, the town was unnaturally still. Everyone was at the park. I wanted to check my phone for the time, but willed myself not to. Watching the clock would make the minutes tick by even more slowly. I went up to my room and grabbed a book from my nightstand.

Back on the love seat, I was soon lost in my book. Before long, I was squinting at the words on the page. I reached up and turned on a lamp.

The problem with starting a romance at the

height of the season was there was no time to be together. I worked every single day at the clambake on Morrow Island. The business had four months to make money and there were no days off. Chris worked three jobs—landscaping, driving the cab he owned, and working as a bouncer at Crowley's, Busman's Harbor's noisiest bar. He'd called in a lot of favors at Crowley's to get the night off, and as time ticked by, I wondered if something had gone wrong. It wouldn't have been the first date he'd missed without calling.

Then, just as I concluded I was being stood up, there was a knock on the screen. I unlocked the door and Chris came through it into my arms.

We were at the early stages of our relationship when everything felt urgent. Not just the sex, though that did, too, but the need to connect in every way. I snuggled into his arms. He was tall and I was small. Sometimes, I'd seen tall women stare at us, with expressions that said, "What a waste of male height." I didn't care. Chris's arms were the one place I fit perfectly.

He was impossibly handsome. His light brown hair somehow always looked like it was just about ready for a cut, and his eyes were a green I swore I'd seen in no other human. And the dimple. Yes, a dimple in his chin, now covered with a light stubble. I thought it was part of what my mother didn't like about him—that he was too handsome.

Chris wasn't a model. He didn't get his body from the gym. His hands were calloused; his face had lines around the eyes from outdoor work. His body had taken abuse from landscaping, hours behind the wheel of his cab, and breaking up the occasional fistfight at Crowley's. Being with Chris made me realize all the whiny stockbrokers, squinty lawyers, and braggart media-types I'd dated in New York were boys. Chris was a man.

"How was your day?" he asked, the irony heavy in his tone. He knew how my day had been.

I burst into tears.

Someone—possibly . . . no, probably . . . Stevie Noyes—had been cooked in my family's clambake stove. During the day, I'd pushed that reality off as often as I could. But safe in Chris's arms, it hit me full force. I cried while Chris held me.

When I pulled myself together, I said, "Binder seems focused on Cabe Stone."

"That kid who works at the fire pit? Not a surprise."

"Because he ran?"

"No. Because he's a kid and he's alone. An easy target." There was an angry edge to Chris's voice.

I personally thought Lieutenant Binder was a better detective than that, but he and Chris had their own bitter history. Binder had arrested Chris for a crime he didn't commit. So I kept quiet.

I made Chris a sandwich and got us beers. I'd just sat back down on the porch when the first firework crested in front of us. It was one of the warm-up types, opening lazily and spilling pink sparkles into the air. The crowd across the harbor oohed appreciatively.

The fireworks kept coming, increasing in size and

intensity—green, silver, gold, red. I loved fireworks. Because the manufacturers kept improving how they were made, unlike other childhood memories, fireworks didn't seem smaller or duller than when I was a child.

"C'mon!" I grabbed Chris's hand and we headed toward our front staircase.

By the time we got to the second floor, the booming was so loud it shook the house. We ran up the attic steps and then up the spiral staircase into the cupola on the roof. It had been my favorite place when I was a child, though I hadn't gone there once since I'd been home. The grown-up me didn't have time to spend hours reading on the window seat and gazing out to the harbor.

We made it just as the finale began, lighting up the sky so bright we could see all of Busman's Harbor in front of us—the footbridge, the harbor islands, the boats at their moorings. As the last bang echoed away, Chris kissed me hard and the urgent feeling returned.

We continued in that vein for a while, then Chris said, "I've got to go."

"What?" *Is he kidding?*

"Your family will be back soon."

"Chris, I'm thirty. They can't tell me who to date."

"It's for the best. I've got an early fare to the Portland Jetport. I've got to be up in four hours."

We were just coming down the stairs hand-in-hand when we heard an impatient knock-knock-knock from the porch.

"Who locked this?" my mother asked, even though

she knew I'd done it. When I unlocked the screen door, Mom and a very tired-looking Page trooped inside.

"Christopher."

"Jacqueline." Chris mirrored her formality. "Nice to see you."

My mother handed me the empty cooler. "Sonny and Livvie decided to go out with some friends."

"Bye." Chris gave me a peck on the cheek.

"Wait!" I called after him, but he'd already melted into the throngs of tourists on the sidewalk, returning from the fireworks to their hotels and B&Bs.

Chapter 6

I was up and out early the next morning, despite a restless night. Images of Stevie, the fire, and the foot had tumbled through my dreams.

As part of my Founder's Weekend committee duties, I'd volunteered to help with the Rotary pancake breakfast. At the Snowden Family Clambake, we served meals to four hundred people a day, two hundred each at lunch and dinner, so feeding a crowd was something I understood.

The Rotary was serving up plain and blueberry pancakes with real maple syrup under a big white tent that occupied the only portion of the town common not already devoted to the art show. Despite the early hour, the Rotary stalwarts were already setting up long tables and folding chairs and prepping the food. In a resort town, all the organizations did their fundraising when there were plenty of tourists and part-time residents to contribute to their coffers. Some summer weekends felt like traffic jams as non-profits vied for time and attention. The Founder's

Weekend committee had to choose carefully who would be honored with plum spots like this one.

Viola Snuggs, my neighbor and fellow committee member, was firmly in charge and already mixing up the pancake batter. She was quite a sight, with her masses of snow white hair piled on her head, wearing, as always, a tailored dress, and most improbably, despite the August heat and grassy cooking area, hose and high heels. A white, starched, bib-front apron was her only concession to the daunting task ahead of her. Usually at the Snuggles Inn, the B&B she owned with her sister, Vee cooked full English breakfasts. Somehow over the years she'd also mastered the art of making perfectly round, light, fluffy and delicious pancakes for a huge crowd. How she did this was beyond me, but she'd helmed the Rotary fundraising breakfasts for as long as I could remember, and I had complete faith in her.

By 7:15 there was a line of hungry tourists stretching down the common and it kept up like that for another two hours. I served pancakes, ladled syrup, poured coffee, and cleaned tables, whatever was needed in the moment. It was another beautiful day. The tent sides were tied back and soft ocean breezes cooled us as we worked. It felt great to be busy, and I could almost forget the events of the previous day, except that news of the murder seemed to have finally, thoroughly reached the tourists. I couldn't help overhearing people's conversations as I cleared their tables.

"He was burned alive."

I shuddered. I didn't believe it. Why wouldn't he

have cried out? Unless he was drugged or otherwise incapacitated.

"It was a local bum."

I didn't think so. Resort towns did attract homeless people, especially in warm weather, but Binder and Flynn would have asked the Busman's Harbor PD to make sure all known panhandlers were accounted for.

"I heard it was the fourth person burned to death in this town this summer."

No to that one, as well. I thought about correcting the speaker, but there had been a murder and a fire on my family's island in the spring. Those events might have caused some of the confusion. I wasn't up to telling that story for the umpteen hundredth time, so I kept my mouth shut.

At quarter after nine, Lieutenant Binder and Sergeant Flynn came through the pancake line. Activity in the tent had slowed and they sat at a table away from the crowd. I poured myself a coffee, piled three of Vee's dreamy pancakes on a plate, two blueberry, one plain, doused them in syrup, and went over to say hello.

"Julia." Binder popped up as I approached.

"Ms. Snowden," Flynn mumbled and stood as well.

"Sit down, sit down." I sat with them, though I hadn't been invited. We dug into our pancakes. Man, they were good. The tart blueberries contrasted perfectly with the sweet maple syrup. We chewed quietly until I summoned the courage to ask, "Was it Stevie?"

"Yes. Thanks to you, we've identified the victim as Noyes. The dental records match," Binder said. Flynn concentrated on mopping up syrup with his pancakes.

I pushed my plate away. "He wasn't, umm, alive, when—" The rumors had gotten to me.

"No, no, no," Binder reassured. "He was definitely dead when he was put under your brother-in-law's clambake contraption. No smoke in his lungs whatsoever. But the medical examiner hasn't confirmed how he died. The damage to the body from the fire—" He looked at my face and said, "Sorry."

I was shocked by how much hope I'd held onto, even in the face of increasing evidence. Stevie Noyes was a funny little man, bald, with what gray hair he had worn in a skinny ponytail. Despite his small frame, he had a distinct potbelly. Ridiculous, really. But he was so full of life, so enthusiastic. He loved every idea anyone had for Founder's Weekend so much, we called him, "I-second-the-motion Stevie." He'd worked tirelessly to make this weekend happen.

I couldn't imagine who'd want to kill him.

"Please keep the victim ID quiet," Binder requested after he swallowed his pancakes and took a swig of black coffee from his cardboard cup. "We haven't announced the identity yet, pending notification of next of kin. We're having a little trouble in that area. Nobody seems to know much about Noyes before he arrived in Busman's Harbor nine years ago. You served on that committee with him, right?"

"Founder's Weekend," I confirmed.

"Did you get to know him? Any ideas where to look for his family?"

I thought for a moment. Plenty of people who moved to Busman's Harbor were like Bunnie Getts. They couldn't shut up about who they used to be back in the world. There were also a small, but significant percentage of newcomers who rolled down the coast as far as the land would take them in an effort to leave their pasts behind. Cabe Stone was one of those. Stevie Noyes must have been as well. I couldn't recall a single time he'd talked about a hometown or a family. Where had he grown up? Who had he been before he arrived in Busman's Harbor? He was in his late fifties. He must have done something before he got to town.

"I really don't know anything about Stevie. Have you tried people at the RV park?"

"Yesterday. We didn't get much out of anyone. Know anybody over there?"

Flynn snorted into his coffee cup. A look passed between him and Binder.

Did Flynn disagree with Binder being so open with me? Asking for my help? It was hard not to take the look personally.

Binder ignored Flynn. "Was anyone else on the committee friendlier with Mr. Noyes? Who did you say was on the committee?"

"Dan Small owns the ice cream parlor. And my neighbor, Viola Snuggs, co-owner with her sister of the Snuggles Inn. You met the sisters this spring."

"I don't remember—" Binder started.

"You met a lot of people last time you were in town.

But the ladies certainly remember you. Sergeant
Flynn made quite an impression."

Fee and Vee Snuggs might be in their seventies,
but they still appreciated a good-looking man. As dis-
creetly as possible, I cocked my thumb over my
shoulder in Vee's direction.

"You're suggesting I send the Sergeant to do their
interview?" Binder laughed.

Flynn blushed and glowered.

"Definitely!" I answered, just to goad him.

"Enough," Flynn said in a voice that bled all
humor from the conversation.

"The other committee members are Bunnie Getts,
head of the Tourism Bureau office and Bud Barbour,
a local ship repairman," I continued.

"We've met with Ms. Getts. Several times. But we
haven't met Mr. Barbour."

"You won't find Bud in town this weekend. He has
a camp way up north where he goes whenever town
is full of tourists." Fourth of July, Labor Day and now
Founder's Weekend, Bud always left for his camp.
"He'll be back on Monday once town empties out."

"Any chance he was close to Noyes?"

"I don't think Bud's close to anyone. He's a bit of
a crank."

"Have you heard from Cabe Stone?" Flynn asked.

"No. Not a word."

"Be sure to tell us when you do."

I noticed Flynn had said *when* not *if*. "Of course,
but I'm not sure I'm the person he'd call." But really,
whom else would he call? Sonny lived on an island
reachable only by radio. Did Cabe have friends? I

couldn't remember him hanging around at the clambake with any of the employees his age. "He's still only wanted as a witness, right?"

"For now," Flynn answered.

That didn't sound good.

"Did you find his employment application?"

I blushed. Somewhere in between Chris and the fireworks, I'd completely forgotten to look. "Sorry. Killer day yesterday." I stopped. "I mean, long, challenging day yesterday. I'll see if I can find it tonight."

"Thanks," Binder said.

At least one of them is civil. I drained my coffee and was about to excuse myself when Bunnie Getts marched up to our table. Ever the gentlemen, Binder and Flynn both jumped up out of their chairs. I stayed where I was.

"Officers. I've been looking for you everywhere. What are you doing here?"

Flynn's face turned scarlet once again, but Binder replied calmly. "We work better when we eat the occasional meal."

"You should be out arresting Cabe Stone," Bunnie responded. "Honest citizens are afraid to sleep in their beds. If I weren't so exhausted from all this work"—Bunnie gestured around the town common taking in the art show, the pancake breakfast, and the thronging crowds—"I wouldn't have gotten a wink."

"Ms. Getts," Binder said, "we're following all leads. Mr. Stone is a witness and every law enforcement agency in the state is looking for him. He is not yet, however, a suspect. We try to refrain from arresting people for no reason."

"But he was right there! He did it. I saw him."

Both cops kept straight faces, but I could swear I saw them mentally rolling their eyes. "You saw Cabe Stone kill someone and put the body in the clambake fire?" Binder's voice was forceful.

"Well, no. I didn't see that, exactly." Bunnie backed down. "But I saw him run away. Why would he run if he wasn't guilty?"

Binder gathered their paper plates and plastic utensils. "Mrs. Getts, running away isn't a crime per se."

Which is a good thing, I thought as I watched Binder and Flynn fast walk out of the tent, *because running away is exactly what they are doing.*

Chapter 7

I walked away from the tent thinking about
Stevie Noyes. I'd met him the same day I'd met the
rest of the Founder's Weekend committee. It was all
Livvie's fault.

I'd moved back to Busman's Harbor to run the
Snowden Family Clambake in early March. In a terrible economy, my mother and brother-in-law had
taken out an unwise loan and we stood to lose it
all—our island, the business, and my mother's house
in town. I'd given up my life in Manhattan and my
work in venture capital for one summer season in an
attempt to turn the business around.

When I'd been back in town a little less than a
month, Livvie decided I needed to get out more. It
was true. Living with my mother and working with
my brother-in-law had been claustrophobic, to put it
mildly, but I hadn't thought a town committee was
the kind of diversion I needed.

March

"Livvie, I don't have time."

"You do. Dad ran the business for twenty-five years and he was always active on town committees."

"I'm not Dad." How often, as I struggled to map a plan forward for the business, had I been aware of that?

"Julia, you need to get out of this house. You need to see people other than Sonny and Mom. You need to talk to people other than seafood vendors and bank loan officers. It isn't healthy."

I knew in my heart she was right. After eighth grade, I'd gone away for school and kept going. I had no group of old friends in town to fall back on. But still I resisted. "I'm not a joiner. You're like Dad, the life of the party. I'm like Mom. I don't fit in here."

Livvie looked me up and down. "You are ridiculous."

My parents always presented the story of their romance and marriage as a great love story, and it was. But my mother had paid a steep price. She'd never fit in. My outgoing father had his sisters and brother, his friends around town and the employees at the clambake. My mother had always been From Away. She'd lived apart, outside the circle.

As a result, I've always felt a little apart, too. Neither a true townie, nor a summer person, I didn't fit in anywhere. I went to elementary school and junior high in the harbor, but I always knew I'd go away for high school. And summers, when the other kids were at Y camp so their parents could work the long tourist hours, I lived on Morrow Island. It wasn't a financial thing. During my childhood there was good money to be made from lobstering, fishing, and construction. I was separated by a mother From Away and my parents' expectations for me.

Livvie had no such qualms. She fought my parents until they allowed her to attend Busman's Harbor High, married a lobsterman's son at eighteen, had Page shortly afterward, and never left town. I envied how sure of herself Livvie felt, but I wasn't certain I envied her life.

Despite my protests, Livvie signed me up. When Bunnie Getts called, effusive in her thanks for joining the committee, I didn't clear up the confusion. I jotted down the date and time for the first meeting, and went.

The Tourism Bureau office was a one-room cottage up the peninsula at the town line, built at the dawn of the automobile age as a place for motorists to stop and get recommendations for lodging and food. In the last decade, thanks to the World Wide Web and GPS, the little cottage had fallen into a deep slumber, like the palace in *Sleeping Beauty*. Running the Tourism Bureau office became the town job where no one expected much to be done. Its tiny stipend was used to supplement the income of some deserving senior who dozed in the cottage for eight hours a day, waiting for visitors who never came. This suited the citizens of Busman's Harbor fine.

Then two things arrived in town at once—the recession and Bunnie Getts. The causes of the recession had been thoroughly hashed and rehashed. The causes of Bunnie were unknown, at least to me. Bunnie was like so many generations of folks From Away who arrived in town "to get away from the rat race," but who nonetheless seemed determined to bring as much of it as they could with them. She decided she wanted the job at the Tourism Bureau and went after it with a vengeance. Somewhere in her late fifties, Bunnie always looked put together, like she could be ready for a yacht club dinner at a moment's notice. She had a limitless collection of the kind of resort wear—colorful shifts and matching shoes—that might have been purchased yesterday or thirty years ago. She was the kind of woman whose style never changed.

"There you are!" She pounced as soon as I came through the door. Though her tone was reproachful, I wasn't late for that first meeting. In fact, I was the only one there. I looked around and had to hand it to Bunnie. The old, dark wood paneling had been painted a gleaming white, there was a clean, attractive beige carpet on the floor and eight new computers sat on eight sleek workstations. "I got some of my friends to donate all this," Bunnie informed me. "Tourists can come here and use the computers to book harbor tours, make hotel reservations, and so on."

I wasn't sure this was a better method than the old one, which involved whoever was working in this office picking up the phone and yelling, "Myrna, do you have any rooms? Well, do you know if Vee does?"

And on down the line until accommodations were found.

"Busman's Harbor needs to be on the Web," Bunnie continued. "We need to be optimized in search engines. We need to harness the power of social media. That will bring the tourists in. That and some exciting new events."

She wasn't wrong. As she spoke, I heard the slamming of car doors in the little parking lot outside and my fellow committee members trooped onto the cottage's big deck and through the door, stomping snow and highway sand off their boots.

"Do you all know one another?" Bunnie asked when we were seated in the semi-circle of crippling folding chairs she'd arranged around the comfortable desk chair she'd put out for herself. I nodded yes, playing along. I didn't know everyone, but in the way of small towns, I knew who everyone was.

"I think I'm the newbie, then," she said. "I'm Bunnie Getts and I moved here from Chestnut Hill, outside Boston where I was involved in multiple volunteer efforts for the Boston Symphony, the Museum of Fine Arts, and so on. Busman's Harbor was quite a change for me," she added in case we didn't get it.

Of course, we got it. We'd seen the same movie hundreds of times, as anyone who lived full-time in a resort town had. Bunnie was rich. She didn't really need to work, but she was bored. She needed a project, and we, God help us, were to be her accomplices.

"I prefer Bunnie. My real name is Minerva, but I don't use it. For obvious reasons."

"Okay, Nervie. Whatever you say," Bud Barbour piped up.

"And we're off," Dan Small muttered under his breath. He owned the town's ice cream parlor and ran it with his beautiful wife and their four stunning teenage daughters. I couldn't tell the leggy blond daughters apart, so they existed in my consciousness collectively as "The Smalls." Dan was good-looking, too. Lean and sandy-haired.

Bud's dog, Morgan, a sleek black lab just past puppyhood, lay curled at his feet. You never saw Bud without Morgan or Morgan without Bud. She always wore a red bandanna around her neck and was never on a leash. Bud ignored the harbor's leash laws, just as he ignored scores of other rules he viewed as infringing or annoying. But Morgan was so well trained, usually no one objected. Bunnie had ignored the dog since she'd come through the door with Bud.

Bunnie ignored Bud's remark as well. "As you know, we're here to talk about Founder's Day." She looked at us expectantly, got no response, and continued. "Founder's Day will be at the height of the summer season. We'll have a windjammer parade and an art show. All the shops can have sidewalk sales. It will bring the tourists flocking."

"I like it," Dan said.

"You would," Vee Snuggs responded. "Your ice cream shop is right on the pier. You're selling an inexpensive, impulse purchase. Any day-tripping tourist is catnip to you. But I don't see how a day-long celebration helps those of us in the hospitality industry."

Her B&B was across the street from my parents' house. I'd been in and out of the inn all my childhood, hoping for some leftovers of the delicious scones Vee always had on hand for their guests.

Bunnie looked momentarily confused, so I clarified. "A one-day event helps the shopkeepers, but for the lodging owners to get on board, the event needs to last the whole weekend, so tourists stay overnight."

"Founder's Weekend, even better. I am loving this." It was the first time Stevie Noyes spoke in the meeting. "Fireworks! I see fireworks and a concert in the park at night. A fabulous reason to stay over. And more events on Sunday." He looked pleased with himself.

I knew he'd come to town From Away nine years earlier and bought the RV campground. The place had a reputation as clean and well managed. My dad had liked him, and that was all I really needed to know.

As much trepidation as I had about this committee, and about whether I could take on another thing beyond saving the clambake, I had to admit Founder's Weekend was a great idea. The economy was still tough and Busman's Harbor needed ways to bring the tourists back. If they came, we all would benefit.

"How much is this shindig going to cost?" Bud Barbour asked. He ran a hand across his face and down his white beard. If he'd had a better disposition, he would have made a great Santa Claus. What was Bud doing on the committee anyway? He had no direct ties to tourism. He owned a small boat repair business on the back harbor used by the local lobstermen and fishing boats.

"We'll have to do a budget, of course," Bunnie answered. "I'm sure we can get donations to cover most of the costs."

"But there will be extra cop details and fire and rescue, extra shifts for the harbormaster. Will my taxes pay for those?" Bud demanded.

"Of course—" Bunnie started to answer.

"Then I object," Bud snapped. "We don't need to spend our hard-earned money to bring even more terrorists to town."

"Tourists," Vee Snuggs corrected quietly.

"Tourists. Terrorists. As far as I'm concerned, they're in the same boat. And hopefully it's sinking." With that, Bud stomped to the door, Morgan at his heels, and slammed it behind them.

Bunnie sat at the front of the room blinking. Evidently, she'd never had the full Bud Barbour treatment before. But she recovered quickly. "I move this committee organize a Founder's Weekend for Busman's Harbor."

"I second the motion!" Stevie Noyes chorused.

"All in favor?"

Reluctantly, slowly, came a chorus of "ayes."

"Who, actually, is our Founder?" I asked.

"That would be a good job for you, Julia," Bunnie answered. "Why don't you figure that out?"

Too late, I remembered the first rule of all committees—keep your mouth shut.

Chapter 8

After the pancake breakfast I was free for a while. Dan Small was overseeing the next event, the B&B Bed Races, where a dozen B&Bs attempted to beat each other in two-bed heats that pitted souped-up double beds-cum-go-carts against one another until a victor emerged. The only rule was the driver had to remain in the bed as it careened down the hill from the library to the dock. It sounded like a great way to get killed and when Bunnie had looked for a volunteer to run it, I'd sat on my hands until they lost all feeling.

With time to kill, I decided to go out to Camp Glooscap. Binder hadn't exactly asked me to find out what I could about Stevie's background, but he'd wondered aloud if I had contacts there. As it happened I did. I hadn't missed Sergeant Flynn's frosty reaction to Binder's suggestion, but I decided to ignore it. Binder was the boss, after all.

When I reached home I asked Mom if I could borrow her car.

"The keys are in it!" she shouted. *Of course they are.*

Driving my mother's twelve-year-old Buick up the peninsula toward Camp Glooscap made me keenly aware, once again, of my transportation problems. The town pier where we loaded the tourists aboard the *Jacquie II* to take them to Morrow Island for the clambakes was a five-minute walk down the hill from our house. When I'd returned to the harbor from my life in venture capital, I hadn't bought a car because I'd be returning to Manhattan at the end of the season. That left me dependent on my mother and her car.

The Buick had only been back a couple weeks after extensive body repairs. That spring, distracted by business problems and the murder on Morrow Island, I'd taken it without telling my mother and wrecked it. Mom had been gracious about continuing to let me borrow the car after it returned from the shop, but I drove extra carefully. I felt like a sixteen-year-old every time I had to ask for it.

Stevie Noyes's RV park was just outside town, twenty acres of hard-packed dirt roads and woods with a rocky shoreline and a little beach on Townsend Bay. I drove under the great wooden sign CAMP GLOOSCAP—RVs ONLY and parked at the camp store and office. A teenage girl was at work in the store, but Stevie's office was locked up tight. I wondered if he'd made any arrangements for his absence, much less his death.

I asked the girl, "Do you know where the Kellys' trailer is?"

"Motor home," she corrected. She pointed to the guest book without speaking. As I signed it, I looked for names I recognized on the lines above my own, but saw none. She gave me a map and I set off on foot.

I'd driven past Camp Glooscap thousands of times, but this was the first time I'd been on the grounds. The park was heavily wooded, well kept, and inviting. Each motor home site had a concrete block fire pit as well as electrical and sewage hookups. Because it was August, every one of the spacious, wooded spots was occupied. The girl in the store had circled a campsite on the shoreline for my friends the Kellys. As I walked, I gained a better understanding of the scale of the map. The well-kept dirt road sloped gently downward toward the bay, so it was an easy hike.

I rounded a bend and saw navy blue water peeking through the bright green leaves on the trees. The closer I got to the shore, the nicer the RVs got. Some had added porches or outbuildings that signaled semipermanent use. Many were strung with colored lights that even in the daytime gave them a cheery appearance. One seemed so long and wide that I was sure the *vehicle* in RV was a misnomer. I couldn't imagine it wending its way down Route 1, the overcrowded, mostly two-lane highway that served as primary access to most of the Maine coast.

The Kellys' gleaming motor home was on an elevated site with a gorgeous view of the bay. Sitting at the far edge of the campground, it had nothing but woods on two sides. I was sure theirs was a primo spot. I climbed onto the RV's wide front porch and knocked on the door.

"Julia!" Cindy Kelly blinked at me. "What a surprise."

Cindy and Chuck Kelly weren't exactly friends. They were good customers. They'd attended opening day at the Snowden Family Clambake religiously for the last fifteen years. As they reminded me, they'd attended far more opening days in recent years than I had. The Kellys came out to Morrow Island several times during the season, usually when they had friends visiting. Over the years they'd developed a fond acquaintanceship with my late father, which they'd just this year transferred to me.

Chuck came to the door behind Cindy. Like her, he was round and soft, with gray hair and glasses. They were retired schoolteachers from Massachusetts who'd been coming to Maine for the length of their fifty-plus year marriage. They were among the first people to move into Camp Glooscap when Stevie started it nine years before.

"Come sit, come sit," Chuck called.

"Yes, of course, dear." Cindy recovered from the surprise of seeing me at their door. "I'll get some lemonade for us."

Chuck settled me on the redwood settee on the porch and sat in a matching chair across from it. While Cindy was in the kitchen, he inquired after Mom and asked me to give her their regards.

"I'm surprised you're not downtown for the Founder's thingie," he said to me.

"I could say the same about you."

"Oh, much too crowded and crazy."

Cindy elbowed the screen door open and carried a tray with a pitcher of lemonade and three matching glasses onto the porch. "We stay away from town on tourist days."

Ah, one of the eternal conflicts of a resort town. The locals, who tended to live, at least partially, off the tourist trade, wanted as many visitors as possible, while the retirees, who had their own incomes, wanted just enough tourists to keep their favorite restaurants and shops open, and no more.

"I've come to talk to you about Stevie," I said, after Cindy had poured the lemonade and handed it around.

Cindy's hand flew to her mouth. "So it was Stevie in your clambake fire!"

"The police told me this morning the dental records were a match." Those same police had also asked me to keep that information to myself, but I didn't see how I could have this conversation if I did.

Cindy began to cry softly. "I knew it."

Chuck went into the house and emerged seconds later with a box of tissues. "Stevie wouldn't disappear in the middle of the season. He hardly leaves this place except to go into town." Chuck perched on the broad wooden arm of his wife's chair and patted her shoulder.

"Did the police talk to you?" I asked.

Cindy nodded. "Yesterday. We told them he was missing."

"Did they ask about his family? I understand they're having trouble notifying his next of kin."

"They did, but we couldn't help them." Chuck shook his head. "We were the first people to rent a site from Stevie. Signed the paperwork and gave him a deposit before the park was even finished. It was a big risk to take, but worth it. We had first pick of all the sites and ended up with this one, which I'll argue is the best at Camp Glooscap."

As he spoke, he gazed beyond the porch, taking in the entire sweep of the campground as well as the water. A couple little boys fished off the long dock that extended into the bay. Kayaks and canoes sat upside down on the beach, their bottoms gleaming. It was an idyllic spot.

"Stevie often joined us in the evenings for a little libation as he made his rounds," Chuck continued. "In the beginning, our conversations were pretty impersonal, but over the years, we became close. We're usually the first ones to come in the spring and the last to leave in the fall."

"We push it right up to the day the water gets turned off," Cindy added. For the moment, it seemed her tears had ended.

"We talked of lots of things," Chuck said. "His hobbies—trains and the Civil War. Politics and the town. Cindy and I told Stevie about our family. He met our three kids and our grandkids over the years and always asked after them. The truth is"—Chuck paused—"I'm embarrassed to say this, but it took me awhile to realize he never talked about his family or where he came from or what he did before he started Camp Glooscap. Once or twice I asked him outright, but he was skilled at changing the subject. Eventually, we understood his past to be off limits."

"He was such a nice man," Cindy said. "We didn't want to press him. But there was a sadness there, I'm sure of it. His life before Busman's Harbor was something he didn't want to dwell on."

"Did anyone here have a problem with Stevie?" Binder definitely hadn't asked me to go down this line of questioning, but I couldn't help myself.

"Why would you want to know?" Cindy asked. "I thought Stevie's murderer was the young man who ran away. The one who works for you."

So even the Kellys, who hadn't been into town all weekend, knew about Cabe Stone.

"Cabe is only wanted for questioning as a witness," I clarified. Chuck harrumphed skeptically, but I pressed my point. "There's no one you know of who had a problem with Stevie?"

I expected more protests about what a great guy he had been, but a look passed between husband and wife.

"Someone's bound to tell her," Chuck said.

"There has been a little problem in the campground," Cindy started. "Such a shame. You see, Stevie has always given out the sites by seniority. The more years you'd been coming and the longer you stayed per season, the better your campsite. If somebody moved on or died, and you were at the top of the list, you had a chance to move up. The system was fair and worked well."

"Until this year." Chuck took up the tale. "The Parkers moved to an assisted living facility and sold their beautiful motor home. They're both in their late eighties. It was just a matter of time."

"It's a lovely spot." Cindy pointed to a campsite on the other side of the little beach from theirs.

I could tell it would have a terrific view of the sunrise over the bay. The camper parked behind its fireplace was pretty barebones, much smaller and more worn than any of the others in the prime waterfront locations.

"Reggie Swinburne, who has the spot behind it, thought he should get the site, because he's next in seniority and he's here half the year, almost as long as we are. But then the Parker kids just moved that, that *thing* into the spot. They claim they're entitled to the site because their parents rented it," Chuck said. "But, it doesn't work that way. They have to go to the back of the line. And, they *only come on weekends.*"

"For *the weekends,*" Cindy repeated. In case I didn't get it. "Weekend people do not get waterfront lots. They're back in their own little area."

Oh geez, I thought, the dynamics of a resort town. The natives looked down on the seasonal homeowners, who looked down on the monthly house-renters, who looked down on the weeklong hotel-stayers, who looked down on the weekenders, who looked down on the day-tripping tourists, who looked down on the natives. In Camp Glooscap, the whole cycle would play out in microcosm.

"This Reggie Swinburne and the Parker children, were they angry at Stevie?"

"They were angry at each other," Chuck said. "There's been a lot of back and forth. Loud music all day and late into night, revving motorcycle engines, reckless riding through the camp on All Terrain Vehicles. Yelling and threats. Reggie expected Stevie to do something about it. And the Parkers said if anyone tried to move their rig, they'd burn Camp Glooscap to the ground."

"Oh my. Did you tell the police about this when they interviewed you?"

"All they wanted was to know if Stevie was missing and the names of his friends and relatives so they could try to locate him. They didn't ask about anything happening at the campground."

When I left the Kellys, I walked over to the dilapidated trailer they'd pointed out on the opposite side of the park's waterfront area. The old camper was rusting and sat slightly askew. Not nearly as nice as the other vehicles in this part of the park.

The well-kept, neighboring RV was set back on its site. A late model, dark-blue pickup truck, one of those huge 4x4s, was parked beside it. The little yard was equally neat, with a well-tended rock garden at the corner of the drive and a neat row of hostas along its front border. Unlike its unsightly neighbor, it would have only a sliver of a view of the bay.

The old trailer had four tents of various ages and conditions scattered around its site. At the edge of the yard stood a tumble of junk—aluminum beach chair frames, propane tanks for a gas grill, a bent bike without its tires. Even a refrigerator with its door removed. The pile was placed so the fancy RV's deck looked directly at it.

As I contemplated the wall of junk, the front door to the sleek RV opened. The man who emerged was in his sixties, dressed in classic outdoorsman style— shorts, camp shirt, socks, and hiking boots. He had a pair of binoculars slung around his neck, a full head of gray hair and an extraordinary handlebar mustache. Unbidden, my mind went to "Colonel Mustard."

"Awful, isn't it?" he asked.

"Amazing. You must be Mr. Swinburne. The Kellys were just complimenting your place."

He stuck out a hand. "Reggie, please."

"Julia."

His bushy eyebrows drew together in a squint. "I know you. You're a Snowden. I saw you at the clambake. Went there with Chuck and Cindy in June."

"That's me." I smiled brightly.

"Terrible thing on the pier."

I nodded. "Had you heard—"

"The victim is likely Stevie? The police were here yesterday."

"I'm sorry to say it was him. The police haven't officially released his name, pending notification of next of kin."

"Damn shame. He was a good man."

"Did Stevie ever say anything to you about his family?"

"No, never. Funny, I had the impression he was from New York, not sure why. Accent, maybe?"

I ran the sound of Stevie Noyes's voice through my brain. I heard a homogenous TV anchor voice, no hint of an accent. "The Kellys mentioned you were having a dispute with the neighbors."

"Ya think?" He smiled. "This monstrosity isn't the worst of it. Weekends, it's like a casino opened up next door. Card-playing, yelling, loud music, people throwing up in my rock garden. I have to use earplugs to get any sleep. To make matters worse, when they arrived Friday, they told me this was their 'family vacation' and they'll be here all week. Heaven help me. Family, indeed. There must be twenty people sleeping on their site. Those tents are against the bylaws. They're not allowed!" Reggie was getting quite worked up.

"Where are they now?" The trailer was silent as a tomb.

"Went off on their motorcycles about an hour ago. Some kind of rally. Damn racket. But they'll be back. I may have to take myself off camping this week to get a night or two away."

The enormous pickup parked in his driveway had a topper on its bed, the kind with the sliding windows. I wondered if he slept in it or just used it to stow his camping gear.

"And Stevie couldn't do anything about the Parkers?"

"He tried. The Parkers absolutely refused to leave,

refused to move their trailer, and refused to follow the community's rules. Stevie was out of options. He was going to hire a crane to drag the trailer out."

"Had he told the Parkers this?"

Reggie grunted at the messy yard. The corners of his mouth, barely visible below the huge mustache, were drawn down. "He had. I stood right on my steps and watched him go in there. I think they thought he was bluffing."

"Had the police been called?"

"The real police? No, we try to take care of most things here in our own little community. No point in bringing people from outside."

If the Busman's Harbor police hadn't been involved, they might not know about Stevie's dispute with the Parker's kids. If I told Lieutenant Binder about it, it might take some of the focus off Cabe.

I said good-bye to Reggie and walked up the road toward my car. Almost back to the little store and lost in thought, I practically ran into a kid exiting a pop-up camper. His features were barely distinguishable behind his long, scraggily hair and bushy beard. The pop-up was hitched to an ancient red Toyota. I wondered if the little car was really capable of pulling the camper. The kid seemed like an odd person for Camp Glooscap, full as it was of retirees and families, but he was dressed like Reggie in a camp shirt and shorts and also wore binoculars around his neck.

Maine appeals to nature lovers of all ages, I thought.

Chapter 9

Since I had Mom's car and wasn't due back to take on any Founder's Weekend duties until after lunch, I drove over to the Busman's Harbor Hospital to visit Richelle Rose. She was sitting up in bed when I entered the room, looking none the worse for wear.

"Julia! So nice of you to come."

"Of course I came. That's a great look for you." I intended it as a joke, but the truth was Richelle was the only person I'd ever seen who looked not just okay, but attractive, in a hospital johnny. Her bed was cranked up and she sat, shoulders straight, back against the pillows. Her light blond hair was neatly brushed, her deep blue eyes bright. She had more color in her cheeks than anyone who'd been conked on the head deserved.

I leaned over the bed and gave her a gentle hug, then sat in the visitor chair. "How are you?"

"Okay, I think. They think. But I've quite a bump. Shook my brain up a little."

"I'm so sorry for what happened. If I hadn't moved, if I'd still been next to you when you fainted, I might have caught—"

"How could you have known?

"What *did* happen?" At the time, I'd been so focused on the foot that had popped out of the clambake fire, I'd been unaware of anything that went on behind me.

"Honestly, I don't know. I've never passed out before in my life. The crowd parted. I saw what you saw, and down I went. The shock I guess. From seeing the body."

The body? All I'd seen was a foot and an ankle and I hadn't been sure of that until Sonny and I bent down to examine it. How had Richelle seen enough from where she stood to be so shocked? It didn't seem appropriate to interrogate someone in a hospital bed, so I kept my questions to myself. I'd ask her some other time.

"When are they letting you out of here?"

Richelle looked down at her blanket. "There's a bit of a challenge there. If all my tests come back okay this afternoon, they'll let me out. But I'm not allowed to travel. I've been phoning B&B's hoping to find an inexpensive place. The town is booked up solid. It's the busiest week of the year."

"Don't be silly. You'll stay with us."

"But your mother—"

"Won't mind," I said with more certainty than I felt.

"I don't know how to thank you. I love Busman's Harbor. I take every tour group here that's offered me, but I never thought—"

"It's settled. Call me when you have a release time."

Chapter 10

Back in town, I put my mother's car in our garage and walked over the hill toward the back harbor and Gus's restaurant. The back harbor is the working part of Busman's, where the shipyard is and where the lobster and fishing boats are moored, away from the hotels and the yachts. The appeal of Gus's springs from its complete lack of charming, touristy trappings. It has an old, round-topped gas pump out front, a candlepin bowling lane inside, and one of the best harbor views anywhere in town.

I climbed down the stairs that led to Gus's lunch counter and dining room. My last Founder's Weekend chore, scheduled for this afternoon, was to judge a blueberry pie-eating contest, which I feared would completely gross me out. I wasn't sure I'd want to eat after witnessing it, so better to grab something while I could.

From behind the counter, Gus raised a hand in greeting. He was skinny, with a great beak nose and a shock of white hair. Nobody except possibly Mrs.

pre-romance so to speak, "happening" to turn up for lunch at the same time three days a week.

Evidently, Binder and Flynn, who'd come to Gus's a couple times with members of the Busman's Harbor PD the last time they were in town, qualified as insiders. They were well into their lobster rolls when I approached their table. Both were too busy chewing to jump up from their chairs, but Binder gestured I should sit down.

I slid into an empty seat. "I just came from Camp Glooscap."

Binder swallowed and dabbed his mouth with his napkin. "Anything about the next of kin?" He didn't reprimand me for butting in, so I must have understood his subtle invitation to help correctly.

"Nothing," I admitted. "I talked to my friends who were the very first residents of the park and who often had Stevie over for cocktails—"

"The Kellys," Flynn interrupted. "Talked to them yesterday." His tone implied he was way ahead of me.

"So they said. I did find out some things going on over there you might want to check into."

"The Parkers?" Binder asked.

"Yes, did you talk to them?"

Binder shook his head. "I don't think they're big fans of the police."

"I talked to the neighbor, Reggie Swinburne. He said Stevie's been trying to get the Parkers off that site. He'd threatened to call in a crane."

"I haven't found any court filings, or even calls out to the campground by the local PD." Flynn addressed

Gus knew how old he was. He, and his restaurant, had looked exactly the same since I was a child.

I was astonished to see Lieutenant Binder and Sergeant Flynn sitting alone at a table. Not because I didn't believe they deserved lunch. It was late by Busman's Harbor standards, and Bunnie Getts had pretty much ruined their breakfast that morning. I was surprised because they were state cops from Augusta and Gus had a strict "no strangers" policy. If he didn't know you, or you didn't arrive with someone he did know, you were politely asked to scram. If you protested, you were told food wasn't being served just then, or there was no room, despite contradictory evidence all around you. If you persisted, a surprisingly strong Gus would usher you out the door.

I had no idea how he got away with this. It certainly wasn't legal for restaurants to arbitrarily decide not to serve certain guests. But all the members of the Busman's Harbor PD ate at Gus's and never interfered with his policy. They probably needed a break from the tourists as much as the rest of us did.

I knew and accepted all Gus's rules. Since I'd returned to Busman's Harbor in March, Gus's had become my home away from home, the place I retreated to when I felt smothered by living and working with family. Even more important, Gus's was where I'd remet Chris Durand all those years after he was a high school god and I was a seventh-grader with a whale-sized crush. And it was where Chris and I had carried on the early part of our romance, our

Binder, even though I was sitting right there and was clearly part of the conversation.

"Reggie told me Stevie liked to take care of things himself. Didn't like bringing in outside resources." I was determined not to be ignored.

"Interesting," Binder said.

"Stupid," Flynn retorted.

"But not unusual around here," I added.

Binder fished out his wallet to pay Gus. "Anything else?"

"Richelle Rose, the tour guide who fainted, is coming to stay at my house for a few days."

"That's nice." Binder wasn't interested in Richelle. She was a witness, no more, and not a particularly good one, because she'd passed out—which meant he didn't wonder, as I did, why she'd fainted. As far as he was concerned, she'd seen a gruesome, burned body. He wasn't standing where I was and didn't understand how little she could have actually seen.

"Did you find the man who was on the balcony with the big camera?" I asked.

"Not yet," Binder answered. "The room was rented by a woman with a corporate credit card from a large Canadian media firm. It will take a while to track it down."

"A woman?" I was momentarily confused. "The person I saw was a big, tall man. Broad-shouldered."

Binder smiled. "Women do, occasionally, share hotel rooms with men."

Flynn hid a grin behind his hand, while I blushed. "Of course, but—"

"Tall. Dark. Handsome. I remember your description."

"Now you're teasing me."

"Maybe a little," Binder allowed. "Is there anything else about him? Anything at all distinguishing?"

I hesitated. I was sure of what I'd seen, but uncomfortable about saying it. I'd just come from living in New York City, the most diverse place on the planet, and I was still adjusting to coastal Maine. I won't say everyone was white, but most people were, which meant when they weren't, you tended to notice it more. Maine was, in fact, the least diverse, whitest state in the union. It was also the state with the oldest population. Some days on the midcoast, it seemed like everyone I met was a clone of Chuck or Cindy Kelly.

But I felt sure of what I'd seen on that balcony.

"Just say it," Flynn snapped.

"I think he was a Native American. That is, he looked like he was. I had an impression—"

"Impression?" Binder prompted.

"That's all it was. I'm not certain. I was fifty feet away and he was three stories up. I could be wrong."

"Thanks," Binder said. "It may help us find him."

"Has your friend Cabe Stone by any chance been in contact?" Flynn asked.

I was surprised he'd addressed a question directly to me. "No. And we're not friends. He's an employee. You're still looking for him as a witness, right?"

"For now," Flynn answered. "But we've found some surprises in young Mr. Stone's past. If you have any influence over him, or anyone you know is talking to him, have them tell him to contact us immediately."

"Okay," I agreed, as much to move the conversation along as anything else. Flynn had an intense stare and an emphatic way of expressing himself that made me feel guilty, even when I wasn't. I changed the subject. "Do they know what time Stevie died yet?"

"The condition of the body makes it difficult to be specific, but Stevie was killed and probably placed under your clambake stove sometime over Friday night into Saturday morning. He was killed elsewhere and moved to the pier."

In other words, during the period when Cabe was supposed to be guarding the Claminator. But he was nineteen, a kid. The odds he got distracted or wandered off were high. Maybe he even fell asleep, though the whole process of moving Stevie's body must have made noise.

"Do you know where Stevie was killed?" I asked.

"No idea yet," Binder answered.

"How do you think his body got to the pier?"

"We're still working on it," Binder said. "Had to be a car or a boat. Mr. Noyes was a small man, but you wouldn't get far carrying or dragging his dead weight."

Cabe was supposed to have been on the pier all night, but he didn't have access to either a car or a boat. Though the foolish way people left their keys in their cars in this town . . . the same with small boats. People were always "borrowing," them. I'd done it a few times myself.

The two cops stood to go. I got up as well. "Lieutenant Binder, have they determined how Stevie died?"

"Yes, they have. Your friend Mr. Noyes was stabbed. Seventeen times."

The news knocked the wind out of me. Poor Stevie. For such a nice man to have been the victim of such a brutal attack.

I was sure the killer couldn't be Cabe. He was a good kid, as Sonny had said. But I also had my own reason to believe in him. He had saved my life.

Chapter 11

July

At the height of the season, I was working thirteen-hour days at the clambake. Chris was landscaping all day, then driving a cab, then working as a bouncer at Crowley's, and then driving drunks home in the cab after closing. It was challenging to find time to get together.

So, several nights a week when the *Jacquie II* brought the dinner crowd back to Busman's Harbor from the clambake, I'd hop off the boat and head for Crowley's.

I didn't normally hang out in bars, but I had to admit, being the girlfriend of a bouncer had a cool, "I'm with the band" vibe. I always sat at a table in the back with the significant others of the bartenders, waitresses, kitchen staff, and of course, the band.

Sometimes during the week, things would be slow enough Chris could take a break and sit with us. The atmosphere at the table was easy and jokey, and the high school geek in me loved sitting next to the handsome ex-football player, an experience I'd never had in my life until then. But when Chris was busy, and I was on my own, I couldn't shake the feeling I didn't quite fit in. I felt like a fraud.

Often Chris would give me a lift in his cab the three short blocks to Mom's house, or even better to the vintage wooden sailboat where he lived in the summertime. But sometimes, duty called, as it did one particular night.

It was a Tuesday and slow. I hoped Chris and I could get together after the bar closed, but just before last call, he took the car keys off a belligerent drunk who was staying in a summer rental way up the peninsula. That meant he'd be driving the guy home in his cab and I was on my own.

I always felt safe in Busman's Harbor at night, particularly right after closing time when the streets were usually crowded with clusters of people heading back to their homes or hotels. But, maybe because it was a Tuesday, the street was empty as I made my way out of Crowley's.

It was still empty when I took the turn onto Main Street and an SUV, big and black, driving erratically with its headlights off, jumped the curb and barreled toward me. My brain couldn't seem to process what I saw. I froze.

Two hands grabbed my upper arms and jerked me backward into the protected doorway of an art gallery. The car roared by, missing me by inches. Brakes squealed and I heard the driver over-correct, then correct again. By the time I looked up, the car was already beyond the short portion of Main Street that had streetlights. It was a dark blur headed out of town.

I turned and threw my arms around my rescuer. Cabe. He too, was pale and trembling.

"Thank you, thank you. If you hadn't been here . . ." I let him go.

"Are you all right?" he asked.

I breathed in deep and blew out slowly. "Yes. I'm fine. Just shaken up. You?"

He smiled. "Same."

"Did you get a license number?"

"It happened so fast."

"Me, neither." I pulled out my cell phone. "But we should call the police anyway."

Cabe put his hand over my phone. "And tell them what?"

"That this guy just tried to kill us. He's drunk, for sure. And dangerous."

Cabe didn't move his hand. "Julia. Really, what will you tell the cops?

"That a black—"

"Dark blue—"

"Maybe dark green, SUV—"

"I thought it was a van."

Whatever it was, it was big and high off the road. It could even have been a pickup truck. I had just the vaguest impression of the back of the vehicle as it careened out of town. The taillights were off, but what else? I wasn't even sure if a guy was driving. It could easily have been a woman. Cabe had made his point. A black-blue-green SUV-van-pickup that we didn't have a license number for, and was already out of town, had done what? Missed hitting us?

"I'll walk you home," Cabe offered.

"I'm okay," I assured him. I was less than a block from my house. "Where did you come from?"

"I'm just headed to my place."

"Thank you." I wanted to hug him again, but didn't. The first time had been spontaneous, a shared reaction to our mutual brush with death. Now a hug would be awkward and inappropriate. I was his boss. A much older woman in his eyes. But Cabe always had a particular vulnerability about him. Despite his strength, he was slight. His dark blond hair fell in his light blue eyes, except when he worked at the fire pit, where he wore it in a samurai-style top knot that I thought of as "Cabe's weird hairdo." His features were regular and still boyish. I wondered how often he had to shave.

It was that vulnerability that made me want to hug him, and I wasn't normally a hugger. It was also what had softened Sonny toward him. Despite his bluster, Sonny was really a big ball of mush.

"It wasn't nothing," I said. "If there's ever anything I can do for you—"

We left it at that.

August

After Binder and Flynn left, I moved to Gus's lunch counter.

"Afternoon." Gus stood in front of me, ready to take my order.

I'd been hungry when I walked in, but suddenly I couldn't make a decision.

"Pie?" Gus offered, as if starting my order with dessert would get me off the dime.

If you were smart, you ordered your dessert when you placed your meal order, choosing a slice from half dozen kinds of pie Mrs. Gus had made starting at four that morning. For one thing, if you didn't order while pie was still available, you might be out of luck by the time you made up your mind. Mrs. Gus's pies always sold out. Also, Gus didn't like surprises. He wanted to know what you were planning to eat, and by extension, how long you were planning to stay, right up front. Gus ran his establishment for the working men and women of Busman's Harbor. Tarrying wasn't encouraged.

Today's pies were blueberry, peach, Boston cream, pecan, and peanut butter. I'd sampled every one of those flavors countless times, and each one caused me to swoon. But I considered the upcoming pie-eating contest and said, "Just a BLT and an iced coffee." Strictly speaking, iced coffee wasn't on Gus's limited menu, but sometimes when he was in a good mood, he'd pour some of the coffee sitting in the pot over ice for you.

He put my bacon on the grill and two slices of Mrs. Gus's homemade wheat bread in the toaster and returned with my iced coffee. I gulped it down, eager for the caffeine blast before I had to run to the pie-eating contest. When I looked over the rim of my glass, Gus was still firmly planted across from me.

"The police seem very interested in our boy."

"Cabe?" I knew who Gus meant. I nodded, yes they were.

"What do the cops know? Why would a young man like that want to kill Stevie Noyes?"

So Gus knew it was Stevie, too. Despite Binder's efforts at keeping the identity of the body quiet, I doubted there was a person in town who didn't know. "The cops aren't obligated to share their theories with me, Gus." It came across crabbier than I meant it to. I was grateful for how open Binder was being with me, even if Flynn suspected me of harboring Cabe.

Gus took my bacon off the grill, sliced a ripe, summer tomato, and assembled my sandwich. "You're going to have to help them."

"Binder and Flynn? Don't be silly. They're professionals."

"They were professionals the last time they were in town when they arrested two innocent people." Gus put my sandwich in front of me with a thump. "And back then it was two grown people who knew how to handle themselves. This is a nineteen-year-old kid on his own."

"Do you know anything about Cabe? Where he's from? Who his family is?"

"I got the feeling he didn't want to talk about that stuff." The counter was empty except for the two of us, but nonetheless Gus moved closer and spoke softly. "He showed up here, hungry, a couple months ago. I gave him some food, had him do some chores. I didn't really need the help, so I sent him along to you."

"I remember. I hired him on your say-so, Gus. You're the one who got me into this mess."

"No, I'm the one who got *him* into this mess. And I'm counting on you to help me make it right."

Chapter 12

Bunnie had given me a neatly typed list of rules for the pie-eating contest, which I followed to the letter. It was a good thing because, despite the threat of pie splatter, she sat throughout the contest in the front row, tapping a pencil on her omnipresent clipboard.

The contest was under the same tent where the pancake breakfast had been held that morning. The tables had been efficiently broken down and the chairs reset theater-style by the diligent Rotarians. At a long table in front of the audience, ten citizens of Busman's Harbor sat with their hands tied behind their backs, ready to consume as many blueberry pies in twelve minutes as they could. I was in charge of enforcing the rules, managing the timer, and declaring a winner. Vomiting, the typed rules told me, was cause for immediate disqualification. *Yuck.*

Vee and Fee Snuggs stood at the ready to shove new pies in front of the contestants as soon as I ruled the previous pie "eaten." Despite the August heat, the sisters wore white rain ponchos over their clothes. The audience whooped when they appeared, their costumes indicative of the amount of mess to come. Obviously, they'd thought through their wardrobes more thoroughly than I had.

And we were off! I ran up and down the row, declaring pies "done," which I admit was kind of a subjective judgment with hands-free eating. Often, several contestants raised their heads to indicate they were finished at the same time, and Fee, Vee, and I ran back and forth in front of the table, their flowing ponchos giving them the appearance of spry ghosts. The audience cheered their favorite contestants so vehemently, I assumed money was changing hands.

The crowd counted down the last seconds on the clock and then roared its approval. While Fee and Vee untied the contestants' hands, I counted the empty pie tins and prepared to declare the winners.

When I named Dan Small fourth runner-up, he rose to accept his prize then pointed to his cheek, indicating he wanted a congratulatory peck. What did I have to lose, aside from the easily replaced Snowden Family Clambake T-shirt I wore? I gave him a kiss on his blueberry-streaked cheek and the audience whistled and stomped. From there, the game escalated, with each runner-up wanting more and more contact, until the winner, a kid from the high school, swept me into his arms, bent me over

Fred Astaire-style and pretended to . . . well, thank goodness he pretended.

I got home looking like I'd murdered a Smurf.

My mother said, "My God," when she saw me as I headed to the shower.

Afterward, I had the joy of telling her I'd invited Richelle Rose to stay with us—without asking permission. Mom took it in her stride. Like most people with a big house in a resort town, she was used to house guests, but she really was a private person and our conversation reminded me once again that I didn't have a home of my own, or a car, or anything else thirty-year-olds normally had. I told myself it didn't matter, I was going back to Manhattan when the clambake closed in the fall.

Right after I talked to Mom, Richelle called from the hospital to say she was being discharged.

"How did the first Founder's Weekend go?" Richelle asked on the ride home.

"Great . . . except for the murder." I had to hand it to Bunnie and the committee. Except for the one incident completely beyond our control, we'd pulled it off beautifully, and in an unbelievably short amount of time.

"And the young man who worked for you? The one who ran away? Have the police found him yet?"

"No," I answered, surprised she'd picked that detail to ask about.

By the time I got Richelle home, it was obvious the

whole discharge process had exhausted her. I put her
to bed in Livvie's old room, which had been done up
pink, princess-style for Page. She had spent many a
night there with Livvie when my father was sick and
after he died as Livvie looked after Mom. Somehow
the decor seemed to suit Richelle's regal style.

I left Richelle with some tea and toast and promised to check in. The next time I did, she was sound
asleep. I closed her door and crept down the hall to
my office.

The office had been my dad's and I hadn't changed
it. As it had in his day, papers covered the big oak
desk and the tops of the old-fashioned metal filing
cabinets. Only this mess was mine. Until the season
started, I'd kept the office tidy, but once I'd starting
working the long days out on Morrow Island, the
place had gotten away from me.

I opened a cabinet and took out my file of employee information. Everyone who had worked at
the clambake in previous years, or who'd been hired
before the season began, was represented in crisp al-
phabetical order. But not Cabe. He'd been hired
later, when I was doing everything I could to find a
financial backer, negotiate with our vendors, and
make the island safe again after the devastating fire.

I attacked the piles of paper. Cabe's employment
application had to be in there somewhere.

I found it on my desk, buried under a mass of in-
voices for produce and seafood. It was even worse
than I remembered.

In small, crabbed handwriting, in light pencil,

Cabe had given me his full name—Caleb David Stone—his high school and graduation date—Rockland Regional High School, spring of the previous year—and a single reference—a Mr. Burford. There was no phone number or e-mail address for Mr. Burford, which meant I definitely hadn't contacted him. But I already knew I hadn't.

Even worse was the information missing about Cabe. I had no address or phone number. No social security number. The Snowden Family Clambake Company would have to send him tax documents in January. I'd thought I'd have plenty of time to get the information later. I remembered Cabe had told me he didn't own a cell phone and was looking for a place to live. I'd never asked him where he'd found a place, not even on the night when he saved my life while he was walking home.

I held the employment application away from me as if it had a bad smell. I was incredibly embarrassed. I tried to give myself a break; it had been a tumultuous time full of loss. I'd been convinced on an hourly basis we would lose the clambake company, and with it my mother's ancestral island and her house. But I was the businesswoman who arrived from New York on a white horse and told everybody how to properly run a company. More than once, I'd chastised Sonny for his slovenly recordkeeping. If he saw Cabe's application, he'd never let me hear the end of it.

I folded the application and stuck it in my tote

bag. I'd take it to Binder in the morning. I assumed the police had most of the paltry information it contained by now, but it was my duty as a good citizen to hand it over.

I stretched and turned off my father's green glass-shaded desk lamp. As I stood, I glanced out the big windows at the lights of the harbor.

What is that? A figure in the shadows looked up at the house. I couldn't make out his face.

"Cabe? Cabe!" I yelled through the window glass.

I pounded down the stairs and threw open the front door. "Cabe!"

I ran across the porch and opened the screen. "Cabe, come back!"

In the middle of the road, I turned in a tight circle. The street was completely silent, not a soul in sight.

Chapter 13

When my cell phone rang at 7:00 AM, I awoke instantly, grabbing it off my nightstand and fumbling to press ANSWER.

"Cabe?" His name leaped from my lips. Flynn's certainty Cabe would contact me must have affected me more that I'd realized.

"Julia, it's Pammie." The kid scheduled to work in our ticket kiosk on the dock today. "I've been throwing up all night. I can't make it to work."

I was usually deeply suspicious of sudden-onset stomach ills, particularly among the college-age staff, particularly on a Monday. But Pammie was the daughter of long-time Busman's Harbor summer residents, and she hadn't been so much as late all summer.

"Pammie, it's okay. Thanks for calling."

"Sorry to call so early. I wanted to give you plenty of notice."

"Go back to bed. Let me know about tomorrow."

"I will. I think it's that twenty-four hour thing that's going around."

First I'd heard of it.

I considered finding a substitute for Pammie, but decided to do the job myself. I left the house before my mother or Richelle were up. They didn't really know each other and I felt badly leaving them alone together, but I had no choice. Richelle's professional tour guide skills included building instant rapport with people, and my mother's upbringing had left her with such a bedrock of ingrained politeness, I was sure they'd be fine.

I spent the morning handing out Will Call tickets from our Internet sales, answering questions from potential customers, and persuading a few prospects to join us at the clambake. The Snowden Family Clambake had been rescued from near financial collapse by a silent partner earlier in the summer. I was very aware he'd entrusted us with his money—a lot of it—and I had an obligation to run the business as well as I could for the best return.

In quick order, we loaded the lunch crowd, two hundred people strong—I successfully sold the last few tickets—and pulled out into the inner harbor.

On a map, Busman's Harbor looked like the head and claws of a lobster floating in a deep blue sea. The jutting head of the lobster separated the touristy inner harbor from the working back harbor. The claws, called Eastclaw and Westclaw Points, embraced the vast bowl of the outer harbor and its six islands. The outer harbor offered every sight

Maine tourists wanted to see—seals, puffins, and a lighthouse.

I worked in the *Jacquie II's* little ship's store, selling drinks and snacks, barely noticing the magnificent scenery. This was my commute. Then, as if to rebuke me for taking the stunning vistas for granted, a minke whale breached right off our bow, and then rolled over playfully showing his white tummy. Captain George made an announcement over the sound system, then brought the *Jacquie II* around, and then around again, so everyone could get a photo. The whale obliged us breaching and diving several times.

Once we passed through the narrow opening of the harbor into the Atlantic Ocean, the sea got a little rougher, the breeze a little cooler. The passengers got quieter. They were ready to be at the island.

In ten minutes, we were there. Morrow Island. Thirteen acres of lawn, pine, oak, and boulders. The crowd disembarked and headed for the bocce court, croquet field, and badminton nets. Some hiked off to find the beach on the other side of the island. A few wandered down to the fire pit where their meal would be cooked. Sonny and his crew, short-staffed without Cabe, already had the lobsters, steamers, onions, corn, potatoes, and eggs on the fire.

I stood and looked up at Windsholme, the great stone summer "cottage" built by my mother's ancestors. The once beautiful building was a burned-out hulk, missing its roof and much of its interior. A horrible, bright-orange, chain-link fence surrounded it to keep the clambake customers out. With its twenty-seven rooms, Windsholme was too expensive to fix up and too expensive to tear down. I felt a little stab in my chest every time I saw the mansion in its current pitiful state. Over the winter, we'd have to decide what to do about her.

I hurried through the covered pavilion that contained most of our seating to the tiny commercial kitchen beyond. There, Livvie and a small group of women made the creamy clam chowder we served as a first course and the blueberry grunt that was dessert. Before I'd arrived, they'd done all the prep work, husking the corn down to one thin layer and wrapping the vegetables in aluminum foil.

The cooks, all considerably older than Livvie, laughed and traded inside jokes. "Yeah, like you're gonna make the chowdah and I'm gonna make the grunt." Evidently, this was a hilarious idea.

I marveled at how seamlessly Livvie had taken command of the group. She'd only been at it since mid-June. She hadn't hired these women. They'd been at their jobs for far longer than she, and had more experience putting out a complicated meal from the tiny space. But it was obvious they not only liked and respected her, they treated her as one of their own. I envied that.

When Livvie turned around, she looked a little green.

"Are you okay?" I asked.

"Queasy. Just came on."

"Pammie called in sick today, stomach bug."

"Who?"

"The kid who works in the ticket booth." Since Livvie had moved to the island, she'd lost track of the shore-side work of the clambake. "She said it's been going around. Can you work?"

"Yeah. I'm sure it will pass. Go do what you have to do."

So I did. My job was to run the front of the house, to be the host, and to make sure the service was impeccable. It had always been my father's role, and I still felt unequal to filling his shoes.

When the ship's bell rang, signaling the start of the meal, the guests gathered at the picnic tables and the waitstaff began running. All the customers had to get their chowder while it was piping hot. Then came the main course. Twin lobsters, steamers, melted butter, clam broth (for cleaning the steamers), corn, a potato, an onion, and a hard-boiled egg, all cooked the way we did it on the island, in a hole in the ground over heated rocks and under a canvas tarp surrounded by seaweed. I circulated to make sure everyone had enough to drink and knew how to eat their shellfish. A hush fell over the crowd because eating steamers and lobsters was both a meal and a workout.

When the mess was cleared away, the blueberry grunt and vanilla ice cream came out. There was a collective groan from the crowd, but to a person they dug in. As they finished their dessert, the diners dispersed to walk along the island paths or just enjoy the view from the great lawn. Within a half an hour, the ship's bell rang again and the guests headed toward the *Jacquie II*. In three short hours we'd be doing it all again for dinner.

I was ready to get off my feet and eat something,

but headed to the kitchen to check on Livvie instead. She and the other cooks were still busy, putting out a meal for our employees and prepping for the dinner crowd.

"Feeling any better?" Livvie's auburn hair, pulled under a baseball cap for work, framed a face that was, if anything greener than before.

"Fine," she answered. And then leaned over and vomited into a trash barrel.

"Livvie—are you certain it wasn't something in the food?" I knew how cold it sounded, but if I'd just put two hundred food-poisoned people on a boat, I had to know. It was my worst nightmare as a restaurateur. Perhaps, in retrospect, my worst nightmare should have been finding someone burned up in the clambake fire, but really, how likely was that?

Livvie shook her head. "Haven't . . . eaten a thing . . . all day."

The women in the kitchen helped her to a stool and gave her water.

"You need to get to bed," I said.

"But the bake—"

"We'll be fine." I looked to the other cooks who nodded vigorously. Even while all this was going on, food was being set out so the employees could eat before the next group of customers arrived. I tucked myself under Livvie's shoulder, positioned her arm across my back, and we left the kitchen.

From the tables where the staff was already gathered for dinner, Sonny and Page spotted me helping

Livvie toward their house and came running. Page's freckled face was puckered with concern. It's upsetting when the strong people who are supposed to take care of you are suddenly weak. In her young life, Page had already watched as my dad had gone from robust to skeletal in the final stages of his cancer.

"Just a stomach bug," Livvie told them. "Nothing to worry about."

Sonny took Livvie's other arm and together we got her into their house and up to the bedroom. We cleaned her up and helped her into her pj's. Page brought a glass of ice water.

"Drink plenty of liquids," I said. "Stay hydrated."

"I've got to get back to the fire," Sonny reminded us. "We're shorthanded."

Livvie turned to me "You have to help out in the kitchen."

"I know. I hate leaving you."

"I'll feel better knowing you're there. You, too, Bug," she said to Page. "All I need is rest. Get back to work." Page and a friend were smalltime entrepreneurs, selling a motley collection of sea glass and shells to clambake customers.

"If you're sure," I said, not feeling sure at all. Just then Le Roi, the island's Maine coon cat, jumped on the bed and gave his hips an Elvis-like shake in honor of his namesake. The people on the island did not own the island cat. At least that was Le Roi's position. He owned the island and looked after the people. He settled his large self on Livvie's bed to do just that.

When I left the house, I spotted Chris tying his motorized dinghy to the dock.

"Hey, beautiful," he called. "Sorry I'm late."

I'd forgotten he was coming.

As a grand romantic gesture, Chris had fixed up the playhouse that was a tiny replica of Windsholme, intending it as a place where I could go in the quiet moments between lunch and dinner to rest, relax, restore. I lived with my mother and worked with my sister and brother-in-law, so sometimes I needed the break. Chris also intended the building, which was deep in the woods far away from the clambake, as a place where he and I might meet—privately.

But it hadn't worked out that way. I hadn't made it over to the playhouse in more than a month. And he couldn't get to the island often, not at all in the last few weeks. Our schedules were so crazy and changeable, even if I'd remembered he was coming, I'm not sure I would have expected him to show up.

Our unlucky streak continued. There'd be no canoodling at the playhouse today. I explained I was needed in the kitchen. Chris gave me a peck on the cheek and let me go. "Do what you have to. I can take care of myself."

That was one of the best things about Chris. I knew he could.

The kitchen was busy, but not chaotic. Chowder was being stirred, blueberry grunt assembled, butter melted, clam broth heated. I grabbed a stool and started husking corn.

Chapter 14

When the ship's bell rang signaling the start of dinner, I took off my apron and ran to do my hosting duties. I spotted Chris down by the fire helping Sonny and his team. Sonny said something to Chris, who threw his head back and laughed. Good. My family's Bad Attitude about Chris was, in great measure, driven by Sonny. They'd been friends in high school and both had reputations for being wild. But Sonny had been a husband and a father for a decade and Chris had continued . . . well, no good could come from speculating about what Chris continued doing.

I was delighted to spy Chuck and Cindy Kelly seated at a picnic table.

"Hello, dear," Cindy said. "Seeing you yesterday reminded us how much we love this place. We're here for the lobster. And for the sunset." Morrow Island offered a gorgeous over-ocean view of the setting sun, a rare sight on the eastern seaboard. Cindy gestured toward the woman seated across from her, "Do you know—"

Bunnie Getts. I couldn't believe it. I'd thought one of the best things about Founder's Weekend being over would be the absence of Bunnie from my life. Yet there she was, seated in front of me. How did she and the Kellys even know each other? I couldn't see Chestnut Hill Bunnie hanging out with teachers of modest means who lived in a motor home.

"Oh! Of course you two know each other," Cindy remembered. "You were on the Founder's Weekend committee together."

"Hello, Bunnie."

"Hello, Julia. I'm glad to see the clambake's association with the young man, the murderer, hasn't hurt your business," she said, more loudly than necessary.

Conversation around us died then surged back again. As I groped for something to say, one of our waitstaff arrived with a tray laden with cups of clam chowder.

"That's the ticket!" Chuck proclaimed. He was as eager to change the subject as I was.

"Leave one more clam chowder," Bunnie instructed the young college kid waiting on them. "My dinner companion will be here at any moment."

Dinner companion? What dinner companion? I looked around to see who might show up.

Bunnie jumped up, waving vigorously to a figure hiking out of the woods at the top of the hill by Windsholme.

Reggie Swinburne! He scanned the crowd and strode purposely toward us. When he arrived at the table, he bent over and gave Bunnie a kiss on the cheek, muttering, "m'dear." Then he stuck his hand out to me. "Miss Snowden. We meet again. Lovely place you've got here. Lovely. I just hiked over to the little beach on the other side of the island."

"Reggie's quite the outdoorsman," Bunnie said, blushing.

Blushing? Really? Blushing Bunnie?

"He's a birder and a fisherman. He loves to hike and hunt and . . ." Bunnie continued on, but I had trouble paying attention.

She and Reggie are a couple? It's improbable that she and the Kellys are friends, but she and Reggie?

Bunnie was still prattling, not a word or an activity I'd ever thought to associate with her. "In the fall, Reggie's taking me duck hunting. He's been teaching me to shoot. He bought me a shotgun."

By that point, I was speechless. Completely blown away. I looked at Bunnie in her Lily Pulitzer shift and ballet flats, her little matching bag sitting on the bench beside her. Did she even have a clue what she'd have to wear to sit in a duck blind in Maine in the fall? *Love is blind,* I reminded myself. *Blind and stupid.*

"Now that our committee duties are over, I do hope you can finally make it to my house for that cup of tea," Bunnie said.

Was she talking to me? It was true, Bunnie had invited me to tea before, but at the time it felt more like a summons to the principal's office.

Chapter 15

April

Vee gave me a ride to the second Founder's Weekend Committee meeting in the well-used maroon Subaru station wagon the sisters shared. Clumps of melting, dirty snow sat by the roadside reminding us that though winter was over, she hadn't gone far and might come back at any moment for one last curtain call.

Bunnie's dark green SUV was already in the Tourist Bureau parking lot when we arrived, as was Stevie's minivan. I was somewhat surprised to see Bud's battered pickup there, too. Dan's bike leaned against the deck rail. At least one of us had we decided it was spring.

Bunnie ran the meeting on a tight agenda, moving from old business to new. She'd booked the windjammers, which had an open Saturday as they sailed from Bar Harbor to Portland for celebrations in those cities. That meant the date for Founder's Weekend was fixed. We were off and running.

"Now the games," Bunnie said, crossing the old agenda items off her list with such force I thought her pencil might go right through the paper and come out the other side of the wooden clipboard. "I've listed trap hauling, lobster crate running, and cod fish relay."

Dead silence.

"Trained seals," Bud muttered. Morgan stirred at his feet, turning her head to make sure he was all right.

More silence.

"Will someone tell me what the matter is?" Bunnie demanded, drumming her pencil on her clipboard. "These are exactly the contests we have every year at the Shrimp Festival."

Finally, Dan Small cleared his throat. "I think, ah, Bunnie, that's the problem. The Shrimp Festival is for us. We have it this month, in April, before the tourists get here. We dash across floating lobster traps and run relay races holding dead fish to celebrate our way of life. Not to amuse a bunch of—"

"Massholes," Bud finished, using the preferred local term for the inhabitants of the great Commonwealth to our south.

Bunnie stopped tapping her pencil, brows knit. "I don't get it."

"Because you're a—" Bud started.

Mercifully, Vee jumped in. "The Shrimp Festival celebrates our *former* way of life. There used to be thirty shrimp boats in this town and two canneries.

Now there are no boats, not full-time anyway. If we don't bring in tourists this summer, ten years from now we'll be having bed-making contests and getting all weepy and nostalgic for our way of life back when we had a hospitality industry."

That shut everyone up. People misjudged Vee based on her ever-present heels and hosiery. Down deep, she was as practical as they come. After some brainstorming, we added the B&B bed races and the pie-eating contest to the list, and agreed to go ahead with the local games.

Vee volunteered to do publicity. Stevie would book the music for the concert and arrange for the fireworks. Bunnie asked Dan and I to organize the food. I was happy with the assignment, something I knew how to do.

"What would you like to contribute, Bud?" Bunnie asked sweetly.

"I'm just keeping an eye on the rest of you," Bud grumbled. "Making certain this shindig doesn't get out of control."

We stood to go and I thought I was home free.

"Oh, Julia," Bunnie said. "How's your research going? Have you discovered who Mr. Busman was?"

"I . . . I . . ."

I had done nothing. It was all I could do to keep the clambake afloat. An acquaintance from New York had just booked the island for her June wedding. I was excited about this new line of business, but it meant more work and more fighting with Sonny.

Growing up, I'd heard at least a dozen stories

about who Mr. Busman was, none of them believable, and I wasn't going to take a chance and blurt one of them out.

"Well, that won't do," Bunnie said. "Julia, get to work. We need this information for publicity and such, and for my opening remarks. Perhaps you'd like to come to my house for tea and we'll work on the project together."

As we were leaving, Dan Small took pity on me. He leaned in and whispered, "Talk to your friend, Gus. He knows more about the history of this town than anybody."

Chapter 16

August

I stayed behind when the *Jacquie II* left the island.
Chris could take me back to the harbor in his
dinghy. I checked on Livvie who was sleeping peace-
fully, Le Roi snuggled in the crook of her knees.
What a loyal cat—giving up cadging lobster from
customers to watch over one of the island's human
inhabitants.

When I came downstairs, Sonny stood in the
living room. "Livvie okay?"

"Sleeping."

"Julia." Sonny stared at his boots. "I've wanted to
tell you. No, that's not true. I *haven't* wanted to tell
you. But I've got to——"

"Sonny, you're freaking me out."

"Cabe was living here."

"In this house?" I couldn't imagine.

"In the playhouse."

"*What?*" My voice shot so high, I thought only

dogs could hear me. "In the playhouse Chris fixed up especially for me?"

"When was the last time you were there?"

Touché. "Sonny, what were you thinking?"

"Cabe hated where he was staying. I needed him on the island early and late. I thought it was a win-win."

"You didn't know anything about him. You have Page here, and Livvie."

"I thought you'd taken care of that, didn't I?" Sonny yelled. "You were supposed to have checked him out." He paused, breathing heavily. "Besides, no one was in danger from Cabe. We both know that."

I did know that. Cabe was never a danger to my family. "Did you tell Binder and Flynn that Cabe lived here?"

Sonny lowered his voice even further. "No. I was hoping you would."

"Me?"

"That way, I don't have to take time off, go into town."

I trusted myself to tell them a lot more than I trusted Sonny. At least, I knew it would get done. When I told them, they'd certainly come out to the island and they could interview Sonny then.

From outside, I heard Chris and Page approaching. They were arguing good-naturedly about something, probably the Red Sox. Page was the only person in the family who had no reservations about my relationship with Chris and that meant the world to me. He was great with kids, meeting them at their level, but never talking down. It was the kind of thing that made a little girl's, and a grown girl's, heart melt.

Chris pushed open the screen door with Page right behind him. "What's going on?"

"How's Mom?" Page asked Sonny.

"She's sleeping."

Chris looked from me to Sonny and back. It was obvious something was up.

"Go get ready for bed, honey," Sonny said.

But Page would not be moved. "Is this about Mom?" she demanded.

"I promise. We are not talking about your mom," I answered.

"Okay." Page trundled up the stairs.

Sonny and I filled Chris in.

"He was staying at one of those boarding houses where they rent to more kids than they have beds. He absolutely hated it," Sonny said. "That's why I offered him the playhouse."

"Do you know which boarding house?" There were a few around town that fit Sonny's description.

"Never asked." He gave me a look that said *let's not get into who didn't ask what.*

"Have you searched the playhouse since Cabe left?" Chris asked.

"Took a quick look. Didn't see anything."

"We should look now," Chris said. "Before Julia talks to Binder in the morning."

"Good idea," Sonny agreed.

I wanted to ask why that would be, though I knew the answer. Sonny and Chris, both convinced of Cabe's innocence, wanted to see if there was anything incriminating in the playhouse before the police searched it. I started to say, "Wai—" but the expedition was unstoppable.

Sonny went to the kitchen and pulled three powerful flashlights off a shelf. "We're going outside for a minute," he called upstairs to Page, then led the charge.

There were outdoor lights around the house, dock, and clambake pavilion, but once we'd walked beyond their influence, you couldn't see your hand in front of your face. I know because I stopped, flashlight pointed at the ground, and tried it.

A million stars were overhead. A meteor streaked across the night sky. The Perseids. I'd forgotten. I loved the clear, open Maine skies. Chris came up behind me and put a reassuring hand under my elbow.

"Look," I whispered. A shooting star plummeted toward us.

"Beautiful." He kissed my neck. The Maine skies weren't the only thing I'd miss when I was back in Manhattan.

"What's goin' on back there?" Sonny yelled.

We hurried to catch up until I ran smack into Sonny, who'd stopped on the great lawn and trained his flashlight on something in the distance.

"Ow! Watch where you're going," he protested.

I grabbed the back of Sonny's belt, Chris kept hold of me, and we crept up the lawn, then through the woods to the playhouse. Even with the flashlights, we had to move slowly. Running into a branch would smart.

Sonny stopped on the porch of the little house, about a foot in front of the door. He mumbled something I couldn't catch.

"What?"

"The screen door opens *out*," he hissed. "Back up."

Chris and I did as requested and soon we were inside the playhouse—our intended trysting place. Where we'd never actually trysted.

Sonny lit a lantern and we spread out to look around. The house was tiny, a small front room and bunkroom. I wondered why all three of us had come. But who would have agreed to stay behind? I hated to admit it, but I was there because I worried Chris and Sonny's unwavering belief in Cabe's innocence might lead them to destroy anything suspicious they found. Sonny believed in Cabe because he knew him, as I did. Chris didn't know Cabe well, but Chris always stood firmly on the side of the underdog. There was nothing that would move Chris more than the plight of a young man without resources, wanted by the police.

"Nothing here," Sonny called from the bunkroom.

"Here, either." Chris and I had searched the cupboards in the sideboard and under the cushions on the settee. There really weren't many places to look.

"That's a relief," Sonny said. "At least I haven't kept anything from Binder and Flynn they'd think was useful."

"But don't you see?" I protested. "There's *nothing* here."

"Exactly." Sonny was losing patience with me.

"But Cabe must have had some things here. He

owned more than one shirt, more than one pair of underwear. If there's nothing here, it means that after the Founder's Weekend celebration, he had no intention of coming back."

"Crap." Sonny said it, but we all thought it.

Chapter 17

Chris took me back to the harbor on his dinghy. We didn't attempt to talk over the noise of its little motor and the sea. We were both shaken by what we'd seen—or hadn't seen—at the playhouse. The word *premeditation* came to mind, though my brain was still unwilling to link the words *Cabe* and *murder*.

Chris tied the dinghy up behind the *Dark Lady*. To make ends meet, he rented out the cabin on a lake he'd bought from his parents and moved onto his boat for the summer. We climbed onto the deck. He kissed me hard, and then, without words, we headed to his cabin below.

Afterward, we lay in his spacious bunk. I loved the way the shape of the *Dark Lady's* bow brought our heads together in the dark. I shifted my position and lay my head on his breastbone, that indentation between the pectoral muscles that is one of the sexiest parts of a man.

"How come you never left town?" I asked. Most young people left. Jobs were hard to come by, especially in the off-season. And most of the jobs that did exist, didn't pay well. Chris strung together landscaping, cab driving, and bouncing—and living on his boat in the summer so he could rent his house.

"I wasn't going to college. You know that." When he spoke, I could feel the hum of his diaphragm, like the bass of a sound system turned all the way up.

"That's not true. You played football—"

"Played football and raised hell." He laughed. "If you think I was college material, you can go over to the high school and ask my old guidance counselor. He still works there. He'll set you straight."

"So you just stayed? Because you had no options?" I sat up on the bunk, facing him, grateful for the dark.

"Jesus, Julia. I'm not pathetic. Is that what you think of me?" I started to protest, but he kept talking. "Of course I had options. The service. A lot of kids joined. Or just leave town to look for work. It's a big world out there. I didn't go because I love it here. That's why I bought my parents house when they went south. I can't imagine not smelling the ocean everyday. I can't imagine being happy where the land is flat, or where the winters are warm. This harbor is my place. I'm dug deep."

I wasn't surprised by what he'd said. I hadn't pictured some *Crocodile Dundee* future where he followed me to Manhattan. Being with Chris was a lifelong dream, but I had to accept it for what it was, the world's most wonderful summer romance.

"Come here." He reached out for me in the darkness and I settled back into his arms.

The sun was barely a glint on the horizon when I rolled out of the bunk and felt around for my clothes.

Chris stirred. "What time is it?"

"Early. Go back to sleep."

"You don't have to go."

"I do."

"Julia, you're thirty. I doubt your mother thinks—"

She probably didn't. Not that my mother's WASPy reserve would ever allow us to discuss such things. But I'd brought my mother a houseguest and then disappeared. I wanted to get back before she and Michelle woke up. The least I could do was make some breakfast and spend a little time with them before I had to run off to work again.

"Bye," I called softly.

Chris was already back snug under the covers, his eyes firmly closed. "Love you," he mumbled.

Wait. What?

Chapter 18

The sun was just coming up over Eastclaw Point as I scurried up the walk to my mother's house. Once inside, I wondered, how far was I planning to carry this charade? Should I mess up my bed and put on pajamas? Ridiculous. As Chris had pointed out, I was thirty years old.

In the end, I took a shower and put on clean clothes, then went down to the kitchen to fix breakfast.

I tried hard not to think about what Chris had said. Or rather mumbled. For a few moments at a time, I convinced myself I'd misunderstood him. It was too soon, too fast, too much. But was it? I'd mooned about him from afar for more than half my life. But we'd only been officially going out for six weeks, if you didn't count the months we'd met for lunch at Gus's. Besides, what good could come of it? I couldn't envision any future for myself that didn't involve going back to Manhattan, and last night

Chris had declared he was never leaving Busman's Harbor—which hadn't come as a surprise.

Mom arrived downstairs before Richelle. If she noticed I hadn't slept at home, she didn't mention it.

"I'm sorry I invited Richelle and then took off," I said.

"Don't be silly. She needed a place to stay. Besides, she's delightful."

"Morning." Richelle was in a nice nightgown and matching bathrobe. She noticed me noticing. "Jacquie took me to Topsham yesterday to pick up some clothes." Topsham was the closest town down the coast offering shopping plazas and big box stores.

Jacquie? No one called my mom Jacquie. Calling our boat the *Jacquie II* was my father's idea of a joke. My mother was Jacqueline, nothing shorter.

"We had a delightful day," Mom said. "A little shopping. Out to lunch."

Hearing that, I was sure I was in an alternate universe. My mom did not have girlfriends. She didn't think shopping was a social activity. She thought it was about meeting basic human needs by making decisions and performing transactions as quickly as possible.

"Did you know Richelle came to Busman's Harbor when she was young?" Mom continued. "Her aunt was Georgette Baker. Remember? The Blue Door?"

I did remember. Miss Georgette Baker had owned a B&B overlooking the back harbor. It was surrounded by a tall fence with a bright blue door. Not a gate, a real door. My memory of her was vague.

Through my childish eyes she'd seemed very old. I wondered how old she'd actually been.

"Well, just the one summer," Richelle said quietly. "She was my great-aunt."

"Really?" I was surprised. "All the times we talked about how much you loved Busman's Harbor and how you tried to lead every tour your company sent here, you never mentioned you'd spent a summer here. Or had a relative who lived here."

"It was so long ago. I didn't think anyone would remember Georgette."

"Of course we remember her," my mother said. "Don't you, Julia?"

I nodded to confirm I did. I took the pan of scrambled eggs off the burner and over to the kitchen table where my mother buttered toast.

"How long do you expect to stay in town?" I asked Richelle. I thought it was more polite than, "How long do you expect to stay in our house?"

"I have a doctor's appointment this morning. Jacquie's taking me. Still not allowed to drive."

"That's very nice of you, *Jacquie*." I couldn't resist trying to get a rise out of my mother, but she just munched on her toast.

When we finished breakfast, I glanced at the digital clock on the stove. I wanted to deliver Cabe's employment application to Binder and Flynn before work. I excused myself, went to our home phone, and called Pammie to make sure she'd be at the ticket kiosk.

"I'm fine," she said. "Twenty-four hour bug."

I walked the block and a half to Busman's Harbor's ugly, brick, fire-department-town-offices-police complex. Inside, the building was quiet. I crossed behind the empty police reception desk and looked into the community room the state police had used the last time they were in town. Binder and Flynn sat at one of the room's central tables, heads bowed, deep in conversation. Around the perimeter of the room were a whiteboard with notes scrawled on it in thick black marker, two computer workstations, and dozens and dozens of cardboard boxes.

"Knock, knock."

"Julia Snowden!" Binder seemed delighted to see me, ready to stop whatever they were doing. Flynn, as always, seemed much less so.

"Come in. Sit down," Binder said.

Ignoring Flynn's scowl, I did. "What is all this? I asked, indicating the scores of moving boxes.

"*This* has to do with the identity of your friend, Stevie Noyes."

"His identity? You mean you found his next of kin?"

"No. We found out who Stevie Noyes actually was."

Actually was? "He wasn't Stevie Noyes?"

"Not always. The dental records you so helpfully pointed us toward got a hit at a federal pen in Pennsylvania. Stevie Noyes used to be T.V. Noyes, big-time stock swindler. He did a federal bill of ten years for a stock con he ran in the early nineties. These boxes contain the trial transcripts, witness lists, and so on. There was a civil suit against him, too, an attempt to recover damages. We're still waiting on that stuff."

"I can't believe it. Stevie Noyes was the nicest person in the world."

"So everyone has told us. He did his time. Apparently, he was a model prisoner. Taught computer classes to inmates. After he got out, he inherited some money from an uncle and bought the RV park. Hasn't had so much as a parking ticket since."

"But that doesn't mean the people he swindled don't still feel wronged." I started to feel hopeful. Maybe Stevie's past would take the focus off Cabe. "Have you found Stevie's family and notified his next of kin?"

"Working on it," Binder answered. "The family situation's a little screwy. We'll release his identity to the press today, regardless."

"A stock swindle, time in prison, and a screwy family. There could be a lot of people who might be interested in killing Stevie Noyes. Maybe finding Cabe isn't so important," I suggested.

"Actually, as the investigation's moved forward, we've become more interested in young Mr. Stone, not less," Binder said.

"He may be in more trouble than ever," Flynn added.

I couldn't imagine why that would be. "How can you say that? You've just told me you have a boatload of possible suspects from Stevie's past."

Flynn folded his hands in front of him and gave me his full attention. "We think you know where Cabe Stone is."

"What! Why would you ever think that?"

"The kid has no resources. He's on his own. Someone's helping him stay out of sight."

"You can't know that. And even if someone is, why me?" I looked at Binder. *Are you going to sit there and let him accuse me?* But Binder said nothing to stop Flynn or defend me.

"Your brother-in-law obviously knows more than he's telling. I'd suspect him, but he lives out on that island with limited mobility and means of communication. We know the kid's not hiding on the island."

How do they know that?

"That leaves you."

I jumped up from the chair, seething with the unfairness of the accusation. "Are you kidding me? I'm *helping* you. I gave you the identity of your victim. I pointed you to the dental records. You told me how helpful I was—like *two* minutes ago!" What a case of what-have-you-done-for-me-lately.

Binder stood up as well. "Ms. Snowden. Julia. This is serious. It's important for Mr. Stone's safety and the safety of anyone he may be with that he turns himself in. If he contacts you, tell him to call us. Now."

Really, this is too much. "He hasn't contacted me, I swear," I insisted. "And I don't appreciate what you're implying."

I pivoted and walked briskly out of the office, and then out the station door.

I was so mad I was shaking. How dare Flynn accuse me. And on what possible basis? And all while Binder just sat there.

I felt in my tote bag for my phone to check the

time. I had to get to the dock in time to board the *Jacquie II.* "Damn." There was the employment application. I'd been so angry I hadn't given it to the cops. Or told them Cabe had been staying on the island. I briefly considered going back, but it was late and I was mad.

When I finally fished my phone out of the bag, an icon indicated a voicemail. I walked toward the town dock, tapping the phone as I went. A single voicemail from a number I didn't recognize. It had come in at 3:04 AM when I was in a deep, well-earned sleep in the bow of the *Dark Lady.* I hadn't heard it ring. I played the message.

"Julia. It's me." I stopped where I stood. Cabe. A tourist bumped into me, excusing herself. I stepped into the sheltered doorway of a shop and replayed the voicemail.

Cabe was whispering, but I understood him clearly. "You said once, if you could ever help me. I think I'm in a lot of trouble. I'm scared. I don't know what to do. Don't tell the police about this call. This guy doesn't even know I'm using his phone. You'll get him in trouble. He's passing through. I'll call you back somehow. Julia, I can't go to jail. I won't survive it. Please help me."

My breath came in ragged gasps. I'd suffered from panic attacks for years and knew what triggered them. They happened when my head and heart conflicted. I knew in my head I should turn around, march back into the police station, and turn my phone over to Binder and Flynn. But my heart wanted to reach out to Cabe, who sounded frightened and alone. Cabe, who had saved my life.

I breathed slowly and deliberately, until the threat of an attack passed. I starting walking again, pressing the CALL BACK icon for the message as I went.

"Allo?" A man's voice answered.

"May I please speak to Cabe Stone?"

"*Qui?*"

"Cabe Stone, please."

"*Désolé, c'est une erreur.*" Click.

Wrong number. The man hadn't sounded suspicious or perturbed. He'd treated my call like any inadvertent wrong number. But what was up with the French? Was Cabe already in Canada? But French didn't necessarily mean Canada. Tons of French-Canadians flocked to Maine for their holidays.

"Cabe, what did you do?" I demanded out loud. I was furious at the universe because I'd missed his call. I wanted to ask him why he'd run.

I'd just lied to Binder and Flynn without knowing it. I'd sworn I hadn't heard from Cabe. How did Flynn know Cabe would reach out to me? More than that, how did he know I wouldn't tell?

I changed course and headed home. I stopped at the end of my mother's front walk, shaky and breathless. I knew I wasn't going to tell. I was going to do anything I could to help Cabe.

Chapter 19

My mother's car wasn't in her garage. She and Richelle must be at the doctor's. I went upstairs to my office to radio Morrow Island.

I didn't know what I was going to say. I was the head of the company. Surely, "I won't be on the boat. Something's come up," should suffice. I hoped Livvie would answer.

Sonny. *Damn.* "Hi Sonny. I'm not going to make it to the island today. I'm really sick." *Coward.* Sonny paused, giving me ample time to feel ridiculous about calling in fake-sick to a company I ran.

"You seemed fine yesterday." He sounded suspicious, like he thought I was lying.

I resented his tone. It was the second time today someone had accused me of lying. It was also the second time I was actually lying. Only difference, this time I knew it.

"Came on suddenly. I think it's the same thing Pammie and Livvie had. I really don't think I can come to the island." I dug myself in deeper. "I'm sorry. I know it's a lot more work."

Sonny relented. "Of course, don't come. We'll manage." There was some warmth in his voice.

"Thanks," I said, and meant it. Partly because he was being nice, and partly because I could see an end to the conversation. "I'm sure I'll be back tomorrow."

"Maybe not," he answered. "Check the weather forecast."

Bad weather? How could I not know? I always knew what the marine forecast was. It was my job, especially if there was any chance we'd have to shut down the clambake. After I finished with Sonny, I called Pammie and told her I wouldn't be going out with the *Jacquie II.*

She gave me a chipper, "No problem."

I fired up my computer. If there was one thing I'd learned in my venture capital job, it was how to do research on the Web. Before our firm put any money into a company, we vetted it thoroughly. Sure, we asked the management for all the information they could give us. But we almost always found the most valuable information independently—a competitor who'd recently made a significant advance, or even information about a management team member he or she would have preferred we didn't discover.

I waved my fingers, warming up like a piano virtuoso preparing for a concert. There were answers inside the magic screen across from me, I was certain of it. I typed T.V. Noyes into a search engine.

Why did Stevie's real name sound fake and his fake name sound real? Floods of information came back. Penny stock swindlers didn't achieve the household-name status of a Milken or a Madoff, but in its time, Telford Vincent Noyes's arrest and conviction had been big news.

He'd run a boiler room operation. A stock scam. They were always with us, but I knew from business school they were particularly prevalent in the early nineties, mostly with unregulated penny stocks, companies too small to be traded on the major exchanges.

Early 1990s stock scams worked in a variety of ways. Since the companies they focused on were so small, the stock was easily manipulated. The scammers would talk up a stock, putting out positive rumors about a company. When the stock was high, the scammers would take money from the gullible people on the end of the phone, but not actually use it to buy the stock. Once the scammers had the money in hand, they spread negative stories about the company and the stock would drop like a stone. The con men pocketed the money and the investor was none the wiser, thinking he'd lost it on the stock.

Noyes had run an operation that did that over and over again. He had a unique variation, too. He'd mail 10,000 people one of two newsletters. Half the newsletters would predict a certain, well-known stock was going up, and half would predict it was going down. If the stock went down, he'd mail a second newsletter to the 5000 people who'd received his first, correct prediction. Half would predict another well-known stock would go up, half down. Then he'd send a follow up to just those who'd received the correct prediction. By the time he was down to 625 people, they'd received five correct stock predictions from him in a row. When his boiler room operators called to say he had a huge winner, his audience was more credulous than any normal sampling of people. They invested with him, and they invested big. Huge sums. People lost fortunes. Some lost everything they had.

Eventually, the Feds swept in. Accompanying one of the articles was a photo of Noyes with a raincoat over his head, being perp-walked out of his elegant Upper East Side apartment building. I couldn't see his face, but I recognized his little body. In the background of the photo, standing under the building's awning, was a beautiful young woman, dark-haired, petite—and obviously pregnant. The caption said she was TV's wife.

I continued clicking on articles about Noyes. There weren't many additional mentions until seven months later when he'd been tried on the criminal charges. Several of his employees had been given immunity to testify against him. His wife sat stalwartly behind him every day of the trial.

The employees' testimonies, along with the rest of the government's case, must have been devastating. Noyes was sentenced to ten years, a long time for a white-collar crime in those days. But when you added in the mail fraud . . . Plus, one of his early victims had killed himself rather spectacularly, diving off the Empire State Building. I didn't even know that could be done.

I sat back in my desk chair and rubbed my eyes. There wasn't much news about Noyes after his sentencing. A short article when he reported to prison included the information that he and his wife had divorced. The civil suit had petered out. Noyes was broke and therefore judgment-proof. There was no point in pursuing the lawsuit.

My mind kept drifting back to Stevie's wife. The look on her face in the arrest photo haunted me— shock, fear, hurt. What was it like to have your whole life come crashing down around you?

The other thing I fixated on in the photo was her great, pregnant belly. I did some fast subtraction. Her child with Stevie would be nineteen years old. Cabe was nineteen years old. No one knew where he came from. He seemed to have no family. Did Binder and Flynn believe Cabe was Stevie's son? Was this the deeper connection Binder had hinted at? The reason the cops were more and not less interested in Cabe?

My mouth felt suddenly dry. I hated to even think about it.

I stood, stretched, then went back to the keyboard. T.V.'s pregnant wife was Carole Noyes. Prior to his arrest, she'd been quite visible in New York— attending charity events and serving on boards. Afterwards, she'd disappeared completely. Or maybe she'd gone back to her maiden name?

I tracked backward and found a 1988 marriage announcement for Telford Vincent Noyes and Carole

Marsh. Moving forward in time got me another marriage announcement, for Carole Marsh and Donald Crane, in December 1993, only six months after T.V. Noyes reported to prison. The marriage had occurred in New Jersey.

There were a hundred Donald Cranes in New Jersey and thirty-seven Carole Cranes. I was grateful for that e. Taking a chance, I searched on "Donald and Carole Crane," and got nothing. But without the quotes, there it was. An obituary for Carole Crane, four years ago in Summit, New Jersey. Survived by her husband, Dr. Donald, and her son, Aaron Crane, still living at home.

I looked at the photo accompanying the obituary. No question it was the same woman from the photo of T.V.'s arrest. Dead at age forty-eight, "suddenly."

Was I looking at a photo of Gabe's mother? Her sudden death might explain the vulnerability we all saw in him.

There was only one Dr. Donald Crane in Summit, New Jersey. I picked up my cell phone and dialed.

"Dr. Donald Crane."

I was momentarily tongue-tied. I'd expected a receptionist or a machine. "This is Julia Snowden in Busman's Harbor, Maine."

"The state police have already called," he said matter-of-factly, not hostile. Letting me know.

"Yes. I'm following up. About your son Aaron."

"As I already told you people, he's not here. I don't know where he is."

He seemed to assume I was with the police. I hadn't said I was, but I didn't correct his misunderstanding.

He didn't say more, but I waited silently. Binder's trick. I didn't think it would work, but then Crane spoke.

"This has to do with T.V.'s death, I assume. If I'd known where the bastard was, I'd have killed him myself. I didn't. T.V. Noyes ruined my wife's life. And my family. I should know. I was Carole's psychiatrist. When she came to me after his arrest, but well before he went to prison, she was broken. Can you imagine, thinking you were wealthy and married to a prominent man, the father of your unborn child, and it all disappears in one day? T.V. spent the cash from the boiler room operation as fast as he made it. When he was arrested, they were destitute."

I couldn't imagine the depths of the deception. That poor woman.

"I wanted to rescue her. As soon as I realized my feelings for her, I resigned as her doctor. But I couldn't forget her. Later, after Aaron was born, and T.V. went to prison, we married and I adopted Aaron.

"But Carole couldn't forgive or forget. No matter how I tried to make her happy, her bitterness and anger overwhelmed all the good in her. Four years ago, she closed herself in our garage and turned on her car. Aaron found her.

"I did my best for him, but he couldn't be rescued, either. He barely attended school. We had truant officers and social workers here. The best child grief psychologist I could find. I hired tutors to catch him up, but he wouldn't or couldn't cooperate.

"All that time, we never heard a word from T.V.

Not even when he got out of prison. He never asked about his son. Initially, I was glad. I thought Carole, Aaron, and I could be a coherent, bonded family. But when Carole killed herself, I couldn't forgive T.V. for not even asking about his son. He'd destroyed his family a second time."

Dr. Crane paused, and I thought about T.V. Noyes, criminal and destroyer of his wife and son. It was hard to reconcile with the happy-go-lucky man I'd known. No wonder he never talked about his past.

"As I told the other officer, Aaron left home on his seventeenth birthday. I haven't seen or heard from him in two and a half years." Crane's voice cracked. "I'm afraid he's dead, but I push back the fear. His car is still in the driveway. His clothes are still in his bureau. I've hired private detectives. Nothing. And since he turned eighteen, the police have had no interest in finding him. Until T.V. died."

Was Cabe, Aaron Crane? For sure, parts of the story fit. If he was, he had plenty of reasons to kill Stevic.

But maybe there was another explanation. Aaron was a runaway who didn't want to be found. If he glimpsed the body in the fire, and realized there'd be a police investigation, he might have taken off in order to conceal his identity. Cabe might be Aaron, and yet still be innocent. I felt a little hope rise.

"Dr. Crane, can you describe Aaron?"

"I e-mailed photos to the state police yesterday." For the first time, he sounded guarded. "Who did you say you were?"

I told the truth. "I'm Julia Snowden. I think I may
be a friend of your son."

Dr. Crane's breath caught, and I immediately re-
gretted what I'd said. I had no right to give him
hope on so little evidence.

"Tell him I love him," Crane said. "Tell him to
come home."

I could tell he was weeping as he hung up the
phone.

Chapter 20

I heard Mom's car in the driveway. She and Richelle came bursting through the back door, talking away. I didn't want to scare them, so I went to the top of the backstairs called down to the kitchen.

"Julia, what are you doing here?" Mom was instantly concerned, her happy chatter with Richelle forgotten.

I came downstairs. "I called in sick this morning." Better to give Mom the same story I'd given Sonny. Mom and Livvie talked at least once a day.

"You don't look sick."

What is this, grade school? Do I have to prove I had a temperature? "I'm much better now. It's a fast-moving stomach virus that's going around. Livvie had it yesterday. I may take the boat out to the island with the dinner crowd."

"Livvie was sick?" My mother used her why-wasn't-I-told tone of voice.

"She's fine. I'm fine. It's nothing."

Reassured, Mom busied herself making tea. I turned to Richelle. "How'd it go at the doctor's?"

"I'm still not allowed to travel. He wasn't happy about my shopping trip. But really, what was I to do? When I left Portland four days ago, I packed for one overnight, and in all the confusion my bus driver took off with that tiny bag. I had nothing."

For the first time, I wondered about Richelle's life in Portland. I was used to seeing her with her cell phone glued to her hand, checking in with her agency, calling about reservations for places up ahead. Yet her phone hadn't rung once at our house that I was aware of. Didn't she have a friend who could bring her some clothes from Portland? It was only an hour and half away.

"So you'll be staying a few more days," I said.

"I hope it's all right with you. Your mom said it was okay. We've been giggling here like girlfriends."

Like girlfriends? Completely ridiculous. I had never, in thirty years, heard my mother giggle.

While I pondered the subject of my giggling mother, Richelle changed the subject. "Are the police still looking for your friend? The boy who worked for you?"

Mom, too, turned from the tea making to hear the answer.

"They're still looking for him, but other evidence has come in." I filled them in on Stevie's former life as a stock swindler and federal prisoner.

Richelle listened intently, leaning toward me. I wasn't sure why she was so interested in our harbor drama. Was it because she'd witnessed the crime, or at least its aftermath, the foot in the fire? "So now they think the boy didn't do it?"

"The opposite. They seem more fixated on him."

Richelle stood up straight and looked at me steadily. "But you don't think he did it." It was a statement, not a question.

"I don't," I confirmed.

She didn't ask me to explain. "I hope your friend's okay. And I hope he turns up soon."

I accepted a cup of tea from my mother, but declined to sit and drink with them. I went back to my office. I'd taken the day off to help Cabe, but what, really, was I going to do? Even if Cabe was Aaron, how could my knowing that help him? Despite my belief in his innocence, I did think the best thing Cabe could do was return to Busman's Harbor and tell Binder and Flynn what he'd seen. Therefore, my best bet was still to find Cabe. But how?

I pulled Cabe's employment application out of my bag and unfolded it. There was so little information on it. Just the name of a school, which gave me a city, Rockland, and the name of a person, Mr. Burford. Had Aaron, with his disrupted education, returned to high school using the name Cabe Stone? The kid I knew wasn't the emotional wreck Donald Crane had described. Perhaps Cabe had gotten his life together.

The way the name was written on the application was the way a student would refer to a teacher. I searched the Web and quickly found an Adam Burford who taught English at Rockland Regional High School. A few more keystrokes and I had his address.

I doubted Burford would tell a stranger much about a former student over the phone. I didn't know if the police had contacted him, but certainly the body in the clambake fire, and Cabe's name as a missing witness, had been all over the Maine media. If I wanted Mr. Burford to open up, I had talk to him in person.

I needed to ask my mother to borrow her car, which meant making up a whole new lie. I told her I had a meeting with a produce supplier and might be gone the rest of the day. She didn't question me, but I knew she'd talk to Livvie tonight and my story would be blown. I just hoped I'd have something to show for it.

Chapter 21

The drive to Rockland was a pretty one along U.S. Route 1, the road that ran 2400 miles from Key West, Florida to the Canadian border. In Maine, the road sometimes clung to the coast. In other places, it meandered through picturesque towns. But I wasn't in the mood to be charmed. I saw license plates from all over the country and felt like I was channeling Bud Barbour as I cursed the slow, uncertain, and sometimes downright lost, out-of-state drivers clogging up the two-lane road.

Finally, I came into Thomaston. The Henry Knox Museum, a 1930s replica of Knox's grand eighteenth century mansion, dominated the skyline. After that came the much less beautiful, but even more imposing Dragon Cement Company, its giant silo rising Godzilla-like on the horizon. Once I passed it, I was practically in Rockland.

I'd always loved Rockland, its Main Street lined with galleries and restaurants, the fantastic Farnsworth Museum with its huge collection of Wyeths. I found the address I was looking for, not that far from Main Street. I parked across the street and sat in my car, figuring out what to say to this man, the only person Cabe Stone felt he could count on as a reference. Of course, there was a good chance the man wouldn't be home. Most teachers had summer jobs. There was no way to know until I tried.

Despite the pleasant temperature, the sun began to heat up the car. With the comforting thought that probably no one would answer the bell, I heaved myself from the seat.

"Hello?" A man not much older than me opened the door. He was handsome, blond, and sunburned, dressed in khaki shorts and a yellow polo shirt. "Can I help you?"

I still hadn't figured out how to ease into the reason for my visit. "Hi. I'm Julia Snowden, Cabe Stone's current employer. He gave you as a reference on his job application. I wondered if we could talk."

The man stood silently, processing what I'd said. I felt a momentary panic. I hadn't even let the poor guy tell me his name. Maybe he wasn't the right person.

He must have decided I was harmless and offered his hand. "Adam Burford." We shook. "There's a picnic table around back. My daughter's down for her nap. Let me grab the baby monitor and I'll come out."

I sat at the table in the backyard. The lawn was lush, but needed mowing. A wild profusion of hedges holding the deepest, bluest hydrangeas I'd ever seen surrounded the yard.

Adam came out the back door, baby monitor in hand. "I think we have a few minutes."

"Thanks for seeing me."

"I feel terrible about Cabe. I can't believe what I've read in the papers."

"He's only wanted as a witness," I said, pushing Binder and Flynn's deeper interest in Cabe to the back of my mind. "Do you know where Cabe is?"

"No," Adam answered without hesitating.

I believed him. He had an honest face and a straightforward manner. "Do you have any ideas? Any places he used to hang out when he was in high school?"

Adam shook his head. "Cabe was a good kid. I taught him senior English. He was miles behind when he started school in September. He'd missed a ton of school. But he had drive, you know? He wanted to do better, and given half a chance, he did. He and I spent hours going over his papers. When I first handed them back, there was so much red ink, it looked like someone had been murdered." Adam paused, realizing what he'd said. "Sorry. But Cabe would rework each paper, and rework it, until it was an honest B, occasionally even an A. The kid was dogged."

"You said he started in September of his senior year. Is that because he'd just moved to the area?" Missing tons of school jibed with Dr. Crane's description of Aaron, but his drive did not. Unless being on his own had caused Cabe to grow up fast.

"Sort of. Cabe lived at Moore House, a group home for troubled kids. Mental trouble, trouble with the law. Some of the kids go to the high school. Others aren't capable of functioning in a public school."

This was new information. How would a runaway from New Jersey end up in a group home in Maine?

"I never felt like Cabe belonged at Moore House," Burford added.

"He wasn't violent?"

"The opposite. Sometimes kids from Moore House got taunted by other kids at school. Cabe went out of his way to avoid confrontations." The sounds of a toddler waking came through the baby monitor. "We've got about two minutes," Adam said, "before she blows."

"Is this Moore House in town?"

"Yes, pretty near the high school." He gave me an address. The baby fussed noisily at the other end of the monitor. "I've got to go."

"Just one more thing. Did Cabe ever say anything about his family?"

Adam climbed out from behind the picnic table bench. "Not a thing. But he wrote about families constantly in his essays and book reports. As Cabe saw it, loss of family was the theme of almost every book the class read and he wrote eloquently about it. I assumed a stable family life was a fantasy for him. I tried to get him to open up about his situation, but he never confided in me. Eventually, I stopped asking. I didn't want to risk the relationship we had."

The baby began to wail. I thanked Adam as he jogged toward his back door.

* * *

It didn't take me long to find Moore House. As I drove Mom's Buick the few blocks to the address, I processed what I'd learned. Cabe was a spottily educated boy, obsessed with loss of family. That fit with Aaron Crane, whose biological father had gone to prison and disappeared from his life, and whose mother was a suicide.

The hardworking kid Burford described, who strove to be better, was the Cabe I knew. He seemed far removed from the troubled kid who'd left New Jersey. What had transformed him?

I was making progress. Adam Burford had led me to Moore House. Perhaps someone there could lead me to Cabe.

Though in a residential neighborhood, Moore House had a distinctly institutional feel. The newish structure looked more like a small professional building than like the older homes that lined the rest of the street. I parked and got out, more confident about taking the direct approach. After all, it had worked with Adam Burford.

A young woman came to the door. For a moment, I couldn't tell if she was an administrator or a resident. "I'm Julia Snowden, looking for the person in charge."

"That'd be me. Emily Draper."

"Oh. I want to talk to you about a former resident here. Cabe Stone."

She looked me up and down, gray eyes narrowing.

Her curly brown hair was cropped short and she wore a casual white T-shirt and a nondescript pair of khaki shorts. "The cops have already been here. Three days ago."

"I'm Cabe's current boss. I want to help him."

"C'mon in."

She led the way to the kitchen at the back of the house. It was an odd mix of institution—professional refrigerator and stove—and dorm room, piled up cases of soda and snacks. She sat at the room's center table and gestured for me to do the same.

"It's awfully quiet here," I said.

"Most of the kids are working. The ones who work nights are probably at the beach."

"How many do you have?"

"A dozen at a time, or so. It fluctuates."

"Adam Burford, Cabe's teacher, told me he didn't think Cabe belonged here."

"The kids who live here can't live at home. They have a whole list of problems, including dysfunctional relationships with any parent or relative they may have. They may have been in an institution—mental hospital, rehabilitation center, jail—but, however bad things might have been for them, they're on the upside. They don't come here until they're on a path to getting better and eventually, to being able to live independently. But most of the kids here are also fragile. Cabe wasn't. He was self-possessed, optimistic."

All things I'd seen in Cabe. "How did he end up here?"

She took so long to respond, I wondered if she

was going to. Clearly, she was struggling, though I couldn't tell if it was something about me, something about Cabe, or some bureaucratic confidentiality restriction that stopped her. "You say you want to help Cabe?"

So it was me. "Yes. As I said, he works for me. And I owe him. He saved my life." She arched an eyebrow at that, but waited for me to go on. "I don't know Cabe all that well, but he doesn't seem like he could kill someone."

Emily stared at the chipped Formica tabletop. "But that's the point. He's already been accused of murder once. His foster father."

Chapter 22

My stomach flipped as if I was on a roller coaster. Binder and Flynn weren't looking for Cabe because he was Stevie's son. They'd fixed on him because he'd been accused of murder before. All my assumptions drained away, leaving me feeling weak, like after an adrenalin surge.

Emily looked up and saw my shocked expression. "What happened?" I finally managed to ask.

"Cabe was adopted as an infant. By all accounts, a good placement with Lilia and Dave Stone. They were older, childless, but up to the task of raising an energetic little boy. Dave was a commercial fisherman, quite skilled. They moved around for his job, but always on the Maine coast. It was a good life."

"How did Cabe wind up in foster care?"

"When Cabe was twelve, Lilia and Dave died within six months of one another. She of breast cancer. Everyone expected Dave would outlive her and end up as a single parent to Cabe. But while Lilia was in hospice, Dave had a fatal heart attack.

There was no one to take Cabe. His parents had been pretty much on their own, which was one of the reasons their adopted child had been such a gift."

Emily gave me a minute to absorb what she'd said. I couldn't imagine young Cabe, a child from a loving home, losing both parents at twelve. My dad had died five years ago, when I was already an adult, yet it was still a staggering loss.

"That's when Cabe went into the foster system. He passed through three foster families in the next year, disruptions that were bad luck and circumstance, nothing to do with him. But by that point the weight of his losses must have been enormous. Then he landed at the Jensens' in Bangor.

"It wasn't pretty. Mrs. Jensen was timid, her husband was a bully—toward her, their biological kids, and the foster kids. He was a yeller. Cabe was a pretty hard-edged thirteen-year-old by then. He wasn't going to put up with anything. He was skinny, but tough as nails. Verbally, he gave it to Jensen as good as he got. It must have been a shock to that big man to have the boy yelling back at him. So he went further with Cabe. He punched him, knocked him flat on his back."

Emily hadn't offered me anything to eat or drink, but I wished she had, so we could take a sip or a bite and break up the relentless flow of her words. I sensed where this story was going. My stomach clenched into a ball.

"Cabe was the first one home after school the day after Jensen hit him. Mrs. Jensen was off somewhere with the younger kids and the older ones had stuff going on after school. Cabe called 911 and calmly reported he'd found Mr. Jensen stabbed to death on the couch in the family room. When the police got there, Cabe had blood on him and George Jensen had a big kitchen knife sticking out of his chest. Cabe claimed he'd found Jensen that way. The blood on his clothes was from checking to see if he was alive. There were no signs of forced entry.

"Cabe was a suspect immediately. It was spring, the windows were open and the neighbors had heard the fight. He was taken in for questioning, given a public defender, and a guardian *ad litem*. He was completely alone in the world."

I sat, thinking about the young man I knew. The young man Emily had just described as self-possessed and optimistic. How did that person arise from this scenario?

"There'd been no incidents in the home," Emily continued. "No police visits, no problems discovered by child welfare, but older kids, adults who'd been in the home before, came forward and told the cops there was bullying to the point of abuse."

"It's nice that those older kids came to Cabe's defense."

"That's not the way the cops saw it. To them, confirmation of Jensen's cruelty gave Cabe motive." She looked at me to make sure I understood. "But the case unraveled before it could begin. Cabe was never formally charged. The state's own blood spatter expert's opinion was that Cabe's explanation for the blood on him was probable and the killer was likely a larger individual."

"How do you know all this?" I asked.

"The bare bones of it was in Cabe's file when he came here. Bit by bit, he told me the rest. And then I checked it out independently. I need to know who's living here. Mrs. Jensen told the cops her husband had a gambling problem and owed money to some bad people."

Emily noticed my quizzical look and said, "I know. Stabbing seems like a messy and unprofessional way to settle gambling debts. But it was enough. There just wasn't the evidence to put together a case against Cabe."

"Was Mr. Jensen's murder ever solved?"

"Never," Emily answered. "Not to this day."

"How many times was Jensen stabbed?" The state police hadn't, as far as I knew, released the cause of Stevie's death.

"I used to know, but I can't remember exactly," Emily said. "Lots though. More than a dozen."

The same MO as Stevie's death. "And after his foster father's murder, where did Cabe go?"

"Obviously, he wasn't going to another foster family. Ironically, he ended up at the same juvenile mental health facility where he would have been sent if he'd been arrested, tried, and found not guilty by reason of insanity, although in a different wing. He hated the place. He ran away repeatedly and stayed on the streets of Portland for months at a time. But he was always found and returned. When he was seventeen, they sent him here."

"He spoke to you about—all of it? What happened?

His feelings?" It was hard to imagine the reticent young man I knew talking about his feelings.

"We talked all the time. He seemed to understand the challenges of my job and he supported my work with the other kids. Honestly, he was a godsend. He told me seeing the kids in that place, the facility where he was sent, hearing the stories of the lives they'd lived, made him grateful for the life he'd had with the Stones. He decided to focus on what he'd been given, rather than on what he'd lost."

"Why did he leave here?" I asked.

"He graduated from high school and aged out of the system. I can't have people here once they're legal adults."

How would I have felt at eighteen if I'd been cast out into the world without family or support? I was relieved Cabe couldn't be Stevie's son. He'd been known to the Maine child welfare and justice systems for years. The horror of his life, the repeated losses, and the nature of the crime he'd been suspected of—a stabbing, just like Stevie's—must be what Binder and Flynn knew and why they laser-focused on Cabe.

"Where did Cabe go when he left here?"

"I don't know. If you're his boss, you know more about where he ended up than I do. Last summer he worked in Columbia Falls up in Washington County in the blueberry camps. You know, with the Mi'kmaq Indians who come down from Canada to pick the crop? I heard from him a few times while he was there. After that, I lost track. It's not like he had a laptop or a cell phone for keeping in touch."

"Did you tell the police what you've told me—including the part about the blueberry camp?"

"They asked if I knew where he was now. I answered honestly, I did not." So Emily, too, was reluctant to give the police more information than she had to about Cabe.

"Do you think he'd go back to the blueberry camp?"

Emily gave me a hard stare, assessing. "You really want to help him, don't you?"

"I do." I held her gaze.

"Yes, I think he might go back. He seemed at home there. Happy. And if you're his boss, you know he's not afraid of hard work."

"Is there anything else you think might help me? Any place Cabe might go? Anything he planned to do?"

She looked down at the table and said in a low voice. "He told me he wanted to find his birth parents."

Chapter 23

Outside Moore House, I started my car and opened the windows. The sun had heated the car to oven temperatures. I sat for a moment and thought about what to do. On the one hand, it was at least a two and a half hour ride north and east from Rockland to Columbia Falls. On the other, I was part way there, I had a car, and I didn't know when I could steal another day off. If there was any chance Cabe was at the blueberry camp, I had to find out. I drove north and east on U.S. 1.

Being alone in the car, a rarity between family and work, gave me plenty of time to think, and my thoughts were much darker than the shimmering summer day outside. I'd thought Lieutenant Binder had made me an unofficial part of his team after I'd proved to him I could solve a murder last spring. I'd been sure all Sergeant Flynn's glowering and harrumphing was because he objected to Binder taking me into his confidence.

But clearly, Binder had been playing me. Telling

me things he wanted me to know. Using me to find out stuff, but keeping an awful lot from me. He must know about the previous murder that had touched Cabe's life. That seemed like a pretty big thing for him to leave out of our conversations accidentally. The more I thought about it, the madder it made me.

Anger kept my right foot pressed down on the gas pedal, though my mother's old car didn't have much of its original power. Within the hour, I'd passed the stately homes of Rockport and Camden, and sailed over the beautiful Penobscot Narrows Bridge, which looked like twin schooners racing over the river hundreds of feet below. I stopped at the Dunkin Donuts in Bucksport to use the restroom and buy coffee, but didn't think to eat. I fidgeted as I waited in the line to pay. I needed to press on.

I roared into Washington County, called "Sunrise County" because it's the first place the sun hits the continental United States. On my right, tantalizing views of the Gulf of Maine appeared and disappeared as the road twisted.

By four in the afternoon, I was starting to lose steam. Blueberry fields appeared on either side of the road. I saw farm workers off in the distance. What now? Why had I thought I could find Cabe in this vast expanse?

I saw a barn-sized geodesic dome painted bright blue. It was surrounded by dozens of round marine buoys that looked like perfectly round boulders, a round water tower, and a fence with round post toppers the size of basketballs, all of them painted

bright blue. WILD BLUEBERRY LAND the sign said. It
seemed like the place to stop.

Inside Wild Blueberry Land, my mouth began to
water. The shop was full of souvenirs—T-shirts, mugs,
pie plates, with blueberries all over everything—but
I was interested only in the goods behind the glass
counter. I didn't know what to choose—blueberry
muffins, scones, pies, cookies, smoothies, milkshakes,
ice cream.

"And they're good for you," the cheerful woman
behind the counter said. "Loaded with antioxi-
dants."

I smiled back at her. Sure, they were good for you
if they weren't surrounded by pounds of butter,
flour, and sugar, but I was way too hungry to point
this out. I finally decided on a muffin and a cup of
coffee to go with it.

"These berries are wild, right?" I asked, while she
served up my coffee and muffin.

She cocked her head. "They're not planted by the
farmers. If you clear a field around here, it will fill in
with blueberries. But the fields are rotated, harvested
one year and burned the next. Fire kills the weeds,
but not the bushes, which are mostly underground.
The part the berries grow on is only six to eight
inches high. That's why they're called low-bush blueberries. The cultivated ones are called high-bush."

I nodded to show I understood. Maine blueberries were a lot like Maine lobsters. A native resource,
not farmed, but carefully managed. I sat at one of
the high tables in the shop. It was everything I could

do not to gulp down the muffin. The sweet and tangy taste of the blueberries was delicious. I closed my eyes and focused on it, determined to savor their flavor, despite the rumblings in my stomach.

After I finished the last bite, I handed the woman a five to pay for my snack. "Can you give me directions to the Mi'kmaq camp?" I asked as she made change.

"The Mi'kmaq work Passamaquoddy land. There are five camps. The nearest one is about ten miles from here." She drew a map on a napkin.

I needed to go back the way I'd come for a few miles, then turn inland. "Great. Thanks." It was already late afternoon. I had a lot of searching to do before I headed back to Busman's Harbor.

When I left Route 1, the scenery changed. Large fields of the low-bush berries were broken up only by single rows of tall trees and the tops of boulders that occasionally broke through the topsoil. Here and there, I saw clusters of cars and trucks and pickers working. I scanned for Cabe's familiar form, but didn't see him.

Farther on, the fields were posted with huge yellow signs. I stopped the car and read PASSAMAQUODDY WILD BLUEBERRY COMPANY. NO TRESSPASSING. ACCESS BY PERMIT ONLY.

What was I doing?

The paved road turned sharply to the left and in front of me was a dirt track. Beside another yellow

NO TRESSPASSING sign was a smaller, hand-lettered sign with an arrow pointing to the camp. My car idled while my natural law-abiding, rule-following tendencies warred with my desire to find Cabe.

I'd always thought of myself as a good person. Someone who'd never lie to the cops or keep things from them. I never parked in handicapped spots. As a kid, I'd never filched so much as a pack of gum, and to this day I grew uneasy in conversations where it was assumed, "everybody did it."

The NO TRESPASSING sign freaked me out. I would never, ever have passed it to get something for myself. But I had to help Cabe. I'd come so far. What if he was just beyond that sign? The story Emily Draper had told me about Cabe's life pushed me forward. Someone should do something for that boy.

Finally, I depressed the gas pedal and pulled forward onto the dirt track, my heart pounding. I passed more fields and considered turning around several more times before the camp came into view.

A dozen or more rough wooden bunkhouses, looking like something out of the Depression, were clustered on a grassy verge. Children chased one another in the space between the houses, laughing and shrieking. Men played cards at tables on the grass. When there were more ruts than road, I steered into a space among the pickups and cars parked at the camp.

I got out of my car into the late afternoon heat. Even just a little bit inland, it was much warmer than on the coast. Was it too much to hope that I would spot Cabe in the crowd? He would stand out, for sure. Though I did see an occasional white person, and black person, and Asian person, almost everyone around me was Native American. The crowd hummed with the sounds of English, French, and another language I assumed belonged to the Mi'kmaqs.

A powerfully built, middle-aged man with a thick thatch of silver hair detached himself from a card game and came toward me. "Can I help you?"

"I'm looking for someone."

"Aren't they all?" he muttered to himself. To me he said, "What's your friend called?"

"Cabe Stone," I answered, giving the only name I had, though I doubted Cabe was using it if he was here. "He's about five foot ten, thin, dark blond hair, blue eyes. Nineteen years old."

"What do you want with this Stone?"

"He's my younger brother." The lie slipped out almost before I knew I'd formed it. The Mi'kmaq man's question gave me hope. Why ask, if my description of Cabe didn't ring any bells?

"Will this brother be happy to see you?"

"Yes. I think so. I'm sure so," I said with more confidence. Cabe had called, asking for my help.

"C'mon," the man said. "Only the younger men are still out in the fields. The rest of us have quit for the day." He headed toward a pickup truck so high off the ground, I wondered if I'd be able to climb into it. Sometimes I hated being short. But after the man opened the passenger side door, I boosted myself onto the running board, grabbed the frame of the open window, and swung myself inside. Despite a lifetime of lectures about stranger danger, I didn't hesitate, even a little bit, to get into the man's truck. He must know where Cabe was. My heart beat wildly.

"Joe Manion, by the way."

"Julia Snowden." We drove out of the camp back along the two-lane road through the blueberry barrens. In the far-off field of another farm, I spotted a hulking mechanical harvester moving slowly down a row of blueberries.

"We have a handshake agreement with the Passamaquoddy. As long as we come to pick, they won't mechanize. Mi'kmaqs have migrated from Canada to pick blueberries for as long as anyone can remember. The last few years, your Feds have given us trouble at the border. Worried we're illegal immigrants. 'You're the illegal immigrants!' I tell them." He laughed. "Though I'm sure it doesn't help matters."

We pulled to the side of the road. Large yellow plastic boxes of tiny blueberries, twigs, and leaves were piled at the edge of the field. "The trucks will be along to pick those up soon," Joe said.

Only about half a dozen people were still working, all fit, young men. "We set our own goals. Number of boxes, dollars per day. When we're done, we head back to camp. We're independent, work for ourselves, make our own rules. That's what we like about working for the Passamaquoddy. They understand our work ethic."

Picking low-bush blueberries looked like unimaginably hard work. Wielding a blueberry rake that looked like a dustpan with a comb at the end, the pickers pulled their rakes through the bushes. The tines of the comb cleaned the berries off the bushes.

Every few minutes, when the rake's scoop was full, the pickers dumped the berries into a plastic tote. Then they moved up their row.

I looked for Cabe among the bent-over figures. The sun was hot, the air still. Sweat formed along my hairline, even though I wasn't moving.

"Want to stand in the bed of the truck, see if you can spot your brother?" Joe asked.

I almost responded, "What brother?" but caught myself in time.

I climbed into the truck bed and scanned the field, searching for Cabe. Nothing. Something drew my eyes to a tall, well-built Native American man. In one fluid motion, he put down his blueberry rake and pulled a camera with an enormous lens from his bag. Pointing it in my direction, he began snapping pictures. In that moment, I was sure it was the photographer from the morning of the murder.

"Hey!" I jumped out of the bed of the pickup and ran. "Hey!"

Chapter 24

The good-looking photographer stood, smiling politely, as I made my way through the blueberry field toward him. "Walk where the berries have already been picked," he called, indicating a row marked with string.

Finally, I made it to the man's side. "I'm so glad I've found you. I'm Julia Snowden."

He shook my hand without hesitation, though he was clearly trying to place me. "Phillip Johnson. You've been looking for me?" He was in his late thirties or early forties, dressed in faded jeans and a sweat-soaked white T-shirt. The cut of his slightly long, black hair looked expensive to my Manhattan-trained eye and I couldn't begin to guess the cost of his photographic equipment. Why was a man like this doing the backbreaking work of raking blueberries?

"That depends," I responded. "Were you on the balcony of the Lighthouse Inn in Busman's Harbor last Saturday morning, taking photos of the activity on the pier for Founder's Weekend?"

"Who's asking?"

"I am. I'm trying to help a friend."

Johnson bent over to put his camera and lens back into their cases. "I think we'd better go somewhere to talk."

I nodded, relieved that he wasn't inclined to blow me off. He handed me his camera case and said, "Be careful. I have to finish my row. Once you start, you're committed." He indicated an area marked off with string.

I watched, fascinated, as he bent and dragged the big rake across the ground under the blueberry plants. "They're beautiful," I said, looking in the plastic tote at the tiny, glistening dark berries and soft green leaves.

"There are naturally fifty to a hundred varieties of blueberry plant in a field. That's why there are different colors from black to light reddish-blue or even albino. They peak for harvest at different times, as well. It's the variety in the type of berry and ripeness that packs them with so much flavor. The ones I'm picking now will go off to be cleaned and frozen tonight. Ninety per cent of them are sold frozen."

He finished his row and picked up the plastic totes containing his blueberries, depositing them at the end of the row. A hundred yards away, two men in a flat bed truck moved along the road picking up the bins.

"Give us a ride back to camp?" Johnson asked Joe Manion.

Manion nodded and the three of us crowded into

the front seat of the pickup. "How many boxes today?" Manion asked Johnson.

"Seventy-five," Johnson grunted. "Got a late start and my shoulder's been bothering me."

"Not bad," Manion allowed. The boxes were enormous, twenty or thirty pounds. I couldn't imagine filling ten of them, let alone seventy-five. I thought the work at the Snowden Family Clambake was physically challenging. I wouldn't have lasted an hour in these fields.

"How much do you get per box?" I asked.

"Two-fifty," Joe Manion answered.

I did a quick calculation. A hundred and eighty seven dollars and fifty cents. A lot of money to many of the people in the camp, by the look of them, but I wondered if it was enough to even pay for Phillip Johnson's haircut.

Back at the camp, Johnson, who asked me to call him Phil, sat me at a table in front of one of the bunkhouses and excused himself to get cleaned up. I still hadn't told him why I was there, exactly. A moment later, the screen door slammed and Phil, towel slung over his shoulder, went off in the direction of the communal shower house.

While he was gone, I watched the people in the camp. There was plenty of evidence, in bent bodies and lined faces, of hard labor and hard lives. Yet the atmosphere was lively, camp-like. It was suppertime and meals cooked on grills and propane rings. I smelled fresh vegetables, meat, and fish.

Phil returned, his black hair still damp from the shower. "Time for you to tell me what this is about."

"Did you know there was a murder that morning when you were in Busman's Harbor?"

He shook his head. "When we checked out of the hotel, all that was known was there was a body in the clambake cooker. I hadn't heard definitely it was a murder." He spread his hands, calloused and covered with small cuts, on the rough wood of the table. "We don't get much news up here."

"That clambake cooker belongs to me. I'm an owner and the manager of the Snowden Family Clambake Company."

"I'm sorry for your trouble, but how can I help?"

"Have the police contacted you?"

His expression went from mildly interested to alarmed. "No. Why would they?"

"How early in the morning did you start taking photos?"

He relaxed visibly. "I'm a photojournalist based in Montreal. I have a contract to do photos for a coffee table book on seacoast celebrations from Cape Cod to Prince Edward Island. At Founder's Weekend, I'd hoped to capture the setup and celebration on the pier—shots from early in the morning when the vendors arrived until midday when there were hundreds of people eating lobster, listening to music, and having a grand time. But the minute the ruckus about the body started, I quit taking shots. For another photographer, a discovery like that might have been a big win. But it wasn't the kind of scene I'd been hired to shoot. I'd wasted my entire trip to Busman's Harbor. Once the body was found, nothing I'd shot was useable."

"How early did you start shooting?"

"Around six-thirty. What time do they think the guy was killed?"

"They don't know. The body was in bad condition due to the fire. In any case, the victim wasn't killed on the pier. So you might have captured someone putting him in the woodpile early in the morning, but you probably don't have photos of the murder."

"Thank goodness. I'm Canadian."

I wanted to laugh at that—like Canadians were too polite to get mixed up in stateside murders—but I knew what he meant. He didn't want to be traveling back and forth to Maine for court appearances.

"I'm sorry about your business, but you haven't actually told me why you're here, or what you're looking for," he said.

"A young friend found the body that morning. He ran away. The police are searching for him as an important witness, but I'm sure they believe he's more involved. I think they mean to arrest him as soon as they find him."

"And you don't think this friend is guilty?"

"I'm sure he isn't. I can't give you a rational reason. I just don't believe he could kill someone."

"Tough break," Phil said. "I'll help you if I can." He stood, scraping the wooden chair across the grass. "I'll get those photos for you."

I was thrilled a stranger was being so kind. To me. To Cabe.

He went to his car, a silver BMW that had been drawing admiring glances from everyone who walked by it, and retrieved his laptop from the trunk. He came back and fired it up.

"Cabe is a white kid, nineteen or so, average height, slight build, dark blond hair. Have you seen him?"

Phil looked away and my heart leaped. For a moment, I thought he would say he'd seen Cabe, but then he turned back to me. "Nope. Sorry."

A teenage boy spotted the laptop and called from the street. "Hey brother, can I check my Facebook?"

"You think we have Internet out here, bro? Go spend time with your family. Unplug yourself. Best thing for you." Phil dismissed the boy with a wave. "Here are the photos from that morning."

We scrolled through the images. They did, indeed, start early in the morning, but not early enough. In the first shot, Cabe was on the pier fussing with the Claminator, but Weezer was also there with his barbecue and Dan Small had his portable ice cream stand. Stevie's body must have already been hidden in the firewood by that point.

Even uncropped and unedited, Phil's photos captured the vibrancy of that glorious morning. The public works guys came to set up the stage and chairs. The sound people came with mikes and speakers. Sonny, Livvie, and Page pulled up in our Boston Whaler and Cabe helped them unload the lobsters and steamers, fresh from the lobster pound, along with more firewood, which they piled to the side. The bakers set out their wares. The members of the high school band trickled in.

"Wait! Stop." I put my hand on Phil's arm. "Can I see that one again?"

He scrolled back to the previous image. I studied it carefully. The pier was quite full at the time it was taken—the vendors, the band, and the tourists. At the edges of the photo, I saw two things that surprised me. The first was the young man with scraggily brown hair and a full brown beard I'd almost run into at the RV park. He looked like a hermit or a recluse. It was hard to imagine Founder's Weekend was his type of deal.

The other thing I spotted was stranger still. In the lower right corner of the photo was the head and neck of a black lab wearing a bright red kerchief. Morgan? It had to be. But Morgan went wherever Bud Barbour went. And Bud was supposed to be at his camp avoiding the Founder's Weekend crowds.

"Can you e-mail this photo to me?"

"It'll be awhile before I'm anywhere where I can e-mail. I'll put it on a memory stick for you." Phil pulled a thumb drive out of his camera bag and moved a copy of the image to it. "Did you see something helpful?"

"Nothing big," I admitted. "Your photos are beautiful, though. Thanks so much for showing me."

We continued looking at the images. There was one of Sonny, face a mask of horror, pointing at the clambake fire, followed by one of the firefighters rushing toward Richelle's prone body. Then the photos stopped. Not the type of heart-warming pictures of life on the North Atlantic seacoast Phil had been hired to capture.

"Anything else you want?" he asked.

I sighed and let my shoulders slump. It was too difficult to disguise my disappointment. "These photos start too late in the morning. I hoped to see what happened before the crowds arrived."

Phil shut down the laptop. "It's a long trip back to Busman's Harbor. Let me get you something to eat."

I protested, but feebly. The cooking smells in the camp were too enticing.

Phil disappeared and came back carrying two steaming plates of food and two wedges of coarse bread. "I hope you're hungry. Dig in."

The food smelled intoxicating, huge plates of the kind of rib-sticking goodness intended for people who'd done hard, physical labor. I dug into the beans.

"My God, these are delicious. They taste something like New England baked beans."

"And who do you think invented those?" Phil smiled at me. "All the tribes in Maine, Nova Scotia, and New Brunswick cooked beans mixed with maple syrup and bear fat in clay pots buried with hot coals."

"The beans in this are bigger than I'm used to."

"Soldier beans. Now grown all over, but they're native to this region."

The bigger beans gave the dish a fuller texture. I took a forkful of the second item on the plate, ground meat mixed with celery, onions, mushrooms, and small pieces of bacon. I recognized tarragon and cinnamon in the seasoning, a distinctive combination common in French-Canadian cooking. The cultures constantly enriched one another, beans from the Native Americans, spices from the Quebecois.

I mopped up the food with a wedge of the bread Phil called lu'sknikn. Cooked at the camp in a large iron frying pan, it was crunchy on the outside, soft on the inside. The closest thing I could relate it to was Irish soda bread. "Who made this?"

"My mom." Phil gestured over his shoulder toward a short, sinewy woman with long gray hair, still cooking over a propane gas ring. She spotted me looking and waved.

"She is dying to know who you are." Phil laughed.

I laughed, too. We ate in silence for a few moments. Then Phil looked up and caught me staring at him.

"You're wondering why I'm here, raking blueberries."

Had I been that transparent? Here was a successful photojournalist, the kind who got contracts for high-end coffee table books, bending, lifting, and sweating as he raked blueberries. Surely he didn't need the work.

"I come because my parents came, and their parents and their parents. No one knows how long the Mi'kmaqs have come to pick blueberries in Maine. Probably since before there was a Maine." He ran a hand through his black hair. "I come to reconnect with cousins and friends, people I don't see enough of as I travel for work throughout the year. I spend two weeks unplugged from the Internet and away from my job and the stress of living in a world where I look different. Here I look the same as everyone." He caught my skeptical look. "Well, maybe a little better off."

And taller and handsomer. But I left those thoughts unsaid. "I get why you come, but why do you rake berries?"

"Partly out of pride, to prove that at forty, I can still rake like a young man. But mostly because I want to be part of all this, a participant. I don't want to stand on the outside and observe. That's what I do for my job. Here I belong."

"You weren't away from the job. You were taking photos when I spotted you."

"That's another thing. Being in camp takes me back to when my photography was a hobby, not a job. No one's paying me to take pictures of the people in the camps. I've been doing it since I was a boy."

When we finished, Phil excused himself to return the plates to his mom. I stood to go.

Phil walked me to my car. "You really think this kid is innocent?"

"I really do."

Phil hesitated, clearly considering. Finally he said, "The images on my laptop aren't all there are. I'd hoped to do a video of time-lapse photographs to promote the book on the publishers' website. Sort of a 'day in the life.' I had a stationery camera set up on the balcony taking photos all night. You know, moonrise, sunrise, the town wakes up and gets ready for its big party."

"That's fantastic!" I couldn't believe the luck. "Can I see those photos?"

"I sent them home with my editor."

His editor? The woman whose room he'd stayed in at the Lighthouse Inn? "Can you get them?"

He considered. "Maybe. If I can get word to her. She's coming to visit. But there are over ten thousand images. If you don't know what time the crime occurred, it would be like looking for a needle in a haystack."

"That's okay. I'll figure it out." I didn't know how, but I'd cross that bridge when I came to it.

"All right. I'll find a way to contact you if I'm able to get my hands on those pictures."

I gave him my cell number and thanked him. By the time I got in Mom's car, big drops of rain splattered the windshield. The weather Sonny had warned me about had arrived.

Chapter 25

It was a three and a half hour drive from the Mi'kmaq camp back to Busman's Harbor. Most people, used to the tiny, crowded states of the Northeastern U.S., didn't realize how big Maine was. It took the same amount of time to travel from Portland, Maine to New York City as it did to travel from Portland to the Canadian border. I was spending the better part of my evening driving across a relatively small part of Maine.

The rain, which escalated occasionally to a downpour, and the fog, which crept in on the stretches where the road hugged the sea, had me sitting straight up in my seat, concentrating on my driving. Radio reception was so spotty, I stopped trying, and my mother's old car offered no way to amplify the tunes stored on my phone. I rode along in the silent car, alone with my thoughts.

I sorted through the jumble in my head. What had I accomplished by playing hooky? More important, was I any closer to my goal of helping Cabe?

Both the teacher Adam Burford, and the group home manager Emily Draper had confirmed my strong impression of Cabe. He was an honest, generally positive kid. He might seem a little closed off, but there were reasons for it. Now that I knew his background—the repeated losses, the false accusation, and the time spent in an institution—I was even more impressed by the strength of his character. Adam and Emily could tell a jury what a great kid Cabe was, but I didn't want it to come to that. Given what Cabe had been through, it was important he never spend a single night in jail.

My mind drifted to Binder and Flynn. I was keeping four things from them—Cabe's employment application, his phone call, the existence of the image on the thumb drive Phil Johnson had given me, and the possibility of more useful photos Phil had sent with his editor to Montreal. Maybe I should give the information to Binder. I wrestled with the dilemma as I drove along. It was my natural instinct to turn it over. But, I was mad. Binder had led me to believe I was part of the team and used me to get information, while keeping me in the dark about what he knew. Maybe Flynn's disgruntled attitude was part of the act, too. No, that was real. The man just didn't like me.

I'd gone to the Mi'kmaq camp to find Cabe, and instead had found the photographer, Phil Johnson. Coincidence? Phil claimed he'd never seen anyone meeting Cabe's description. But he'd looked away from me when he said it. Could I trust him? Perhaps

Cabe was at another camp. The woman at Wild Blueberry Land had said there were five.

What had I learned from the photo Phil had put on the thumb drive? Two things, admittedly neither of them big. The hairy kid had been on the pier in the morning before the body was found. That could be completely meaningless—there'd been at least a hundred people on the pier by the time the shot was taken. And Bud Barbour had been there, too, or at least, Morgan was. Bud was supposed to have been at his camp up north, avoiding the Founder's Weekend crowds. He'd sworn to us all he wouldn't be on the pier for the opening ceremonies.

As I drove on through the rain, I thought about Bud.

May

The day before the third Founder's Weekend committee meeting, I went to Gus's in the late afternoon. There weren't many customers at that time of day and Gus was known to be more expansive. I scraped the mud off my boots before I walked down the stairs to the restaurant. In New York it was springtime, with lunches outside and beautiful, flowering shrubs in Central Park. In Maine it was cold and wet. The day and a half we'd later remember as "spring," was a month away.

I sat down at the counter. Bud Barbour dawdled at the other end. Morgan lay quietly at his feet, red bandanna around her neck as always. Gus had all kinds of rules, including, "No Animals," though he, like everyone else, made an exception for Bud's black lab.

I tried to out wait Bud and Morgan, but finally gave up. "I hear you're the expert in the history of our peninsula," I said to Gus.

"Ayup." Gus didn't go in for false modesty. He was more about accuracy.

"Can you tell me," I asked, desperately hoping for a shortcut, "who the founder of Busman's Harbor was?"

Gus waggled his a bushy white eyebrows at me. "Which time?"

"Which time what?"

"The first founder of Busman's Harbor was a Wabanaki Chief. The Wabanaki tribes called this land Ketakamigwa, 'the big land on the seacoast.' They came here seasonally and farmed, fished, lobstered, and traded with other tribes, and eventually with the French."

"And their village was right where the town is?"

"Probably not," Gus conceded. "The steep, protectable harbor wasn't needed by people who didn't have enemies. They would've wanted a sheltered beach for drying fish and clamming. Archeologists think their longest seasonal settlement was where Camp Glooscap is."

I wondered if Stevie knew that. "And this founding chief's name wasn't, by any chance, Mr. Busman?"

"Alas, his name's been lost to the misty dawns of time."

Gus poured me a cup of coffee I was sure had been sitting on the burner for hours. I didn't want it, but I didn't protest. Another of his rules was you couldn't come to Gus's just to sit and yak. You had to buy.

"The first European settlers," Gus continued, warming to his subject, "were fishermen. In those days, for cod to be sent home to England, it had to be dried on wooden racks. There was fierce competition among the fishing crews for the best areas for drying operations, and it didn't take long for captains to figure out that if they left a small group of men over the winter, they'd have a huge advantage come the spring."

"When was this?"

"1615."

"Before the Pilgrims?"

"Definitely. Those Massachusetts-come-latelies are always claiming the credit."

"Massholes," Bud interjected. It was the first time he'd looked up from his coffee cup.

"These fishermen, was one of them was named Busman?" I asked, not particularly hopeful.

Gus laughed. "Not too many auto-buses in the early seventeenth century."

"Maybe he was French? *Bisou* man? Perhaps a bit of a kisser? I'm sure it got lonely staying all winter."

"Ha-ha," Gus said. "By the way your French is terrible."

"Well, do you know his name?"

"Nope," Gus answered. "But that doesn't mean he shouldn't be recognized as our founder. Imagine how lonely and cold it was in that fishing station.

How long the days were, and how heavily time weighed. The nameless people do all the hard work."

"Ayup. You tell it, brother," Bud called from the end of the counter. He got up and moved to the stool next to mine to join the conversation.

"The first permanent settler arrived in 1642. Like most Maine settlers, our founder wanted nothing more than to be left alone with his family and servants to farm and fish. Of course, that made the Puritans to the south deeply suspicious and set up years of conflict between them, especially after Maine became a colony of Massachusetts."

"Massholes," I said before Bud could, just to vex him. He gave me a gap-toothed smile through his Santa Claus beard. "I suppose it's too much to hope that this man was named Busman?" I asked Gus.

Gus shook his head. "His name was Town. Edward Town. He named the settlement after himself."

"He named the town, 'Town'?"

"Of course not." Gus laughed. "He named it Town's End. But without a doubt, he was our founder. Just like the anonymous cod fisherman and the Wabanaki chief."

"Message received." I didn't want to think about how Bunnie would react to the idea of multiple founders, not one of them named Busman. "Keep going," I said, hoping we'd eventually get to the answer.

Gus then did something I'd never seen. He came around the counter and sat on the stool to my left. He never mingled with the customers.

"Edward Town's descendants lived on the land for three generations, but eventually they were burned out by the natives. After nearly fifty years of Indian wars, there were no Europeans left permanently settled on the mid-coast. England tried to reclaim the land from Massachusetts, saying Maine was no longer a colony because it wasn't colonized. To repopulate, the English sent the toughest, fiercest, most independent people they could think of—the descendants of the Scots that England had used to colonize Northern Ireland. They were as different from the wealthy Massachusettsans, who thought they held title to the land, as they could be. The Massachusetts proprietors thought of the settlers as tenant farmers who owed rent. The settlers thought of themselves as free farmers who owned their own land. They quickly learned to distrust anyone From Away who came calling."

On my right, Bud grunted, making it clear he still held that sentiment.

Great. My father's forbearers were practically genetically wired to hate my mother's ancestors. *No wonder I'm a mess.*

"And the Scots-Irishman who settled this harbor, was his name Mr. Busman?" I asked.

Gus looked at his watch. "Will you look at the time? Mrs. Gus will be wondering what happened to me. Time to close up. I'll tell you about Busman the next time."

"Gus, you are killing me." But I knew better than to argue.

When I admitted my failure the next day at the at the Founder's Weekend committee meeting, Bunnie's brows knitted together so tightly I feared they'd form a vortex and swallow her whole face.

She tap-tap-tapped on the ever-present clipboard with her pencil. "Well, that doesn't really help us, does it?" she concluded. "Why don't you come to my house for tea some afternoon this week, Julia, and we'll talk about it?"

Another invitation I'd have to figure out how to avoid.

But everything else was going swimmingly. Bunnie had made some "important connections" with the Busman's Harbor Art League and our art show was going to be juried. I suspected making "important connections" was as difficult as walking into the Art League gallery on Main Street and introducing herself, but everyone seemed excited, so I kept my opinion to myself.

There was a discussion about whether crafters could have tents at the art show or just artists, which lead to a discussion about "What is art?" Mercifully, Bud cut this short by miming slitting his throat, falling off his chair, and twitching on the floor of the Tourism Bureau office as he fake bled-out.

At least I didn't totally disgrace myself. Dan and I had done a good job of lining up the meals. We were just waiting for permits so there could be food trucks at the concert.

Stevie had taken on the job of finding the band with his usual enthusiasm. It was late in the season to be booking, but he'd collected a few dozen demo CDs. He wanted some of us to go on a series of outings to hear the finalists. Vee and Bunnie had agreed to go with him.

"Come along, Julia," Stevie said. "It'll be fun."

I worried about what kind of music that group might choose, but the Snowden Family Clambake Company was set to open in less than a month and we still had so much to accomplish. I threw Dan a look. I was fifteen years younger than he was, but he was almost fifteen years younger than the others.

"I'll go along to hear the bands," Dan said, receiving my silent message.

"Great!" Stevie boomed. "We're going to have a blast."

Chapter 26

August

It was after ten-thirty when I got back from the blueberry camp to Busman's Harbor. Chris was working his bouncer job at Crowley's, and ordinarily I would've gone there automatically. But I hesitated, worried about what Chris had said in the early hours of the morning. *I love you.* A long day had gone by with no communication between us. If I did go, would it be awkward? Or worse, if I stayed away, would he take my absence as rejection, or at a minimum as a freak-out? Maybe it was.

My back was stiff from the hours in the car, plus Chris and I hadn't spent much time sleeping the night before. The stress and the sleeplessness and the driving caught up to me. I stood for a moment outside the car, undecided. Then I thought about Chris, his handsome face, his lips, and last night. I pulled my mother's umbrella from the backseat of her car and headed to Crowley's.

Chris wasn't in his usual spot at the door. I asked the burley substitute bouncer where he was.

"Dunno. Got called in last minute. I'm missing my girlfriend's birthday party." He didn't seem happy about it. He handed my ID back to me and I passed through the front door. The bar was crowded and noisy, as I'd expected. Tonight's band seemed particularly raucous.

"Where's Chris?" I shouted to Sam, part owner and bartender.

Sam said the same thing the guy at the door had. "Dunno." Then he added, "You know Chris. Thinks he's Australian. Goes on walkabout. No notice, nothin'. I'd fire his ass if he wasn't so good." Sam handed me a draft. "I thought for sure you'd know where he goes. It's different with you, different from all the old girlfriends."

My cheeks went red, though I couldn't have said for sure which I was more embarrassed about. That I didn't know where Chris was, or the reference to "all the old girlfriends."

I took the beer and looked around for an empty table. I didn't want to sit with the significant others of the staff members, where I'd have to field more questions about Chris's whereabouts. I saw someone waving frantically from a corner table. Reggie Swinburne sat with a man whose back was to me. I waved back, hoping that would be enough, but he countered with the universal gesture for *come over here*. I crossed the room toward them.

Reggie jumped to his feet and pumped my hand. "Julia." His Colonel Mustard mustache danced as he spoke. "Join us. This is my young friend, Zach. Zach, meet Julia Snowden."

Zach's eyes widened at the mention of my last name, but caught himself and resumed his pleasant expression. A lot of people reacted to hearing the name Snowden. They knew the clambake company, or they knew my family. Or they'd heard about the murder this spring on Morrow Island. Or maybe, lately, they'd heard about the Snowden Family Clambake's connection to Stevie Noyes's body.

Reggie had a half-full mug of beer in front of him. Zach, confirming my impression he was under twenty-one, had a soft drink. The band thanked everyone and took a break. It was still noisy, but at least we didn't have to scream.

"I've been teaching Zach here the joys of bird-watching," Reggie said.

Zach was a good-looking kid, square-jawed with dark hair, deep brown eyes and long, dark lashes. Even sitting, I could tell he was short and slight. There was something so familiar about him. Especially around the eyes.

"Bunnie's not with you?" I asked.

"Not her kind of scene," Reggie said.

I wasn't surprised.

"Those Parkers came back," he continued. "Such a racket over there, with the music and the parties and the revving of the motorcycles. I persuaded Zach here to come along for a drink to get away from it all."

It was hard to believe Crowley's on a rainy August night was any quieter.

"If it keeps up, I've a mind to call the cops," Reggie continued. "Stevie wanted those Parkers out. Maybe they or some of their motorcycle cronies had something to do with his murder."

Zach looked alarmed at this idea. I couldn't say I blamed him.

Reggie called out, "There's a cop now!" He waved in the direction of my childhood friend, Jamie Dawes, familiar from his many traffic details around town.

Jamie waved back, but didn't come in our direction, thank goodness. Zach excused himself and went to the men's room. I finished my beer, said good-bye to Reggie and headed for the door.

"Julia." Jamie came up beside me. "Join me for a beer?"

It was absolutely the last thing I wanted to do. For one thing, he was a cop and I still had Cabe's employment application and the thumb drive Phil Johnson had given me. For another, my sister believed Jamie had a crush on me, but I had chosen Chris, and Chris was, at this moment, I-had-no-idea-where. Things had been awkward between Jamie and me for a couple months, since we'd sort of accidentally, drunkenly kissed, and I felt terrible about it. I sensed graciously accepting the offer of a beer would go a long way to smoothing things over.

We sat on stools at the bar and ordered drafts, which we both sipped slowly. I asked after his parents; he asked after my mom. The band returned from its break and started up again, which made conversation difficult.

"How's the investigation going?" I shouted.

"Okay, I guess. Progress."

"Do you know where Stevie was killed yet?"

Jamie looked around and hunched toward me. I did the same, which brought us nose-to-nose. Uncomfortably close.

"Unofficially? No," he said.

"Officially?"

He grinned. "Still, no."

"Lieutenant Binder told me the body was brought to the pier by car or boat." I wanted to show I was already the recipient of inside information, so it was okay to talk to me. "Could a woman have moved the body?"

Jamie considered. "Possibly. If she came by car and pulled up real close." He sat up on his stool. "Enough shop talk. How do Livvie and Sonny like living on Morrow Island?"

I'd just started to answer when I realized who Reggie's friend Zach was—the hairy guy from the RV park. I kicked myself for not recognizing him, even without the scraggly beard and hair. I knew he looked familiar. I wanted to ask why he'd been on the pier in the morning before Stevie's body was found. When the kid looked hairy and crazy, it hadn't seemed like the kind of place he'd want to be. But now that I'd seen him looking perfectly normal in a crowded bar, that seemed like a ridiculous conclusion. I looked over at the table where they'd been, but there was a new group of people there.

Jamie and I finished our beers and I stood to go. I was glad we'd been able to chat casually about mostly inconsequential things. I hoped it would help make things more comfortable between us. I didn't suggest that he walk me home, and he didn't offer.

Chapter 27

The house was quiet when I got in. I guessed Mom and Richelle were long in bed and I was relieved. I was exhausted physically and emotionally. I climbed into bed, but knew I wouldn't sleep.

Away from the curious eyes of Jamie, Sam the bartender, and the significant others, I gave in to my emotions about Chris. I rocketed from fear to despair to fury.

Where was he?

Was he in some kind of trouble?

Had he run off because he'd told me he loved me and I'd remained silent?

How dare he disappear without a word.

Of course, I'd played hooky and driven over two hundred and seventy miles today without a word to him. Let she who is without sin . . .

I wanted to ask Chris what, for him, the saying "I love you," meant. Did it mean, "I want to spend my life with you?" Or did it mean, "It's been great. See you later!" Maybe he said it to all the women who climbed out of his bed before sunup. Though I'd done that before, and this was the first time he'd said it. What if he really meant it? What if he'd told me he loved me and I'd run away?

I wasn't naive about the rumors about Chris. He'd been a bad boy in high school and some people around town claimed he was a bad man still. In the spring, there'd been rumors he'd supplied drugs to a friend of Livvie's. She'd made a plea deal with the state and supposedly given them evidence, but nothing had come of it, so I didn't give any credence to the rumors. Nasty, small-town gossip.

More important to me, though, in our time together, I'd never seen a single indication Chris wasn't what he appeared to be. An honest citizen, a small businessman, a warm and caring man.

Focusing on these thoughts, I calmed myself and drifted off to sleep.

I didn't miss the next call when it came in the middle of the night. I shot up out of a deep slumber on the first ring of my cell phone. The display showed the time as 3:07, the number as BLOCKED.

"Julia?"

"Cabe! Oh God, Cabe. Where are you?"

"I'm safe. I'm fine. For now."

"Tell me where you are. I'll come and get you. I'll go with you to the police station. I'll get you the best criminal lawyer in Maine. You're only wanted as a witness."

"But they think I did it, don't they?"

I didn't respond. Lieutenant Binder had boxes and boxes of evidence in his office attesting to how many people had reasons to hate Stevie, yet even in the face of all that, Binder continued to focus on Cabe.

"I can't go to jail, even for one day. I know you won't understand, but I just can't." He sounded so young.

"Cabe, I know about the last murder you were accused of."

"I didn't do that, either! I wasn't even indicted."

"I know. What I am trying to say is, I know why you don't want to spend any time in jail. I understand. I want to help."

There were muffled sounds from the other end of the phone. Cabe was sobbing. It broke my heart. I had to do something for this poor kid. "Tell me what happened that night, Cabe. I'm trying to help you, but I don't know what I'm looking for."

I waited. Finally, he spoke, his voice steadier. "Sonny and I came on the Whaler from Morrow Island after the clambake dinner on Friday night. We set up the Claminator on the pier and unloaded the wood for the fire. Sonny went back to the island to sleep. He was going to come back in the morning with Livvie and Page, the food, and another load of wood."

"What time did Sonny leave?"

"Around one in the morning."

This all jibed with what Sonny had said. "Then what happened?"

"As soon as Sonny left, I piled the wood under the

Claminator. I was in a hurry to get the fire laid. I knew it would be much harder in the morning when the pier was crawling with people."

"Was there anyone else around? Did you see anyone?"

"No, it was quiet. The other vendors had set up their rigs to some degree like we had, but they were gone for the night. There were a few people out on their balconies at the Lighthouse Inn, sitting out talking or having a smoke. I didn't pay too much attention. "

"What did you do after you put the logs under the Claminator?"

Only the sound of his breathing traveled through the night air.

"Cabe?"

"I went to the boarding house where I used to live and slept for a few hours." He exhaled. "Please don't tell Sonny."

The kid was probably facing a murder charge, yet he was afraid Sonny would be mad. I didn't want to scare him off. "Of course not," I assured him, like the two of us were talking casually, no consequences. "What time did you leave the pier?"

"Around two, I guess. I was back by five-thirty." He paused. "Julia, I am so sorry. This never would have happened if I'd stayed with the Claminator like Sonny asked me to. No one could have left a body there."

Or Cabe could have been surprised by a killer and perhaps been another victim. "Did you know it was a man named Stevie Noyes in the fire?" Would

Cabe ever have met Stevie? I tried to think where and when.

"Yes. It was on the news today."

"Did anyone see you at the boarding house?" Since the police didn't know exactly when Stevie had been killed or when he'd been put in the woodpile, an alibi would be only partially helpful to Cabe, but it seemed better than the nothing he had now.

"I don't think so."

"Give me the address." As soon as Cabe told me where it was, I knew the place.

"I'm sorry," he repeated.

"Sonny shouldn't have asked you to stay on the pier all night. It was wrong. Of course you had to sleep." He was silent. I tried again. "Tell me where you are. I'll come."

"Sorry, Julia." He was gone.

Chapter 28

I awoke the next morning straight out of a vivid dream. I'd chased Cabe across a rain-drenched blueberry field. The low bushes ensnared my boots and every time I got close to him, he disappeared, only to pop up far across the field. I'd chase him again, shouting his name, which he didn't seem to hear, and the whole cycle would repeat. I was seething with frustration when I swung my feet onto the wooden floor and climbed out of bed.

Wind-driven rain hammered my bedroom windows. Outside, the harbor was shrouded and hushed.

I went down the hall from my bedroom to my office. The foghorn bleated from Dinkums Light, clearly audible through the closed windows. Sonny and I held a brief consultation over the radio and decided to cancel the lunchtime clambake. The marine forecast was terrible. He'd been on the radio since dawn, and most of the working boats in the harbor weren't going out. With our covered pavilion, we could run the clambake in almost any weather, but guests who came for lunch wouldn't leave with happy memories.

Sonny was optimistic the weather would clear up in time for dinner service. I let the staff know we'd be closed for lunch and asked Pammie to persuade the lunchtime ticket holders to switch their reservations to dinner.

I never thought I'd be grateful for a storm in August, but I was. Half a day off would give me more time to help Cabe. Thank goodness it was Wednesday, our second slowest day of the week. The financial hit, while meaningful, would be modest. I showered and dressed, then took the backstairs to the kitchen.

Richelle was already up, fully dressed and staring out the window at the rain. "I'm so bored, Julia! I'm going stir crazy. Please, come out to breakfast with me."

"It's miserable out there."

"I don't care. I'm miserable in here." She caught herself. "Not that I don't appreciate . . ."

"You're not supposed to travel." I couldn't help but feel sorry for her. She was used to being on the go, waking up most mornings in a new location. She'd been basically confined to our house for three days.

"There must be plenty of places to eat within walking distance."

Of course, there were. I looked at the clock on the stove. "Okay, let's do it. But we have to be quick."

Richelle jumped up and grabbed her bag. "Quick it is."

I found an old slicker of Livvie's hanging on a peg in the kitchen entrance way and handed it to Richelle. Nothing of my mom's or mine would have covered her long arms. We trudged over the hill to Gus's, sometimes walking backward to keep the stinging rain, with its briny, sea-smell, off our faces. The howling wind made conversation impossible.

Gus's was a mob scene of fishermen and lobstermen and half the public works department, all temporarily sidelined by the storm. Slickers were draped on every chair.

I dreaded bringing a stranger into Gus's. He practically required a pedigree and a certificate of good health and sanity from a doctor. I looked in vain for a table in the back of the dining room, finally deciding we had to grab the last two seats at the counter. Let the third degree begin.

Gus advanced to fill our coffee cups. "Morning, Julia."

"Morning, Gus. This is—"

"You don't need to tell me who this pretty woman is. I'd know her anywhere. She's Georgette Baker's niece."

Richelle seemed as stunned as I was. "I can't believe you remember me!"

"'Course I remember you," Gus said, pouring her a generous cup. "You stayed here one whole summer. With your aunt."

"Great-aunt," Richelle corrected. Still, it was astonishing. Richelle had been a child.

"Gus Farnham." He reached across and shook her hand. "Glad to have you back in town."

"Richelle Rose."

Gus shook his head. "No, that's not it." It was typical of Gus to insist he knew your name better than you did.

"Quite a reception," I said when Gus had turned back to the grill.

We settled into a nice breakfast. Gus's special oatmeal served with a dollop of Maine maple syrup for me. Blueberry pancakes with a side of bacon for Richelle. Her appetite was healthy and there was color in her cheeks. I could tell she was on the mend. We ate in silence for a moment, enjoying Gus's simple, good food.

"Can I say something to you, honestly?" Richelle asked.

I nodded. Where was this heading?

"It's about your boyfriend."

My boyfriend. How did she even know about—? *Mom.* Mom must have shared her disapproval with Richelle. I wasn't sure I liked this version of my mother, gossiping with girlfriends. "What brought this up?"

"Your mother mentioned him."

Uh-huh. "I'm sure she didn't have anything positive to say."

Richelle didn't deny, but she didn't confirm, either. "I've seen him around town before, at the cab stand by the pier. Quite the hunk."

What was I supposed to say to that? Thank-you? It's not like I'd invented him.

"Is it serious?" She asked the very question I was avoiding.

Richelle looked straight into my eyes. When she realized I wasn't going to answer, she went on. "I had a great passion once. I was much younger than you are now." She put down her fork to give all her attention to the subject at hand. "But a person can fall head over heels at any age and do foolish things. Crazy things that mark their life forever. Be careful, Julia. Be careful who you give your heart to. Love can lead you to make terrible decisions."

I studied her to see if she was teasing, but she wasn't. It was serious advice, seriously given. Did she know? Did she know I was teetering on the brink of declaring my love for Chris? "I'll be careful, Richelle. I promise. I understand how much I could screw up my life."

"I doubt you do," she responded. "Truly. Follow your head, and not your heart—or any other part of your body. That's all I'm saying." She smiled to show the difficult topic was closed and changed the subject. "Any news about that young man you were looking for?"

"Lots," I answered, "but none of it good." I told her about the deaths of Cabe's adoptive parents, the murder accusation, the institution, and group home.

Richelle pushed her half-finished plate of blueberry pancakes away. "That poor, poor kid."

"I know. I can't stop worrying about him. Listen, do you think you can get home on your own? I have some things to do in the back harbor here."

Richelle nodded that she could. She insisted on picking up the check, but then couldn't because Gus doesn't take any form of payment except cash. He'd demand gold coins if he could get away with it.

Chapter 29

I walked the short distance to Bud Barbour's small boat repair business. His home and boathouse were on the water, accessed by a narrow dirt lane that led behind another small house. I slipped and slid down the dirt road, a river of mud. My boots were caked by the time I reached the house and I stood for a moment wondering what to do.

A string of expletives exploded out of the boathouse. A lobster boat I recognized as belonging to one of Gus's customer's was in the shop, hoisted out of the water on a set of rails. Bud was somewhere inside it, and judging by the banging and the swearing, not having much luck with whatever he was attempting. As I listened, I felt myself blush. I wasn't a prude by any stretch—I'd spent my whole life on the water and in boardrooms, two places where people used more swear words than regular ones, but the verbal combinations Bud put together were so colorful and so anatomically impossible, I didn't know whether to laugh or retch.

"Bud!" I called, hoping to interrupt the flow of words. "Bud, it's Julia Snowden!"

Morgan poked her head out of the boat first, her red kerchief blazing. Wagging her tail, she jumped out and sniffed my hands in greeting.

"What?" Bud's head poked up from below deck.

"I want to talk to you."

Bud sighed. "Give me a minute." He wiped his hands on a dirty rag, then climbed down the ladder on the side of the boat. When he reached my side, he repeated, "What?"

There was no way to ease into it. Mainers of Bud's age and disposition didn't go for small talk. "Bud, why were you on the pier the morning Stevie's body was found?"

Rain dropped off his white beard onto his flannel shirt. "Who says I was?"

I moved under the shelter of the boathouse roof and motioned for him to do the same. "I saw a photo of Morgan on the pier. If Morgan was there, you were, too. You told the committee you'd 'rather be dead and buried in a New York Yankees' uniform,' than participate in the opening ceremony. You told the cops you were at your camp up north. *I* told the cops you were at your camp up north."

Bud put a greasy hand out. "You have a photo of Morgan, you say. Let me see it."

I hadn't thought to print a copy before I came. A few of Bud's colorful curses ran through my mind.

"I thought so," he said. "You're bluffing."

"Bud, I can go get the picture if necessary, but

why don't you answer the question and save us both time?"

"There are a load of black labs on this peninsula." He climbed the ladder, headed back to work. I was dismissed.

I debated whether I should follow him up and corner him, but no good could come of it. Better to go home, print a copy of the photo and come back another time. As I made my way up the ribbon of mud toward the main road, I noticed two things about our conversation. Bud had accused me of "bluffing," not "lying." And he hadn't actually denied being on the pier.

I was nearly opposite the little house at the top of the lane when I heard a rapid tapping, accompanied by a muffled shout. It was hard to tell over the sound of the rain, but the noise seemed to come from the house. Morgan barked a blue streak from Bud's yard below, adding to the cacophony.

Bunnie Getts's head stuck out of the partially opened screen door on the back deck of the house. "Julia! I was banging on the window to get your attention. Everyone comes through the back door at this house. Have you finally come for tea?"

After the months of summonses, I was trapped. Though I'd been innocently passing by, I decided the time was right to have tea with Bunnie. I had something to ask her.

This was Bunnie's house? It was a neat, but tiny Cape. And in the back harbor, the least fashionable part of town. I'd assumed Bunnie lived out on East-claw or Westclaw Point, where the rich people lived.

But sure enough, her dark green, full-sized SUV was in the driveway, the car I'd seen so many times parked in front of the Tourism Bureau office. I climbed the steps to her back deck. I was glad I could busy myself taking off my slicker and muddy boots while I adjusted to this new idea of who Bunnie might be.

"Sit down, sit down." She bustled around the kitchen, putting the kettle on and setting out things for our tea. "You look nearly drowned. Let's get something warm in you." She put a plate of blueberry scones on the kitchen table along with two bowls, one of clotted cream and the other blueberry jam. "I made them myself. The scones, the jam." She waved airily, taking in the whole of her kitchen. Another new idea of her.

While she brewed the tea, she talked a blue streak. Bunnie, stripped of her clipboard, agenda, and neat checkmarks, turned out to be a yakker. It was going to be tough to get a word in edgewise. She talked on about our fellow committee members. She had positive things to say about all of them. I tried to remember any time over the months of planning she'd said anything positive to someone's face. When we came to the subject of Bud, she said, "Oh, that Bud," in the same affectionate way the old-timers around town did. "And poor Stevie" she added, shaking her head. "Just so sad. In the prime of his life."

Is she going to cry?

As she talked on, I looked around. The house seemed as small on the inside as it did from outside.

Just the eat-in kitchen and a sitting room on the first floor, crowded with furniture much too big for the home's tiny scale. It was a Cape and I bet there was just one bedroom or at most two upstairs. Was Bunnie one of those Yankee misers, or was it possible she was living in the harbor on very little money? Maybe she actually needed her job with the Tourism Bureau. Who would have ever thought it?

I looked out the picture window beside the kitchen table. The view, over the top of Bud's boathouse, was beautiful. In the back harbor, fishing and lobster boats bobbed in the rain.

I remembered back to the first meeting of the Founder's Weekend committee. I could have sworn Bunnie introduced herself to all of us, including Bud. And Bud, too, seemed not to have previously met Bunnie. Was it possible they didn't know each other? He lived essentially in her backyard.

Bunnie put the teapot on the table and sat across from me.

"Beautiful view," I said.

"Yes. That's what sold me on the house. Although I had no idea the harbor would be so noisy early in the morning. I can't leave my windows open at night, or I'm awakened before dawn by boats going out and men shouting to one another."

A typical sentiment by someone From Away. They buy a house on a working harbor because it's charming, and then complain because the lobstermen make noise. I sighed and broke open a scone. I was still full from Gus's oatmeal, but felt I had to be polite. I spread the clotted cream on the scone, followed by the jam, and took a big bite. Man, it was good. I savored the sweet of the jam and cream, balanced by the dense texture of the scone.

I heard the name "Reg" float by and realized Bunnie was talking about Reggie Swinburne. "How long have you and Reggie been a couple?"

Bunnie ducked her head like a bashful virgin. "Just a little while. My late husband . . . well, he died rather tragically. I was quite young."

"Bunnie, I'm so sorry." I'd never given a thought to what had happened to Mr. Getts.

"After he died, I didn't think I'd ever get involved with a man again, much less—" She stopped.

Much less what? Much less a man who lived in a camper?

"I was on the library fundraising committee with Cindy Kelly, and she introduced Reggie and me at the annual gala."

The "gala" was held at the Grange Hall and involved lots of gelatin-based salads. My conception of Bunnie continued evolving.

"Reggie is so"—she hesitated—"reliable. Steady. My husband was, I guess you would say, impulsive."

Bunnie spread clotted cream and jam on a piece of scone. "But what about you? I've seen you around town with that good-looking cabbie. What's the story there?"

What is this? National Interrogate Julia about Her Relationship Day?

"Is he . . . reliable?" Bunnie asked.

Was he? Yesterday, he'd disappeared with no

explanation. But then again, on the same day, I'd taken off on an eleven-hour round-trip without a word to him. As far as Chris knew, I'd been working at the clambake. More important, in the larger sense, Chris was reliable—in his work ethic, his concern and support for the underdog, his love of the sea and this harbor.

I had no intention of saying any of this to Bunnie so I simply said, "Yes."

Managing for the first time to take control of the conversation, I asked the question I'd come inside to ask. "Why are you so convinced Cabe murdered Stevie?" She'd been bleating about Cabe from the start, and I wanted to know why.

Bunnie sat back in her chair. "It makes sense, doesn't it? The boy was tending your clambake fire and he ran away."

"That's not really evidence. You're talking about putting a young man behind bars for life."

"Well, there is one more thing. I was around quite a bit the morning of the opening ceremonies, checking on things at the pier. Before the cooking even started, that boy was acting strange. Like a scared rabbit. I remember clearly. I came up behind him to ask a question and he jumped a mile."

Bunnie could have that effect on people. And, neither Sonny nor Livvie had said anything about Cabe acting strangely. But it had been a busy morning, their attention would have been elsewhere. They might not have noticed.

"Did you tell the state police about Cabe being nervous?"

"I certainly did. They were very interested, let me tell you."

There didn't seem to be much sense in arguing with her. I stood and thanked her.

"I hope we can do it again," she said.

I went to the back hall, climbed into my muddy boots, and slipped into my soaked slicker. As I stepped out onto the deck, Bunnie stuck her head out the door to say good-bye. The minute she did, Morgan began barking.

"That damn dog," Bunnie said. "Always making a racket. I can't even enjoy the deck."

Morgan hadn't barked when I first went out, only when Bunnie appeared. Bud had his dog so well trained, she wouldn't have barked like that unless he'd taught her to.

When Cabe told me the address of the boarding house where he'd lived, I knew the place exactly. Old Man Carver had inherited the big Victorian just off Main Street from his grandparents when I was a kid. Rather than sell it or fix it up for summer rentals, he threw two or three mattresses on the floor in every room and rented it to as many college students as he could, kids wanting cheap lodging so they could work low wage summer jobs. Usually, there were more renters than mattresses. He counted on shift work, along with summer hook-ups, to make up for the shortage.

I stood on the street in the rain, looking at the crumbling building. An overgrown lilac bush hid the front porch and grew into what was left of the gutters. I climbed up the rickety front steps and opened the sagging screen door. Like every other house in the harbor, the door was unlocked, though in this case I understood. Far too many kids coming and going. Besides, if Old Man Carver started giving out keys with his first renter, there'd be hundreds in circulation by now.

Inside, I was nearly bowled over by the smell of unrinsed beer cans, old pizza boxes, and marijuana. Like every kid in town, I'd been to parties in this house during my college years. It hadn't changed a bit. Not even the smell. There was a metal pot in the front hall positioned to catch water that dripped steadily from the ceiling, but no one had thought to empty it, and the water had overflowed in a big, wet ring. I didn't bother to take off my boots.

In the front room, two guys, one brown-haired and one blond, sat on a mattress playing a video game on an enormous flat screen TV. Neither looked up when I entered.

"Excuse me." I said it. And then shouted it.

The brown-haired one looked in my direction. He was dressed in a white button-down shirt and black pants, which marked him as a waiter, bartender, or busboy. Had he worked a breakfast shift or were these the clothes from the night before?

"Yeah?"

"Do either of you know Cabe Stone?"

Blank looks, but they did pause the game.

"Cabe," I prompted. "Five foot tenish, skinny, dark blond hair. Worked at the clambake."

The blond kid shook his head, no. But the brown-haired one recognized my description. "Oh, that dude. The cops have already been here, yo."

The cops had no doubt been there because some-one had told them Cabe had lived in the house. What the cops couldn't know, because they hadn't talked to Cabe, was that he'd slept there the night Stevie was murdered.

"He moved out," the brown-haired kid said. "He was weird. Paranoid."

"Paranoid? How?"

"He kept accusing people of going through his stuff. We don't want your crappy stuff, weirdo. Didn't seem like he had anything worth taking anyway. So he moved out, like I said."

"After he moved out, did he ever stay here? Like when he needed a place to crash in town?"

The brown-haired kid shrugged. "How would I know?"

I tried one more time, because I had to. "Did Cabe Stone sleep here the Friday night of Founder's Weekend?"

Blank looks.

"The night before the fireworks." They couldn't have missed those.

More blank looks.

"The night before the guy was found burned up on the town pier."

"Oh," Brown-hair said, comprehending. "Dunno."

"Are we playing this game or what?" the blond kid asked, indicating the TV screen.

I wandered through the rooms of bare mattresses, piles of laundry, and half consumed bags of chips. I found a girl asleep in a back bedroom.

"Mom, *go away*," she said when I tried to wake her.

On my way back to the front door, Brown-hair called out. "I remembered something."

I walked into the front room and looked at him.

"Like I said, the kid was paranoid. Always asking if people had come to the door looking for him. Then after he left, someone did come."

Who could that have been? "Did he leave a name?"

"It was a lady."

A woman? "What did she look like?"

"Old."

"Old like your mom, or old like your grandma?"

"Yeah," the kid said, "old like that."

Chapter 30

Back at the house, I asked Mom for her car. The rain was lightening up. It looked like Sonny was right and we might be able to run the clambake for dinner. I had to get as much done as I could before I went back to work. I wanted to find Zach and ask what he was doing on the pier the morning Stevie's body was found. I was still mad at myself that I hadn't recognized him at Crowley's the night before until it was too late.

After going through the "Can I have the car?" ritual with Mom, which Richelle watched with interest, I drove over to Camp Glooscap.

At Camp Glooscap, I signed the guest book, then got back in my car and drove through the gate. I found my way to Zach's old pop-up trailer easily. It was closed up tight, and the little red Toyota I'd seen the first day I'd been at the camp wasn't anywhere in sight.

"Damn."

I drove along toward Reggie's motor coach,

hoping he might know where Zach was, or could at least tell me something about him. I passed the Kelly's RV, then drove down along the shore and looped back, heading for Reggie's place.

Reggie stood outside the Parker's trailer, red-faced and screaming. I rolled down the car window and understood why he was yelling.

There was a party in full swing at the Parkers. Heavy metal music blared at ear-bending decibels, even though it wasn't yet noon. There were motor-cycles and ATVs littered across the wet dirt that served as the dilapidated trailer's front yard.

Reggie stopped yelling and paced back and forth on the muddy road. He was soaked to the skin. I wondered how long he'd been out there.

"Do you believe this?" he demanded when I pulled up beside him. "Camp Glooscap has always been a family place, each of the nine summers I've lived here. And now," his face turned even redder as he struggled to put his anger into words. "Now *this*!"

I looked at the old trailer. The sounds escaping it were no more sinister than people having a good time, but it was undeniably disruptive for the other residents of the RV park.

I started to speak, but didn't even squeeze out Reggie's name before he picked up a baseball-sized rock and whipped it toward the trailer. It hit a screen, shredded it, and continued on its trajectory through the window.

The music stopped. A mountain of a man dressed in motorcycle garb banged through the trailer's screen door. "What the hell!" He stood, arms tensed at his sides, ready for combat. Behind him, partiers peeked out the door and windows. "Swinburne!" he roared.

"Parker!" Reggie shouted back.

The motorcycle man walked down the steps and he and Reggie faced off in the yard like a couple gunslingers in the Wild West. I couldn't imagine what was going to happen next. For one thing, though this particular Parker had forty pounds on Reggie, I was astonished to see that the men were the same age. Somehow in my mind, the partying Parkers were my age or younger. Though the man's age made sense, when I thought about it. The Parker parents, who'd ignited this whole conflict when they went off to the assisted living place, were in their eighties, so their children would be closing in on senior citizenship.

Reggie made the first move, lunging at the larger man who grabbed him by the shirt. There was a lot of scuffling and shoving and some very bad words, though neither of the men had Bud Barbour's creativity in that department.

"This is a family place!" Reggie yelled, swinging ineffectively at Parker.

"And that's what I'm doing. Enjoying my vacation with my family."

"And preventing everyone else from enjoying theirs."

The members of the Parker clan spilled out of the trailer and crowded into the little yard. Other residents of Camp Glooscap filtered out of their RVs and gathered on the road. It looked like we were set up for the oldest gang fight ever seen.

"If Stevie Noyes were alive, you wouldn't have a site in this camp!" Reggie screamed.

"That's a lie," the huge man sneered. "He told me the night before he died he'd decided we could stay on this site. And when he left, he went to inform you. I saw him go into your place." Parker hauled off and slugged Reggie.

As Reggie went down, he kicked out a leg and took Parker down with him. They rolled in the mud, each trying to get a grip on the other.

"Stop!" I yelled. "Stop this instant!"

The big man had already stopped, as if startled by what he'd done, so by yelling, I hadn't actually stopped anything. But I had called attention to myself. Everyone in the crowd stared at me.

"You are neighbors," I insisted, saying the first thing that came to mind. "You are neighbors and adults." I stared down at the two mud-covered men.

Reggie picked himself up and rubbed his jaw. Parker got up and moved off. As the circle of on-lookers backed up, I put my shoulder under Reggie's arm and helped him back to his RV.

Inside, I sat at the dinette table in Reggie's RV, unable to avoid the sounds of him showering and changing in the bedroom just beyond. The inside of the camper was luxurious, with granite countertops, leather banquettes, and wide mechanical window bays that expanded its narrow footprint. The decor was exactly what I would have expected for Reggie. A locked gun cabinet was large enough for rifles and shotguns and a frame on the wall held mounted trout flies.

The RV couldn't have been more different in style, but the motor coach reminded me of Chris's sailboat in its tucked-up, everything-in-its-place efficiency. Outside, big drops fell from the trees. I couldn't tell if it was still raining, or just the aftermath.

"Do you believe the nerve of those Parkers?" Reggie asked as he came out of the bedroom wearing a clean version of his outdoorsman uniform—camp shirt and shorts—a purple towel around his neck.

"Is it true Stevie came here on the night before he died to tell you he'd given the campsite to the Parkers?"

"Balderdash!" Reggie protested. "You only have to look at those people to see they're lying snakes."

Who did I believe? If the Parkers were telling the truth, I was in a confined space with possibly the last person to see Stevie Noyes alive. I put my hand on my chest to register my heartbeat. Nothing extraordinary. Just the slow, familiar thump-thump. I wasn't afraid of Reggie Swinburne. But I could be underestimating him.

"Tell me about your friend Zach," I said.

Reggie rubbed the towel across his gray hair. "Nothing much to tell. He turned up here in the spring, just a little after I got here for the season. He started coming by, asking me the names of various birds, plants. I had the impression he was a city kid. Didn't seem to know much about nature. From there, we became friends. I took him on some day hikes and some overnights, tried to teach him a few things."

"Didn't it strike you as odd, a young man alone in a campground full of retirees and families?"

"I'm here on my own."

"But you're retired. How does Zach live? Does he have a job?"

"It's inexpensive to live here if you own your own rig. Both his car and the pop-up are older."

"Does he have any connection to this part of Maine? Family in the area?"

"Not that he ever said. He does go off, occasionally. Usually during the day. I thought he was sightseeing on his own. Why the third degree anyway? What's Zach to you?"

I sat back on the banquette, trying to convey casual interest. "No reason, really. I noticed him the first time I came to Camp Glooscap. I didn't recognize him right away last night because he'd cut his hair and shaved."

Reggie smiled. "He was going for the mountain man look. I finally persuaded him only bugs and nettles love it. It's not comfortable for a human male in August, even in Maine. He just shaved and got his haircut yesterday morning."

"You said you're here on your own, but that's not strictly true. You're with Bunnie. I just came from having tea with her."

He cocked a bushy eyebrow. "So you finally had your tea. I'm glad. Bunnie likes you. She said you were a joy to work with on the committee. She thinks you're both cut from the same cloth. Natural leaders."

Bunnie likes me? She had an awfully funny way of showing it. I tried to think of one word of praise she'd given to my work on Founder's Weekend.

"Bunnie doesn't have many friends," Reggie continued. "She's had a hard life. Her late husband lost all their money. She was one of those trusting wives who never asked her husband how he was managing their investments."

That explained a lot. The tiny Cape house. And Bunnie's warning not to be too trusting in my relationship.

"After he lost the money, Bunnie's husband jumped off the Empire State Building. Poor girl, she's had such a rough time of it."

Jumped off the Empire State Building? Hadn't one of T.V. Noyes victims jumped off the Empire State Building?

I wrapped up the conversation and hurried home to do more searching on the Web.

Chapter 31

I put Mom's car back in our garage and hurried up the front walk to the house. The rain had stopped. I was sure the clambake would be open for dinner, so I wanted to do my research before I had to run down to the pier.

"Yoo-hoo, Julia!" Vee Snuggs called from across the street. "I need to speak to you."

"Can it wait? I'm kind of in the middle of something."

"No, dear. The time is now."

Viola and her sister Fiona had run their bed and breakfast, the Snuggles Inn, in the gingerbread Victorian house across from my parents' house for as long as I could remember. Though a generation older, they'd been close friends of my parents, and unofficial great-aunts to Livvie and me. The Snuggles had been a sort of second home, where I could always find Vee's delicious scones along with the sympathetic ear of a grown-up who wasn't my parent.

A few years ago, the sisters asked me to call them Vee and Fee instead of Miss Snuggs. I'd agreed reluctantly, but it didn't make us equals. When Vee said, "Come over now," I went.

I took off my muddy boots for the third time that morning, and Vee led me to her old-fashioned, homey kitchen, one of only two rooms off-limits to guests at the Snuggles. The other was the small former sitting room at the back of the house the sisters shared as a bedroom in the summer, so they could rent out all the rooms on the second and third floors. I sat at the familiar table with its cream-painted legs and red linoleum surface. Vee didn't offer me food. I was grateful, because I'd just eaten. Consuming Bunnie's delicious scones made me feel a little bit like I was cheating on Vee.

"I know you've been keeping company with that young man, Chris." Vee opened the conversation.

I tried not to look too stunned. First Richelle, then Bunnie, now Vee. Why was today the day everyone wanted to counsel me about my relationship?

"Yes," I admitted, and stopped there, wary of what was coming.

"I just wanted to say, I think it's wonderful." Vee smiled beatifically.

Well that made a change. But I was still suspicious. Why was this conversation so urgent?

"I've been wanting to say that to you, and I wanted to say that when my sister wasn't at home." She took my hand. "I wasn't always on the road to becoming an old maid. I had a great love once, and I let him go. It's my biggest regret."

Her declaration didn't surprise me. Her sister Fee was a plain woman, far more interested in her succession of Scottish terriers than in any male. But there'd always been rumors about the glamorous Vee, with her masses of white hair and her proper hose and high heels. The kind of rumors talked about among the grown-ups, which a certain type of big-eared child, like I had been, was bound to hear.

What did surprise me was what came next. Vee burst into tears.

I reached across the table with the hand she wasn't holding and patted her arm. "Don't talk about it, if it's too painful." I truly did not want to talk about it.

Vee let go of my hand and took a perfectly pressed handkerchief, embroidered with tiny pink flowers, out of the pocket of her apron. "I wanted to spend my life with this man, but there would have been scandal. He was married, you see. My parents disapproved. My sister disapproved. I listened to them. I never should have." Vee snuffled into her handkerchief. "I sent him back to his wife. For my trouble, I got to see them have three children together and bring them up, while I sat on the sidelines and watched my life go by. They were never happily married, and he and I never stopped loving one another."

This was new information. The proper Vee involved in a scandal. I could imagine the pressure her parents and sister applied.

"Vee, do you know why my mother objects to Chris?" I knew why Sonny objected. That was history.

And why Livvie objected—because she was fiercely loyal to Sonny. But I couldn't figure out what my mother's problem was. I worried the rumors about Chris's supposed criminal activity had reached her. It was true Mom didn't have girlfriends per se, but if she'd confided to anyone about the heart of her issue with Chris, it would have been Vee.

"She hasn't told me, and I haven't asked. I've just sensed her reluctance to embrace him. And I've sensed something holding you back as well." She grabbed my hand again. "Do not make my mistakes, Julia. Don't be an observer of your own life. I regret it every day."

Chapter 32

I stayed with Vee until she was calmer. She wiped her eyes for the last time just as Fee walked in the door with an armload of groceries. Then I hurried across the street to my house, hoping I could still get in an hour or more of Web searching before I had to be on board the *Jacquie II*.

Mom and Richelle were in the kitchen.

"You're home! Perfect timing," my mother called. "Come join. Richelle has prepared a delicious late lunch for us."

Oh please, not more food. Bunnie's scone still sat heavy in my gut. I started to refuse, but my mother glared at me, so I sat down. "I'll just keep you company."

Richelle put a bowl of tomato salad on the table, along with a bowl of tuna and white beans and a loaf of crusty bread. I watched while they each spooned the salad into bowls, the tuna onto their plates, and took slices of the bread. The smell of the tomatoes was overwhelming. It brought back memories of childhood when Livvie and I, playing in the vegetable garden on Morrow Island, had eaten tomatoes straight off the vines.

"What's in this?" I asked.

"Tomatoes, garlic, salt," Richelle answered.

"That's it? No oil?"

"The salt causes the tomatoes to create their own juice. Try it. It's good for you."

I rationalized that I needed to add vegetables and protein to the crazy amount of carbohydrates I'd consumed that morning. I helped myself to the tomatoes and the tuna, and I ate. The tuna was deliciously simple—canned tuna, white beans, onion, salt and pepper. It had a clean, cool taste. The burst of flavor from the tomatoes knocked me over.

"I had no idea you were such a good cook."

Richelle smiled, pleased by the compliment. "I'm hardly ever home, so when I am, I eat in. I like dishes that are simple and seasonal. I love to improvise, though these are two of my standbys. When there are tomatoes at the farmers market, I cannot—"

There was a sharp knock at the screen door on the porch. I peered through the front hall. Binder and Flynn. *Great.* "Come in!" I called. "It's unlocked." I stood to greet them. "Can this wait? We're eating, and I have to go to work soon."

"We're not here to speak to you." Binder's voice was abrupt, not his usual calm tone. "We're here to ask Ms. Rose to accompany us to the station."

Richelle stood, too.

"If it's another witness interview, Lieutenant," my

mother said, "perhaps you can wait a few minutes for us to finish? You're welcome to some—"

"Ms. Rose knows what this is in regard to. I'm sure she's been expecting us. Will you come along?"

I turned to Richelle, who moved toward the door, regal as ever.

"I'm coming with you," I said and followed them out.

They wouldn't let me in the interview room. I hadn't expected them to. I sat on the bench across from the civilian receptionist and waited. I didn't have my tote bag or phone. I fidgeted and wiggled. The minutes ticked by on the big clock behind the reception desk. Several times, I considered leaving, worried I would literally miss the boat, but I couldn't desert Richelle. The clambake staff was more than competent to get the dinner guests on board the *Jacquie II*, but I couldn't leave Livvie and Sonny alone to run the clambake yet again, and with no prior warning.

Just when I decided I had no choice but give up, Richelle emerged, red-eyed and red-nosed, from the conference room.

"Are you all right?"

"Let's get out of here." She rushed outside and I followed.

"I'm sorry, Richelle. I have to go to the boat. I just wanted to make sure you were okay."

"I'm fine. I've just been forced to relive one of the most humiliating, awful times of my life, but I'll get over it." She saw my questioning look and said, "I'll walk with you."

We started down the steep hill from the town office complex to the pier.

"I want you to hear this from me," Richelle said. "Twenty years ago, the man you know as Stevie Noyes, was my boss. I worked as his secretary. I knew how his whole operation worked. I was the one who typed, copied, and mailed the newsletters, which predicted a stock would go up or down. I kept track of which people got the accurate ones, so we could send only those people the next prediction."

"You were in on the stock fraud!" It wasn't an accusation. It was an expression of pure astonishment.

"I didn't understand it at first. I was a dumb, twenty-year-old kid, fresh out of secretarial school. It took me awhile to put all the pieces together—the ever-smaller number of newsletters and the stock selling operation going on in the next room. By the time I figured it out, I was in too deep. I'd committed mail fraud. Besides there was something else."

Tears oozed from the edges of Richelle's eyes. She snuffled. "Everyone is going to know this now." I waited while she fought for control. "I had an affair. I had an affair with T.V. Noyes."

Good grief, how much more could there be to this story? "He was married," I said, trying to keep the censure out of my voice.

"I was such a stupid kid. He was charismatic, flattering, powerful." She began to cry out loud, great, gulping sobs.

Tourists stared. We were almost to the dock. I

tried to imagine the Stevie I knew as charismatic. If he was still exuding excess pheromones in the months before he died, I had missed them. I tried to picture his little self next to the Amazonian Richelle. The image was disturbing.

"I testified against T.V. in his criminal trial in exchange for immunity. I left New York, changed my name. That's why Gus recognized me, but not my name. I almost died this morning when he told you I wasn't Richelle Rose."

I'd missed it entirely. I'd thought it was Gus being Gus.

"Is that why you kept coming to Busman's Harbor? Were you in contact with Stevie?" Had he been the one great love of Richelle's life? Did she regret leaving him, as Vee did her married man? After all, Stevie's wife had divorced him when he went to prison.

"Good grief, no! That's all behind me. I had no idea he was here. But once the police figured out who Stevie really was, I knew it was just a matter of time. My name, my former name, is all over the transcripts of the criminal trial."

The *Jacquie II*'s whistle sounded.

I put my arms around her. "I've got to go. I'm so sorry. Go back to the house and take a warm bath and have a stiff drink. The worst is over. You've told them. It will all be better in the morning, I promise."

I went off to do my job and left her standing on the pier.

Chapter 33

I was the last one to board the *Jacquie II*. The crowd was light, perhaps a hundred people. Despite the lower revenue, I was glad for the smaller group. It was going to be a busy evening. Normally, we had the quiet time on the island between lunch and dinner to get ready for the next boatload of tourists. Now, most of the staff members were aboard the *Jacquie II* with me. The moment we disembarked, we'd have to run to get set up.

On the boat ride over, the murder was still a topic of conversation, but not the only one. The locals were all talked out, and as last week's tourists left and people who hadn't been in town for the grisly events took their place, the chatter became more distant and speculative, lacking the "where were you when they discovered the body?" immediacy.

When we reached the island, I ran to the kitchen to check in with Livvie.

She saw me approach and came into the dining pavilion to greet me. "How are you feeling?"

"What?" I'd forgotten about the lie I'd told just the day before. "Better," I said, recovering. "Twenty-four hour bug. Same thing you had."

Livvie's worried features softened into a smile. "Julia, I wasn't sick. I'm pregnant."

It took me a moment to understand what she'd said. "What?" I shouted so loud several of the wait-staff, busy setting the tables, turned to stare. In a lowered voice I stammered, "I never thought . . . I just assumed . . . but Page will be ten!"

Livvie laughed. "It's not *that* crazy. We were so young when Page was born. So we waited, and then Dad got sick, and then he died, then the business was failing. Close your mouth." She placed her index finger on my chin and closed it for me.

"How do you feel? When are you due?"

"March. Pretty okay. Some queasiness, as you saw."

"I'm so happy for you. Does Mom know? Does Page know?"

"You're the first. And don't tell either of them, please. Mom will hover and tell me to move off the island—despite the fact she was pregnant here herself—twice. And as for Page, seven months is an impossibly long time to wait when you're nine. We'll tell them both soon."

Great, just what I needed. More secrets.

Sonny, emerging from the kitchen, came up behind Livvie, and put his arms around her. "You told her."

"Congratulations," I choked out.

"Should I congratulate you, too? You said you had

the same thing as Livvie. Does slippery Chris know he finally got caught?"

I let that one go by.

Sonny kissed Livvie's neck. "The best thing I ever did was marry your sister and have Page. I'm so happy. I think I'll have a kid every decade!"

Livvie rolled her eyes. "We'll see."

It wasn't out of the question. She'd only be thirty-eight in ten years.

Sonny went on his way and Livvie and I walked back toward the kitchen. "So where were you really yesterday?" Livvie asked.

"Trying to help Cabe."

"Any progress?"

I sighed. "Not really. Stevie's not Stevie, which means there might be plenty of people who'd like to kill him. But Cabe's been suspected of killing someone before." I told her what I'd learned.

She listened, head bowed, brow creased. "Can you help Cabe?" she asked when I finished.

"I think so. At least I hope so. I'm certain he's innocent."

"Of course he is. Take whatever time you need. Sonny and I can handle the clambake. Really."

As she turned to enter the kitchen, I put my hand on her shoulder. "Wait, there's one more thing I need to tell you." We'd only spent one day apart, our first separation of the summer. Was it possible so much had happened? She turned back toward me, a little impatient. There was still a ton of work to do.

"Chris said he loves me."

"That's wonderful!" Livvie threw her arms around

me. "Isn't that what you've been wanting? You've loved him half your life. What did you say to him?"

"I pretended I didn't hear."

"Julia!"

"What kind of future could we possibly have? Besides, you all hate him."

Livvie laughed. "Did you like Sonny when I first brought him around? Or for that matter when we got married? You thought I was too young. You thought he was a lobsterman's son."

"How can you say that? I'm a lobsterman's granddaughter."

"And a college professor's granddaughter. And a captain of industry's great-granddaughter. And let's face it, you've always been more their descendant than the lobsterman's."

Was my sister calling me a snob? I'd spent most of my life having an unrequited crush on Chris, thinking *I* was the one who wasn't good enough for *him*.

"That's not fair. Besides, there's no future in it. I'm going back to New York in the fall. Chris will never leave this harbor."

"You won't even consider staying? I would love it. Mom would, too. Even Sonny. It would mean so much to me if you were close by for Page." She put a hand on her flat stomach. "And for this little one, too."

"Livvie, you know I can't stay in the harbor. I'd never be happy. I've never fit in."

Livvie didn't say anything for a moment. "What does that mean, you don't fit in?" she asked softly.

I struggled to find the words. It was a feeling I'd

had all my life. That my parents' marriage, a summer person and a local boy, doomed me never to have a place. It was like I was on the outside looking in. Phil Johnson had said at the blueberry camp, "I don't want to be an observer. I want to be part of it." I wanted to be part of it.

"I don't have any friends here," I finally said, though it was so much less than I meant.

"What are you saying? That Gus isn't your friend? That Fee and Vee Snuggs aren't your friends?"

"Great, I have three friends over seventy."

Livvie had the grace to laugh. "What about the clambake? The gang at Crowley's? The Founder's Weekend committee? You talk about them all the time."

"Here, I'm the boss. At Crowley's, they're Chris's friends."

"Did you ever think, Julia, that if you weren't so standoffish, they could be your friends, too? You have to give a little of yourself." She paused again and I thought the conversation was over, but it wasn't.

"Julia, You need to ask yourself, is it the town that's holding you back from telling Chris you love him, or is there some other reason?"

"Livvie," I answered, ignoring her last point and the troubling questions it raised. "I've tried to fit in here. I'm not a local. I'm not a summer person. We've been caught in between our whole lives."

"I haven't," Livvie said. "I made a choice. Maybe now it's time for you to make one, too. What kind of life do you want, Julia?"

* * *

I waited impatiently as the dinner service ended and most of the guests drifted off to the island's westernmost point to watch the spectacular sunset, amplified tonight by the last, lingering clouds of the storm. Before I left the island, I was determined to search the playhouse again. The approach Sonny, Chris, and I used the last time, seemed, in retrospect, more like the Three Stooges than any forensics team. I hoped that we'd missed something, anything that would help me figure out where Cabe had run.

I walked up the path and let myself into the little house. I waited a moment while my eyes adjusted to the gloom inside. A quick look around confirmed our impression from two days before—there was nothing obvious in the playhouse. All four bunks were stripped bare. I lifted the mattresses, searching for something Cabe had left behind. Nothing.

The sitting room was equally barren. There was nothing in the cushions of the rustic settee or in the sideboard that served as a kitchen cupboard. I opened a lower door of the sideboard and stuck my hand into the darkness. Why hadn't I brought a flashlight? The cupboard was cool and damp. And empty.

I wasn't sure what I was looking for. Cabe had cleared everything out. My only thought was, when he'd lived here, Cabe might have hidden something in the little house he wouldn't want Sonny, or some lost stranger, to walk in and find, and then forgotten when he left.

I knelt in front of the fireplace. Though the nights could be cool in Maine, even in August, I doubted Cabe would have made a fire. He would have returned, late in the evening, exhausted from working at the clambake. By that point, he'd have been standing by a fire all day. I didn't think he'd want one at night.

I stuck my hand up the chimney and felt around. When I was a child, the bakemaster and his family had lived in the playhouse in the summer. But Livvie and I had played there in the spring and the fall, and I remembered a small shelf in the chimney where we'd hidden messages as a part of our games. Sure enough, the shelf was there and something was on it. Not a note, but a metallic object the size of a wallet.

I knew before my hand even came out of the fireplace the object was a camera. When I saw it, I realized that despite its small size, it was expensive, with a powerful zoom function. How would a young man, too broke to have a cell phone or a laptop, own something like that? I wondered if someone else put it there. I wondered, but then felt terrible about wondering, whether Cabe had stolen the camera from one of our guests. I was supposed to be on his side.

I found the power button and the camera whirred to life. The battery was still good. It took a bit of monkeying around to figure out how to view the stored images. I accidentally took a photo of my own work boot-shod foot. But finally, I got it.

My heart beat faster. Surely, the camera could contain some hints about where Cabe might have gone. Photos of friends or places. The first image I saw was my foot. I clicked back. The next one was of Stevie Noyes. And the one before that, and the one before that. And the one before that. I clicked for what seemed like hours, but was only minutes. Every single photo was of Stevie. Stevie in town, Stevie in the office at the RV park, Stevie at his trailer, Stevie going into Gus's restaurant. There was even a picture of Stevie coming out of the Tourism Bureau office after one of our committee meetings. I caught a glimpse of my hair in the background of the shot.

My hands shook when I finally turned off the camera. *Cabe, why were you stalking Stevie? And why on earth would you pack up your worn jeans and ratty T-shirts and leave this behind?*

Chapter 34

I felt miserable on the boat ride back to the harbor. The clambake guests held lively conversations, and normally I loved overhearing raves about the food and the beauty of Morrow Island. But I couldn't enjoy them because I knew as soon as I got to shore I had to give the camera to Lieutenant Binder.

I hadn't told Sonny or Livvie about what I'd found. I knew Sonny would try to talk me out of turning it over. "It could have been *anyone's*," he'd insist.

I hadn't told the cops Cabe had called me. He hadn't said anything about where he was. I hadn't told them I'd found Phil Johnson, either. All he'd given me was a photograph of Bud's dog and the hairy guy from the RV park. I was able to convince myself neither were worth mentioning.

But I couldn't keep quiet about the camera.

And I couldn't stop turning my mind over the question Livvie had asked. Could I not tell Chris I loved him because I didn't see a future for myself in the harbor? Or was there some other, much deeper, much less circumstantial reason? I hadn't told Livvie about Chris's disappearing act the day before. We hadn't had time for one thing. Dinner service was upon us. But I also hadn't told her because I knew what she would say. And I didn't want to hear it.

As we pulled into the harbor, there was Chris on the dock, obviously waiting for me. I should have been delighted to see him, but my stomach clenched. *What now?*

"I didn't expect to see you," I said when I disembarked. "Aren't you supposed to be at Crowley's?" *You weren't there last night, either.*

"Slow night. We had two guys on and I wasn't really needed. So I thought we should take this opportunity to discuss the elephants in the room."

"Two elephants?" I asked, all innocence, though I dreaded where this was going.

"One elephant where I told you I loved you. And the other elephant where you took off like a shot right after I said it."

Oh, those elephants. As I feared. *And what about the third elephant, the one where you disappeared?* "We should definitely talk. But I need to do something first." I told Chris about the camera.

"I'll walk you there." As we walked, he accommodated his long-legged stride to my own. He had wanted to talk right away. I'd insisted we go to the police station first. And still he supported me, even without words. I leaned in close to show my appreciation.

He said he had no need to see Lieutenant Binder and waited outside the station. I marched in.

I wasn't surprised to see Binder and Flynn still at work. Flynn sat in a pool of light at the end of the conference table, reading documents. Binder was on his cell phone. He motioned for me to come in. Flynn continued to examine the papers in front of him. There were new stacks of boxes on the other side of the room, unopened. I assumed they were from the civil litigation against T.V. Noyes.

"Did you go into the ocean today?" Binder spoke into his phone, obviously talking to a child. "Uh-huh. That sounds like fun." He listened some more, then said, "You go to bed now. Let me talk to your mom." There was some more muttered conversation. Binder said, "I hope to be there by the weekend," followed by, "Love you, too." He clicked off the phone and turned his attention to me.

"You have kids." I realized we'd never had a personal conversation.

"Two boys. Six and eight. We have a cottage in York for these two weeks. My wife's having trouble getting them settled down enough to sleep."

"I'm sorry about your vacation."

He shrugged. "It happens. What brings you here at this time of night?"

I pulled the camera out of my tote bag and set it on the table. That got Flynn's attention and he came and stood next to Binder.

"Why is this important?" Binder asked.

I explained where I'd found the camera—which meant I had to explain Cabe had been living in the playhouse. A little spot began to pulse on Detective

Flynn's neck as I talked. I stepped back from the table in case he blew. Then I told them what I'd seen on the camera.

"You looked at it?" Flynn was furious.

"I hoped it would help us find Cabe . . . ." My voice trailed off. I had no excuse.

"Us?" Flynn said. "There is no 'us.' There's you, apparently doing whatever you want. And there's us, the state police."

Binder put on gloves and turned the camera on, examining its display. "What's this?"

"My foot." I'd thought about deleting the photo, but figured I was in deep enough already. If they had a professional look at the camera and he told them I'd deleted an image, I'd be in even bigger trouble.

Silently, Binder scrolled through the rest of the photos with Flynn peering around his shoulder, so close they could have been embracing. There had to be more than a hundred pictures. When they were finished, Binder put the camera down on the table.

"Thanks for bringing this in, Ms. Snowden. Come in tomorrow and we'll take a formal statement as to where you found it and fingerprint you so we can eliminate your prints and see what's left. That way, when we bring your young friend in, and believe me, we will, soon, we can match the prints on this camera to his. We'll take it from here."

I was dismissed.

* * *

Chris and I walked from the police station across the town common. He listened sympathetically as I told him what had happened at the station. He knew how hard it was for me to turn in evidence that looked bad for Cabe.

We sat down on a wooden bench halfway across the common. There were people around, strolling along with ice cream cones from Small's, but the bench felt private. The feel of Chris next to me was intoxicating—his power, his rock steadiness, his certainty about who he was, who I was. I breathed it in, savoring our closeness in the moment before the conversation to come.

"About those elephants," I joked. "Where did you go last night?"

"I took my boat out. I had to clear my head. Figure out what I wanted to say to you."

If what he said was true, then I had hurt him, just as I'd feared. But somewhere in my gut, I didn't believe him. He wasn't telling the truth, or at least he wasn't telling all of it.

He sensed my doubt. "Julia. I went for a sail. You trust me, don't you?"

"Yes," I answered. "Of course I do." *But did I?*

"My turn," Chris said. "I love you."

Even the ten seconds I hesitated was too long. It felt like a million years, a million miles.

"What can come of it?" I asked.

"What do you mean? We'll be together. Maybe, someday, we'll move in together. That's what people do." His tone was matter-of-fact, like what he was proposing was the most logical thing in the world.

Not in the least bit angry. Not needy. Chris was never needy.

"I never envisioned a future that didn't involve going back to New York." When I finally got the words out, my voice was so quiet I was afraid he would ask me to repeat myself, which I didn't think I could do. I felt like a creature was inside, tearing my guts up. This was the man I had wanted half my life.

"Okay, Julia. I understand. I'm not asking you to commit your life or even think about the future. But in this moment, I need to know. Do you love me?"

I hesitated again. I thought about the look of pure joy on Livvie's face that afternoon when she told me she was pregnant. I thought about Vee Snuggs telling me to go after passion, not to be an observer of the life that could have been. Then I thought about my mother. She had her one great love, but ended up living a life where she was always viewed as an outsider. I thought about Chris and how I didn't know where he'd been yesterday, and didn't believe what he'd told me about it.

I hesitated too long.

My cell phone rang. I looked at it. A blocked number. "Chris, I think this is Cabe."

"Take it." He smiled to show he wasn't angry. I almost wished he were.

I answered the phone. "Cabe, wait one second."

Chris stood up from the bench and bent to kiss me on the forehead. "I'm sorry things turned out this way," he said and walked off into the night.

Chapter 35

"Cabe, where are you? Things have gotten really complicated here." I watched Chris walk away. I wasn't talking only about Cabe. "You need to come back."

"I can't."

"Then why call me?" I hadn't asked for this.

"I wanted to make sure you were okay."

"Of course I'm okay. But you're not. You're in real trouble, Cabe, and you're only making it worse by staying away."

He didn't respond, but he didn't hang up. I tried a different tack. "Cabe, why did you come to Busman's Harbor in the first place?"

"I was looking for something."

"Your birth parents." Emily Draper at Moore House had told me this.

"Yes."

"Did you find them?"

He let out a long sigh. "One of them. I always knew I was adopted. When I moved to Moore

House, I decided to figure out who I was. I'd seen so many kids in the institution, and even in Moore House, who had such terrible families, but I still wanted one. I thought maybe I had a second chance to have parents. When I turned eighteen, I applied for my birth certificate from the state. I kept the birth certificate in a little box in my room at the boarding house. In the box was a photo of me with my parents, the Stones, and their wedding rings. That box was the only thing I'd been able to hold on to through all the moves, the foster families, and the group home. While I was at the boarding house, someone went through it. I could tell because they refolded the birth certificate and left the photo upside down in the box. That's why I moved to the playhouse on Morrow Island."

The idea of Cabe, clinging to a tiny box holding a photo of his parents and their rings, stabbed me in the chest. I thought about Page, who's every significant moment since birth had been recorded, and then about Cabe, who had so little.

"I was born in Busman's Harbor Hospital," he continued. "I looked at pictures of the town on the Web and imagined my mom living there in a cottage by the ocean. When I finally got to the harbor this June, it was as beautiful as I'd imagined. I instantly felt like I'd come home.

"The father's name on my birth certificate was Telford Vincent Noyes. There were tons of articles on the Web about the stock swindle and the trial. I was desperate to find the man, but he'd changed his name after he left prison. It took me a long time

working in libraries and Internet cafes to figure out
Stevie Noyes of Camp Glooscap in Busman's Harbor
was actually T.V. Noyes. I thought it meant something he'd come back to Busman's Harbor after
prison. Like maybe he hoped I'd find him."

My mind struggled to keep up. Cabe was T.V.
Noyes's son, but he wasn't Aaron Crane. Cabe had
been given up for adoption as an infant. "How did
Stevie react when you told him you were his son?"

"I hadn't yet. As far as I knew he was a con man
and a criminal. I wanted to get to know him, the way
he was today before I decided whether to tell him
who I am." Cabe's voice faltered. "Now I'll never get
the chance."

We didn't talk for a moment while he collected
himself. I was afraid he would hang up. "Is that why
you took all the photos of Stevie?" I asked.

"What photos?"

"Cabe, you didn't take about a hundred photos of
Stevie and leave them in an expensive camera on a
shelf in the chimney of the playhouse on Morrow
Island?"

"I don't even own a camera."

My throat closed a little. I'd just turned over the
camera to Binder and Flynn, along with the information that Cabe had lived in the playhouse. "Then
how did you get to know Stevie?"

"One day, just after I got to Busman's Harbor, I
saw him coming out of the post office. I'd looked at
so many photos from the time of his arrest, I was
sure it was him. So I spied on him. It was easy. It
turned out he had a fairly regular routine. He'd

come in every weekday morning about eleven, go to the post office, the hardware store, do whatever he needed to do, and then have lunch at Gus's."

"That's when you started hanging around there."

"Gus gave me a job, but it was obvious he really didn't need the help. So he introduced me to you. I was grateful for the job on Morrow Island."

Maybe not so grateful now. "But you never talked to Stevie?"

"Oh, I talked to him. Casual stuff about the harbor and the campground. I liked him. I was almost ready to tell him who I was. But when I took the job at the clambake, I wasn't hanging around in the mornings anymore, and once I moved to Morrow Island . . ." His voice trailed off. "I thought there'd be plenty of time in the fall. When the clambake was closed for the season."

He thought there'd be plenty of time. The poor kid. Even with all his losses, he still had that human belief there'd be more time.

"If you didn't leave the camera in the playhouse, who do you think did?"

"That's just it, Julia. A few days before Founder's Weekend, somebody went through my things at the playhouse. They took the box with the rings, the photo, and my birth certificate in it. It freaked me out so much, I planned to move again."

"That's why you emptied out the playhouse and brought all your stuff to Busman's Harbor that evening."

"I thought about trying to move back to the boarding house, but once I stayed one night, I knew

I couldn't do it. It was like the group home only without Emily there to kick butt."

"Cabe, Stevie was your father. Who did your birth certificate say your mother was?"

"I never got far in looking for her. I only know her name."

When he told me the name, I didn't recognize it, though it didn't really matter. I was sure I knew who she was.

"Julia, I can't thank you enough for trying to help me. I know how bad my situation looks."

Help him? I'd just turned over a damning piece of evidence to the state police. "Of course, I want to help you, Cabe. I know you didn't kill Stevie. Besides, you saved my life."

"No, Julia. I didn't. I put your life in danger. That car was aimed at me."

"Cabe, what are you saying?"

But he was gone.

Chapter 36

I walked home, but didn't go directly to bed. I was too restless and roiled and sad. The look on Chris's face after he'd kissed me on the forehead haunted me. Why hadn't I grabbed his hand so he couldn't walk away?

The abrupt end of my conversation with Cabe frustrated me to the point where I wanted to scream in the night. What had he meant, the vehicle that had almost run me down was aimed at him? Did Cabe honestly believe he was in danger?

If he did, it explained a lot. Why he'd moved out to Morrow Island. Why he'd been too afraid to sleep out in the open on the town pier with the Claminator the night of Stevie's murder. Why the guy at the boarding house said he was paranoid. And why he'd cleared out his things on Morrow Island, intending to move again or even leave town.

Who would want to intimidate Cabe, a poor young man with no connections to the town? Was Stevie's entire murder a setup intended to hurt Cabe?

It made no sense. Stevie, a liar who'd swindled thousands of people, was a much more obvious target than Cabe.

I climbed the stairs to the second floor. My mother's door was closed, her room dark. But a thin line of light showed out from under Richelle's door.

I knocked and pushed the door open slowly. Richelle sat up in bed, a book propped on her knees, though she didn't seem to be reading. She stared off into space.

"Richelle?" I spoke softly, hoping not to startle her. When she turned toward me, I saw her face was streaked with tears. I said, "I think it's time you told me the truth."

She gave into the tears. "Oh Julia, I've made such a mess of things."

I sat on the bed and handed her tissues from a box on the nightstand. She was ten years older than me, and ten inches taller, but, with her child-colored, corn silk hair, she looked young and vulnerable in the pink princess bed decorated for a nine-year-old.

"Would it be easier if I say it?" I asked.

She nodded, wiping her tears.

"Cabe Stone is your son. Your son with Stevie Noyes. The reason it was so traumatic for you to testify against Stevie wasn't just because he was your beloved boss. He was your lover, and you were pregnant with his child."

"He was married. It was wrong. I regret it every day."

"You and his wife were pregnant at the same time?"

"Her son was born six months before mine. When

T.V. was arrested and their whole lives came crashing down, she threw him out. She sat behind him every day of the trial, but their marriage was over. When he was out on bail, he lived with me. That's when I conceived Cabe." She stopped, too overcome with emotion to go on.

I waited. It was her story to tell.

"One day, early in my pregnancy, federal agents arrested me as I left our apartment. They offered me a deal. They'd drop the charges if I testified against T.V. I hadn't even told T.V. I was pregnant. That night I did, and we agreed that I should take the deal. We both cried. In the morning, he moved out. Sitting in the witness stand testifying against my lover, my friend, the father of my unborn child, was the second hardest thing I'd ever done. The hardest was giving our baby up for adoption."

"You came to Busman's Harbor to stay with your great-aunt during your pregnancy." I'd assumed, when Richelle said she'd spent one summer here, it had been when she was a child. But Gus had recognized her, which meant she was probably older. And Cabe had been born at Busman's Harbor Hospital.

"I thought I was giving my baby a good life," she wept. "I was young, jobless, penniless, disgraced. I didn't know if I'd ever work again. His father was in prison."

"You did give your baby a good life," I said. "At least at first. Cabe had a happy childhood. The Stones were good parents. Even later, after all the awful things that happened to him, Cabe had a reservoir of resilience left from his early years. By the time he got to the group home, he'd focused on what he'd had, not what he'd lost."

Richelle nodded and even managed a tiny smile, like she wanted to believe me.

"Did you know Stevie was in Busman's Harbor? Is that why you came here so often?"

"Not for years. I'd moved on with my life put my affair, the trial, and Cabe's birth behind me. I'd moved to Portland, became a tour guide. I came to Busman's Harbor, believe or it or not, because those months when I lived here with Aunt Georgette, waiting for my baby to come, were my happiest in that whole period. The trial was over, T.V. was in federal prison for ten years. I know it sounds crazy, but by then, I could only look forward. I didn't look for Stevie, as you call him, at all, anywhere, ever."

"But then you saw him."

"Early this spring. I was on a research trip, investigating new places to take our tours. Through the window of a shop on Main Street, I saw him walk by. I would have known him anywhere."

"Did you approach him?"

"No, but I began to consider the possibility. All those years I wasn't with him, and didn't even know where he was, it didn't bother me. I had a happy life. But once the possibility of T.V. existed again, I couldn't stop thinking about him. He was the great love of my life. I wasn't sure how he would react to me. I did some research and found out he'd never married again, was completely unattached, just like me. I began to fantasize about our reunion."

Richelle sighed and looked down, picking at the

bedspread. "I built it up so much in my mind, made it so romantic and idealized, I kept chickening out. I knew reality would never come close to the scene in my head. But whenever I came to Busman's Harbor with a tour, when my groups had free time, I would be on the lookout for him" She looked up from the bedspread. "I discovered he had quite a reliable routine."

The same thing Cabe had said. "You realized you weren't the only person watching him."

"Once, in the spring, when I brought a group to town, I saw a young man following T.V. I wish I could say I recognized him, that there was some instant, magical connection with my son, but there wasn't. I saw him again, the next time I came. I followed T.V. to Gus's and lingered in a shop across the street, pretending I was interested in marine fittings." She laughed at herself. "T.V. came out Gus's front door and seconds later, a young man wearing a white apron came out the kitchen door and watched T.V. walk away. That's when it clicked. I asked around about the young man, looked into his history."

"You went to the place where he lived."

"He was the right age and from Maine. His housemates said he'd told them his parents were dead. I figured it had to be him. I thought he looked a little like us."

I hadn't thought of Cabe as the physical combination of Richelle and Stevie. He didn't look like either of them, but he had Stevie's slight frame combined with most, if not all of Richelle's height. And his light blue eyes somehow mirrored Richelle's darker ones.

"You didn't tell either of them what you knew?" I was skeptical. How could she hold it inside?

"If I wasn't sure how T.V. would greet me, I was even more worried about Cabe. T.V. and I had agreed about everything I'd done, even my testifying against him. But Cabe hadn't asked for any of it. That's the reason I asked you about Cabe when we were standing on the pier at the Founders Weekend celebration. I wanted you to introduce us."

"It's also why you fainted."

"I heard you talking to that lady about Stevie Noyes not turning up for the ceremonies and how odd that was. I could tell you were concerned about his absence. When I saw Cabe running away, I thought he must have hurt T.V. because he was so angry about what we'd done to him. I didn't really see the body in the fire. I knew T.V. was missing; there was a big kerfuffle around the clambake fire. Then I saw Cabe run away. I put the ideas together and panicked."

Richelle took a clean tissue and dabbed at her eyes. "When you said you didn't think Cabe was guilty, you gave me such hope. Please help him, Julia. Please help my baby."

I moved quietly across the hallway to my office and sat at my computer. I was too keyed up to go to bed. I had to do anything I could think of to help Cabe. And it was easier than thinking about Chris.

Reggie had told me Bunnie's husband jumped off the Empire State Building. One of Noyes's victims had also. Could they be the same person? I looked for articles about Empire State Building suicides. I knew from my years in New York, taking visiting family and friends on tours, it wasn't easy to jump from the 102nd floor. There were high barriers and guards on duty. The 86th floor observatory appeared to be the place for suicides, though others had bought tickets to the observatory and then jumped from open windows they found throughout the building.

Incredibly, not all the jumpers were successful. One woman jumped from the 86th floor, only to be blown back by a strong gust of wind through the windows on the 85th, safe with only a bone broken. I wondered what had happened to the woman, but this wasn't the time to use my mad skills to find out. It had been an emotionally exhausting day and I was going to crash soon. I had to keep moving.

I concentrated on the computer screen, trying unsuccessfully to push all other thoughts out. Chris had said "I'm sorry things turned out this way." Did that mean it was over between us? The loss seared me, starting at the place on my forehead where he'd kissed me and traveling throughout my body, leaving an empty ache in its wake. My eyes teared up, blurring the images on the monitor.

I pushed the thoughts away, refocused on the task at hand and moved on.

I zeroed in on suicides in the late eighties and early nineties, when Stevie's boiler room had been active. I added the surname *Getts* to the criteria and up it came. The story of Bunnie's husband's suicide. It happened well before Stevie's arrest. Walter Armbruster Getts jumped to his death on December 23, 1989. He left behind a widow Minerva, a mother, and a circle of grieving friends. The cause was unknown. He left no note, though one article did refer to "recent financial reverses."

Was Walter one of T.V. Noyes's victims? If he was, did Bunnie, who had let her husband manage their money, know it? And, did Bunnie know T.V. was Stevie?

I thought back to that first day when the Founders Weekend committee met. Bunnie hadn't seemed to know Stevie, but then she had also pretended not to know Bud, her closest neighbor. And who had recruited Stevie for the committee anyway? Had he received one of those won't-take-no-for-an-answer calls from Bunnie, like I had?

I looked to see if the documents from the civil suit against Stevie were available online. If Bunnie had been a plaintiff, it would prove a connection between her and Stevie. But the case was too long ago to be on the Web. Binder and Flynn had the civil suit documents, but I wasn't about to ask them. When I'd seen them the previous night, the boxes had appeared unopened. Binder and Flynn were still reading the documents from the criminal trial. It might take them days to get to the civil case. I didn't think I had that kind of time. Binder had said they were close to finding Cabe.

The last thing I did before falling into bed at 4:00 AM was print the photo Phil Johnson had given me and tuck it into my tote bag. I set my alarm for 7:30.

Chapter 37

My eyes flew open before the alarm went off. There was nothing to do but get up. By 7:30, I was showered and fully dressed. The house was quiet. I wondered what time Richelle had finally fallen asleep.

I paced in the kitchen while the coffee brewed, which seemed to take forever. If I left my house in twenty minutes, I would be at Bunnie's house at eight, the earliest possible time for a visit. At 7:45, unable to contain my nervous energy, I set out for Bunnie's. The haze over the harbor was the kind that would burn off with the morning sun. Today would be a workday.

Reggie's out-sized pickup was in Bunnie's driveway. I don't know why I was surprised. They were adults. I climbed the stairs to the deck and banged on the door.

Bunnie opened it right away. She'd obviously been in the kitchen.

"Julia, what brings you here so early?" She wore a bright summer robe . . . and makeup. Her never-out-of-place hair was perfectly in place. I wondered if all this was for Reggie's benefit, or if she put her face on every morning before she came downstairs.

I'd been rehearsing my speech since the wee hours of the morning, but I was flummoxed for a moment. "I'm here to talk to you about your prior relationship with Stevie Noyes, or T.V., as he was known then."

She didn't seem surprised by what I said. "You better come in."

"What's going on?" Reggie entered the kitchen, fully dressed in his usual outfit. His tone was jovial, but his eyebrows were drawn together in the beginnings of a scowl.

"Julia is just asking me about Stevie," Bunnie explained. "From before."

"Have a seat." Reggie pulled out one of the kitchen chairs. I was so fidgety, the last thing I wanted to do was sit, but I thought the conversation might go better if I did. Reggie sat, too. Bunnie fussed with the coffee pot, her back to us. I waited, my mouth clamped shut, until she turned around and spoke.

"I assume you've discovered my late husband invested all of our money with T.V. Noyes. And lost it." I nodded. "Then you'll know once the money was gone, Walter committed suicide."

"Actually, I told her that part," Reggie said.

"Why would you—"

He held his hand out, palm forward. "I thought it would help. I knew you wanted Julia to like you. It helps explain who you are."

Bunnie looked like she wanted to argue. What Reggie had said was wrong on so many levels. What if Chris felt he had to go around "explaining" me to others? Though given what Livvie had said the day before about my standoffishness, maybe he did.

Bunnie seemed to think better of taking Reggie to task for something that was, however wrong-headed, intended as a kindness.

"Did you know Stevie was T.V. Noyes?" I asked.

"I had no idea. When I read about who he really was in the paper, I couldn't believe it."

"You never recognized him?"

Bunnie brought the coffee pot over to the table and sat down. "I never met him back when everything happened. I didn't attend his trial or anything like that. I knew who he was, but I never saw anything except a few grainy photos in the newspaper and even then, it was so painful for me, I had to look away. At the time and afterward, I protected myself by staying away from anything related to T.V. Noyes."

"But you did join the civil litigation against him."

"My lawyer's idea. It turned out Noyes didn't have any money, so it was pointless." The money Stevie had bought Camp Glooscap with had been inherited after he got out of prison. Much too late for people like Bunnie.

"Have you told Lieutenant Binder about your history with Stevie?"

"No. Why would I? I had nothing to do with his murder."

"The state police have all the files from the civil litigation. It's just a matter of time before they find your name."

Bunnie's head dropped into her hands. "I thought all that was behind me. Finally. After Walter died, I sold our home and moved to a small condo. But I stayed in the same neighborhood outside of Boston where we'd lived. I believed I could keep my old life, my old friends. It was denial, I suppose. I couldn't grasp that my life had been so profoundly changed. And by something I'd never paid the slightest attention to. Money.

"I watched, year after year, while my friends travelled and went to their summer houses. Their children went off to school and then married. Grandchildren started to come. But I stayed exactly as I was. When I thought about what had happened to me, I was angry at some abstract idea of T.V. Noyes. But mostly, I tried not to think about it, to pretend nothing was wrong."

She stood and moved to the counter where she took three mugs off a wooden tree. She poured coffee for each of us, then set out cream and sugar. Was she avoiding telling more, or just following her ingrained instincts as a good hostess?

She sat down again and continued. "In the end, it became too much to bear. I had a nervous breakdown. Exhaustion, the doctors called it. Exhaustion from pretending my life was something it wasn't. When I got well enough, I made a new life here in

Busman's Harbor where I didn't have to play the tragic widow."

"Why Busman's Harbor?"

Bunnie seemed surprised by the question. She gestured toward the picture window and the back harbor outside. "Because it's beautiful. And because if I lived in town, instead of on the Points, I could afford it on the proceeds from my condo. Believe me, I didn't know T.V. Noyes was here. I didn't know until I read it in the paper two days ago."

"But he was," I said.

"I didn't kill him. As I said, I didn't even know it was him." A tear left a track in the powder on Bunnie's cheek.

I took a swig of coffee.

"Enough," Reggie said. "You've upset Bunnie. It's time for you to leave."

I didn't disagree. I hadn't learned much and I'd made Bunnie cry. Reggie was clearly angry. Nothing would be gained by antagonizing him further. I didn't want to end up rolling around in the mud with him the way Parker had.

Bunnie surprised me by following me out to the deck. As soon as she walked out the screen door, Morgan began barking from down in Bud's yard. The black lab was so loud Bunnie had to shout through her sniffles. "Don't let Reggie bother you, Julia. He's trying to protect me. He wants me to be happy in my new life. To fit in." She stared toward Bud's yard in exasperation. "That damn dog."

"Bunnie, do yourself two favors. Tell the cops

about your connection to Stevie before they find it. And then take a plate of your delicious scones to Bud. Tell him you're happy to be his neighbor."

"He's never so much as come to my door," Bunnie sniffed. "Aren't the established people supposed to welcome the new neighbors?"

"Maybe in some places. But if you understood the history of Maine better, you'd understand how wary local people are about people From Away. They're proud Mainers. They don't care how much money you have. They reject you first because they're used to being judged and found wanting."

"I have never done such things to Bud!"

"Maybe you haven't, but too many have. Let him know you respect him and his business. Scones and polite, respectful conversation will work wonders. It's what neighbors do." I gave her hand a squeeze. The poor woman. Maybe she wasn't so bad.

I let myself out of Bunnie's back gate, only to run into Bud. He'd wandered up the lane to see what the commotion was about. "Oh, it's you," he said when he saw me. "I thought you were what's-his-name, her overnight guest."

Why had I just been defending Bud to Bunnie? I pulled the photo out of my tote bag. Morgan was in it, beautiful and sleek, with her bright red kerchief. "Tell me one thing, Bud, and tell me the truth. Why were you on the town pier the morning Stevie's body was found?"

Bud looked embarrassed. I could tell he would

give me the truth this time. "I wanted to see," he muttered, "how all our hard work turned out."

June

Having learned my lesson, I went to Gus's several days before the next Founder's Weekend committee meeting. I went at the same late afternoon time, and Bud Barbour was at the counter again, Morgan asleep at his feet. I wondered if they visited Gus most afternoons.

"Tell me about Mr. Busman, Gus," I said when he'd poured me a sludgy cup of coffee.

Gus dumped the remaining coffee in the sink, filled the pot with soapy water, then sat on the stool next to me and picked up exactly where he'd left off. "Even though the Towns were driven off by the natives, the harbor was called Town's End for almost two hundred years. The town thrived for years on fishing, ice cutting, shipbuilding, canning, and packing salted fish. But after the Civil War, the axis of the country changed. Trade was no longer ruled by ships sailing north and south along the coast. It was driven by railroads going east and west. In some ways, Maine's economy never recovered.

"So the locals were glad to see the earliest vacationers when they started coming in the 1870s. For the most part, they were wealthy. Came here on their yachts and settled on Eastclaw and Westclaw Points and on the islands." Gus aimed his great, white eyebrows at me. "Like your mother's people.

"The summer people didn't come into the town. They objected to the smells from the fish salting, the canneries, and the noise from the shipbuilding. The Points were booming, but the town was dying. Ordinary people couldn't come to the harbor for their vacations. There was a railroad, but it was way up the peninsula, along where Route 1 is now.

"Then in 1895, a young man started meeting every train with a horse-drawn carriage, an open coach that sat twelve people in rows. He called it an omnibus and took all comers on a first-come, first-served basis, as long as they had a nickel. He called everyone, rich or poor, by his or her first name. Visitors began to come to the town.

"The people in the harbor loved the Busman, and turned their big, old sea captain's homes into lodgings. The money from the weekly boarders in the summer kept many people in their homes through the winter."

Morgan stood and walked in circles, tapping her nails on the wood floor to let Bud know it was time to go. I thought he'd excuse himself and shuffle off, but he commanded the dog to settle.

Gus glanced at Bud and went on. "In 1906, the Association of Working Women bought one of those grand houses in town to offer vacation housing to twenty women of low income per week. The girls came from the mills, up on the train and down the peninsula with the Busman. They didn't care about the smell of drying fish. The air was the cleanest they'd ever breathed. They swam in the harbor like children. For most of them, the first time they came here was the first vacation of their lives. Some returned year after year, even married local fisherman. Their descendants are with us still.

"The Busman's son took over the route. He brought the first horseless bus here in 1926. When his father died the next year, the community voted at the next town meeting to change our name from Town's End to Busman's Harbor. The business continued until 1936, killed off by the Great Depression and the automobile."

"Okay, Gus," I said. "Time to give it up. Who was the Busman?"

"His name was Harold Barbour the first. That's Harold Barbour the fourth, sitting down the counter from you, the Busman's great-grandson."

Bud tipped his Red Sox cap and smiled his gaptoothed Santa smile. "At your service."

Two days later, I was afraid Bud wouldn't show up for the Founder's Committee meeting, but he was there, nodding as I told the story. When I was done, he pulled a photo from his greasy satchel— his grandfather with the horseless omnibus, which looked the Model T version of a stretch limo.

"This is wonderful!" Bunnie proclaimed. "Bud, you'll be in the opening ceremonies."

He demurred.

Despite that, the committee was in good spirits. We'd accomplished so much. We were going to pull Founder's Weekend off. This would be our last formal meeting. Soon, the Tourism Bureau office would be crowded with visitors. Small's Ice Cream would go to its summer hours—10:00 to 10:00.

Already a dozen RV owners had arrived for the summer at Camp Glooscap, and, according to Vee, four couples celebrating a birthday were checking into the Snuggles that afternoon.

The clambake would be open in less than a week. Our first private event, a wedding, was the next Saturday. It had been an enormous amount of work, but I'd held the bank at bay and we were ready for the season. All we needed was a little luck and good weather to save the clambake.

"We picked a band for the concert," Stevie announced. "Take a listen." He popped a CD into an old boom box and the room came alive. A swing band. Perfect.

The music played and Stevie began to dance. He was a funny little man, with his potbelly and skinny ponytail. Not a picture of grace, but his joy was infectious. He pulled me from my chair and swung me around. Dan danced over to Bunnie and Bud took Vee's hand.

We danced until the music stopped.

August

I left Bud and jogged out of the back harbor. In ten minutes, I had to be at the dock for the start of my workday.

My cell phone buzzed. I extracted it from my tote bag as I ran, then stopped dead. A strange number, but not a blocked one. When I answered, there was a moment of echoing quiet, and then a deep, familiar voice said, "Julia? Phil Johnson. I have the storage device."

The photos on that device were the one thing that might exonerate Cabe. "Have you looked at the images? Can you see who left Stevie's body under the firewood?" I was breathless from the anticipation and the running.

"I have the storage device to give you, but it's a longer story. I need to explain. Can you get up here, right away?"

I could. "Where are you?"

"I spent the night at a B&B here on the coast with my . . ."

I waited him for him to decide whether to use the word *editor* or *girlfriend*.

"With my girlfriend," he finally said, "which is why I can reach you by cell phone. But I'm headed back to the blueberry barrens. There are just a few more days of raking." He told me which field he'd be working in and gave directions.

"On my way."

I rushed home and left a note for my mom that I was taking the car. I ran to my office and radioed Morrow Island. Livvie answered.

"Did you mean it when you said I could take a day off whenever I needed to help Cabe?" It would be a much heavier workday at the clambake than the day before. The early morning haze had burned off and I could tell the afternoon would be beautiful. Sonny and Livvie would have lunch and dinner to cope with.

"Of course. Take whatever time you need. We have everything under control."

"Thank you, Livvie. And thank Sonny. Are you feeling okay?" That should have been my first question to my sister. Today and for the next seven months.

"I'm fine. Good luck."

I left the house and hit the open road.

Chapter 38

On Route 1, traffic headed Down East was light. The morning's fog still hovered in a few areas along the coast. I tried to remember to breathe. I had three hours alone in my mother's car to think about my problems. Not good.

I'd left things in such a terrible place with Chris. He wanted to know if I returned his feelings. If I loved him. It was a reasonable request.

The irony wasn't lost on me. I'd been the school-girl with the crush. My feelings for him had been unrequited for years. I'd been on his boat, in his bed. And now, I was the one who hesitated.

There was no future in it. This is what I'd told myself over and over. Chris was a creature of the harbor. He loved the wild Maine coast. He'd do anything to stay. It was impossible to imagine him away from it. He belonged.

I didn't. I never had. Though Livvie seemed to think that had more to do with me than it did with

Busman's Harbor. Could she be right? Did my sense that I didn't belong come from inside me? I'd just told Bunnie to extend herself to a neighbor in order to be accepted. Was I talking to myself?

That gave me something to work on as I sped along.

Chris hadn't asked me to marry him. All my ruminating about where we'd spend our future was profoundly premature. He'd asked me if I loved him. In the moment. Why couldn't I at least answer yes to that? My knees went weak whenever I saw him. His touch took my breath away. I couldn't be near him without wanting to touch him. I lusted for him, that was for sure. And he lusted for me. Not just generically, as all men lust, but he lusted specifically for me. I knew it. I could feel it. I trusted my feelings. My feelings toward him physically were unambiguous.

But my attraction to Chris was so much more than physical. He was the person I told everything to. Not just my problems, but also my triumphs. Both were hard for me to share with people. I had more of Mom's Yankee reticence than I cared to admit. Chris made me feel safe.

Except for one thing. The thing that couldn't be ignored. The thing that wrapped itself like a python around my heart. He had a reputation as a bad boy. He occasionally disappeared without explanation. My openness with him wasn't reciprocated, in one critical way. He had asked me to trust him, but could I?

I thought about Cabe's situation and immediately felt like a self-involved child. Cabe was about to be accused of murder, and I was worried about my *boyfriend*.

I passed through Ellsworth and hit the open road, going as fast as Mom's old car allowed. So fast, I almost missed my turn onto the Route 182 bypass. So fast, I definitely missed the state cop parked just before the turnoff.

His light bar blinked on and his siren blared.

"Damn." I pulled to the side of the road and stopped.

"License and registration, ma'am," the cherubic-faced trooper said through my driver's side window.

I pondered my excuses as I flipped through my mother's glove compartment for the registration. *I didn't know I was going so fast*, sounded idiotic, compounding inattention with excessive speed. *I'm in a hurry*, I thought he might have heard before. I turned over the registration and my license without saying a word.

"Is this your vehicle, ma'am?"

"It's my mother's."

The trooper looked at me doubtfully. I was about a decade too old to have to borrow my mother's car.

"See." I pointed to the two documents he held in his hand. "Same last name."

"You're a long way from home. Does your mother know you have the car?"

"Of course she does," I answered, a little too vehemently. I hoped Mom had found my note.

"I need to check to make sure this vehicle hasn't been reported stolen."

"Oh, for heaven's sake."

"Did you say something?"

"Nothing." He went to his vehicle while I sat and steamed in the August heat. How bad could it be? I didn't think Mom's old Buick could even go that fast.

"Here's your citation. You're free to go."

"Two hundred and fifteen dollars!"

"I clocked you at sixty-two in a forty mile an hour zone."

He got back into his patrol car and watched while I gingerly pulled Mom's car onto the road and set off a couple miles an hour below the speed limit. If I'd been unhappy with the state cops before, because of Binder and Flynn's behavior, I was furious at them now.

As the road turned back into Route 1 and curved toward the coast, the mist returned in the form of a low ground fog. I cursed my bad luck. If the fog had come up sooner, or the cop had been positioned later, I wouldn't have been speeding. Following Phil's directions, forty minutes later, I pulled to the side of the road, grateful to get out and stretch. Yellow totes full of blueberries lined the field, waiting for the truck to pick them up.

Out in the blueberry barrens, the pickers moved in the mist like ghosts, swinging their rakes like Death's scythe. As I wondered how on earth I was going to find Phil, a tall figure walked out of the fog and met me at the edge of the field.

"You made it," he said.

"Have you got it? The storage device?"

"Yes." Phillip reached into his camera bag and pulled out a plastic box about the size of a smart phone. "But I don't think it's going to help you. There are over ten thousand photos. Since you don't know what time the body was dumped, it may take days to go through them."

I nodded to show that I understood and slipped the device into my tote bag. I did have some sense of the time frame. Cabe had said that he'd left the pier around 2:00 and returned before 5:30.

"She'll know what to do. I know she will." A slender figure appeared out of the mist almost next to me.

"Cabe!" I threw my arms around him.

My joy morphed to anger. "Why didn't you tell me you were here?" I whirled back to Phil. "Why didn't *you* tell me he was here?"

"Hey, don't yell at me. I'm the one who persuaded him to see you."

I turned back to Cabe. "You need to come to Busman's Harbor with me and meet with Lieutenant Binder. Right now, he still only wants to interview you as a witness, but I'm not sure how long that will last." Behind me, a vehicle door slammed.

Cabe didn't respond. He turned and ran.

"Outatheway!" A hand struck me in the back, pushing me to the side.

I lost my balance, twisted around, and fell flat on my back. Sergeant Flynn leaped over me and brought Cabe down.

"You're under arrest!" he screamed at Cabe. "Do you understand me?"

Chapter 39

"You okay?" Lieutenant Binder and Phil Johnson stood above me, looking down. Binder stuck out a hand.

I grabbed it and started to get up. As soon as I put weight on my left foot, pain seared up from my ankle. "Yowza!"

Binder grasped both my forearms and pulled me to my feet.

"Ow. Ow. Ow. Ow."

"Sorry about that. As a policy, it's a bad idea to get between Flynn and a suspect."

"I didn't know Cabe was a suspect. And I didn't know I was in between. Did you follow me up here?" I demanded.

"Of course not."

"The speeding ticket! You knew I was on Route 1 because of the speeding ticket. And then you tracked me here."

"You got a speeding ticket?" Binder chuckled, adding insult to actual injury.

"You know damn well I did."

"When?"

"About an hour ago."

"Julia, what do you think this is? *CSI: Pine Tree State*? How would I get here from Busman's Harbor in an hour? Do you see a chopper anywhere?" He took off his dark glasses and wiped the lenses with a handkerchief. "This kind of operation doesn't come together in a day. The blueberry fields are tribal lands. State cops don't come busting in here without letting local law enforcement and the Passamaquoddy leadership know." He let that sink in. "Honestly, I didn't know you were here. I wasn't even completely sure you knew where young Mr. Stone was. It was a bit of a shot in the dark when Flynn accused you."

"I didn't know where Cabe was when Flynn accused me. I just found him." Really, I hadn't found him. He'd let Phil summon me, but I didn't say that to Binder. Nor did I tell him about the storage device in my tote bag.

Phil, standing nearby, also said nothing.

"I've been helping you. I gave you the camera, for goodness sake. You used me to get information, yet told me nothing. You treated me like a fool."

Binder put the sunglasses, completely unnecessary in the morning mist, back on. "I never thought you were a fool. I'm sorry if that's the way it came across." He pointed down at my ankle, which was swelling rapidly. "You'd best get that seen to. I'll have one of my people run you to the ER in Machias."

"My car—"

Phil said, "I can drive her over."

I handed Phil my keys and they helped me hobble to my car. "Geez," he said when he tried the door handle. "Did you *lock* this thing out here?"

We spent two hours in the ER waiting room while my ankle blew up to the size of a softball. People came and went, some obviously in worse shape. A cable news show was on the TV in the corner, its sound turned off.

"What do you think is happening with Cabe?" Phil asked.

"I'm sure Binder and Flynn are taking him to Busman's Harbor for questioning. I should have reminded him to ask for an attorney." The moments from when Flynn pushed me down until Cabe was loaded into the state police car in handcuffs were a blur.

"Excuse me," I said and dialed Chris on my cell. I wasn't even sure he'd answer. We'd left things in such a weird place. *C'mon, c'mon, c'mon, Chris. Pick up.*

"Julia, are you all right? Why aren't you at the clambake?" He knew my cell phone didn't work on Morrow Island.

"I came out to Washington County to get those photos I told you about from the night on the pier. Cabe was arrested."

"What happened?"

I took Chris step by step through the events of the day so far. I left out the part about my ankle, because if I told him, he'd want to come get me. Or he'd go over and punch Flynn in the nose. Neither was productive. I needed Chris to be in Busman's Harbor, helping Cabe.

"Where are you?" I asked him. "I forgot to tell Cabe not to say anything without an attorney present."

"I'm in my cab. I can swing by the police station. What time do you think they'll get here?"

"I doubt they'll let you see him. Can you call that lawyer, the one who represented you when—"

"I was arrested in the spring," he finished. For the murder on Morrow Island he hadn't committed.

"Yes, please. Tell him I'll pay."

"I'm sure he'll help if I can find him. We can work out how he gets paid, later."

"Okay, and Chris—"

"What?"

I heard him breathing. There were so many things I wanted to say. I hated this gulf between us. But we couldn't talk now. Phil was sitting next to me, and I was in no shape to get up and move away. And, I wanted Chris to find the lawyer and get him to the station house. "Nothing. Good luck with Cabe."

"Drive safely."

"I will."

When I hung up, Phil looked at me curiously. "You're really looking out for that kid. He told me he isn't your brother. Why are you in this?"

"He saved my life once."

"Is that so?" Phil looked at the silent TV where pundits yelled at one another like a bunch of mad mimes. Then he looked pointedly at the ancient magazine in his lap. "I think you better tell me the whole story."

Why not? He was involved after all, and we had to pass the time. So I told him about how Cabe pulled me from the path of the oncoming vehicle. And how the body was found in the fire under the Claminator, which he knew because he was there. I told him the dead man was Stevie Noyes, and about Stevie's two identities, and about how even though two women had loved him, and had each born him a child, he'd ended up alone.

"Wait, what did you say this guy's RV campground was called?"

"Camp Glooscap."

"You know what that is?"

I shook my head.

"In my culture, Glooscap is the first being. The name means, 'man created from nothing,' or 'man created only by speech.'"

"Which Stevie Noyes was." It made perfect sense. "When he left prison, he wasn't T.V. Noyes anymore. He created Stevie, the nicest guy in the world."

The nurse finally called me.

"Does this hurt?" the doctor asked as he manipulated my ankle.

Tears sprang to my eyes.

"Not broken," the doctor said. "A significant sprain. We'll bandage you up. Elevate. Ice. No weight-bearing for at least three days."

Three days! I had a business to run. And Cabe had just been driven off to jail in handcuffs, a place I couldn't let him stay.

Once my foot and ankle were wrapped, a process that caused me to bite my hand to keep from screaming, the doctor said, "I'll provide you with something for the pain."

"No pain meds. I have to drive back to Busman's Harbor right now."

"Don't be silly. You can't drive."

I couldn't stay. Cabe was in jail, afraid and counting on me. "Why not? It's my left ankle. I don't use it to drive."

The doctor wrote something on my chart. "All right. I'll give you the prescription. You don't have to get it filled."

They gave me crutches and made me practice with them. Walking with crutches was a lot harder than it looked. I hobbled out the ER exit. Phil had gone ahead to bring the car around.

Phil pulled up.

"Get out," I said.

"What?"

"Move to the passenger side so I can practice driving with someone in the car. It's a long way back to Busman's and I don't want to fly solo on my first time out."

"You can't drive home."

"I can't stay here. After all I just told you, do you think I'm going to sit around for three days with my foot in the air? I have to get home."

Chapter 40

The trip back to Busman's Harbor was long and painful. I drove with my teeth clenched, my back tight against the throbbing pain. At times, I thought I wouldn't make it, but what would I do if I stopped? When I finally pulled into our driveway late in the afternoon, I sat for a moment, uncertain if I could get out of the car. It wasn't only my ankle that hurt. I'd landed hard when Flynn pushed me, and the long ride had magnified every ache.

Mom and Richelle rushed out to the porch when they saw me making my way gingerly up the front walk on crutches.

"Julia! What happened? Are you all right?" Concern etched deep worry lines into my mother's face.

"I'm fine," I answered, though anyone looking at me could tell I wasn't.

Mom and Richelle helped me up the porch steps and settled me on the love seat, my left foot up on the ottoman. Mom ran to get me something to drink and an ice pack.

"And some ibuprofen!" I called after her.

"They arrested Cabe," I told Richelle.

Her sharp intake of breath told me what terrible news this was for her. "What can we do?"

"I've asked my friend Chris to find Cabe a lawyer."

"But there must be something more. Julia, please. I've never done anything for my son. Please help me do something for him now. You still don't believe he's guilty, do you?"

I didn't. In spite of the mountain of evidence, the camera, the running away, even the previous murder accusation, I did not believe Cabe Stone had stabbed Stevie Noyes seventeen times and put his body in the clambake fire.

I wiggled on the love seat to get comfortable and felt the weight of the storage device Phil had given me shift in my tote bag. If Cabe wasn't guilty, someone else was. And if I could figure out who, maybe I could spare Cabe the trauma of an extended stay in jail and a trial. I just might have the answer on the storage device. As Richelle wiped her eyes, I extracted my cell phone from my tote bag and called a number on my contacts list.

"Bunnie? It's Julia. I have a favor to ask. I'd like to use the computers at the Tourism Bureau office. And I need some people to work on them. Can you call the committee members for me? Just tell them I need help. Yes, right now."

Bunnie assured me, with probably more politeness and enthusiasm than I deserved considering the tone of our last conversation, she would do as I asked.

"Great," I said. "I'll meet you at the Tourism Bureau office in twenty minutes."

"I'm driving, " Richelle said.

I looked at my swollen ankle resting on the ottoman. "You're not allowed to drive."

"Oh, Julia. The doctor cleared me to travel four days ago. I just couldn't leave town when my son was in so much trouble."

Bunnie's big SUV was already in the parking lot at the Tourism Bureau office when Richelle and I arrived, as was Vee's Subaru wagon. Dan Small's bike leaned against the deck rail. I was shocked when Bud Barbour pulled up in his ratty old pickup.

Inside, I asked them to take a seat at a computer. The Bureau's computer workstations were paired so two people sat facing one another, though the monitors blocked the sight of the person sitting opposite. Everyone was quiet. It was the first time we'd all been together without Stevie and I had a little lump in my throat. I could tell we were all feeling it.

"Cabe Stone was arrested this afternoon for the murder of the person we knew as Stevie Noyes," I said for the benefit of anyone who hadn't heard.

"What happened to you?" Dan looked from the crutches I'd leaned against a desk to my bandaged ankle.

"I got pushed in the arrest."

"Police brutality!" Bud yelled.

"Bud," I warned. "I was in the wrong place at the

wrong time. It was an accident." I took Phil Johnson's storage device out of my bag. "I believe Cabe's innocent, and I think this could help prove it."

I heard a vehicle door slam and caught a glimpse of Reggie's Swinburne's giant, dark blue pickup in the parking lot outside.

"Bunnie called me. I'm here to help," Reggie said as he came through the door.

"Of course. I'm just explaining what we're going to do." I waved the storage device in front of them. "This device contains pictures of the pier taken by a professional photographer on the night of Stevie's murder. I believe it includes photos of the real murderer placing Stevie's body under the clambake stove. There are over ten thousand photos on the device. I'm going to divide them up and give each of you a group to go through. Ideally, you're looking for a series of pictures that capture our killer in the act. But if the group of photos you get doesn't contain anything conclusive, look for anything out of the ordinary."

Each of them sat quietly as I moved a large block of photos off the storage device and onto their computers. I showed them how to open and scroll through the photos. The files were enormous and took time to open. It was going to be a long, tedious process.

When I moved the first batch of photos, time-stamped 8:00 PM to 10:00 PM, to Vee's computer, I saw exactly what I expected. Sonny and Cabe were setting up the Claminator. Weezer worked on his barbecue. Dan fussed with his portable ice cream cart. The sun was down, but in the first few photos there was still plenty of twilight.

I gave the second set of photos, 10:00 PM to midnight, to Bunnie. They were taken in full darkness and were disappointingly shadowy. Two streetlights on the pier threw a little light on the Claminator. The moon over the harbor was a slim crescent. In the first photo, I could just make out Cabe's familiar body stacking wood.

I gave the third group of photos, midnight to 2:00 AM to Dan Small. I kept the ones from 2:00 AM to 4:00 AM for myself. Cabe had said he'd left the pier to go to the boarding house and sleep between 2:00 and 5:30, so I thought this group was the most likely to contain the images I was seeking. I gave 4:00 to 6:00—daybreak—to Richelle.

I gave 6:00 AM to 8:00 to Reggie and 8:00 AM to 10:00 to Bud. "Your assignment is slightly different," I told them. "These photos were taken after sunup and probably after Stevie's body was hidden. People will have started coming to the pier, so look for anyone acting suspiciously."

"Cabe Stone acted suspiciously," Dan pointed out. "He ran."

"That's not the only kind of suspicious. Look for people doing the opposite of running. Hanging around. Staring at the fire. People who are a little too interested."

They were all pretty comfortable with their computers. I wasn't surprised. Vee and Dan ran small businesses. Bunnie ran the Tourism Bureau. Richelle used a computer all the time with her tour guide work and Reggie had retired relatively recently. The only one I wasn't sure about was Bud, but he caught on right away.

"World of Warcraft," he muttered in response to my quizzical look. "The winters are long."

I hopped back to my computer and starting scrolling through my group of photos. They were maddeningly dark. I could see what Phil had been trying to do. In a time-lapse video, the constantly changing photos would be lively, but looking at them one at a time, they were uninteresting and worse, uninformative.

In the very first ones, I could just make out a figure lying on the pier, head propped on something. At first I thought it might be Stevie, but then the figure moved and I realized it was Cabe, trying to sleep on the hard concrete. I assumed the darker patch beneath him was a blanket he'd taken from his bunk in the playhouse, brought over in the backpack he used as a pillow. I was angry at Sonny all over again for asking Cabe to sleep with the Claminator. I scrolled on.

"Can you look at this, Julia?" Reggie asked. I got up, hopped behind him, and looked over his shoulder at his monitor. In the sequence of photos he showed me, the vendors arrived and continued setting up. Cabe was there. So were Sonny and Livvie. Off to the side, a man stood, apparently staring at the Claminator. As Reggie scrolled forward, the man stayed still for several frames.

"Can you enlarge that?" I asked.

Reggie did. I bent over his shoulder to get a better look. "I don't think it's meaningful," I said, pointing to the wires that trailed from the man's headphones to the bulge in his shirt pocket. "He's on the phone or listening to music. It looks like he's staring at the clambake stove, but I think he's staring off into space."

"I think you're right," Reggie agreed.

"Are you sure?" Richelle pleaded from her desk, which was across from mine.

"Just in case, can you mark the number on those photos?" I asked. "And print them?" I wasn't hopeful, but the committee members were working hard and I didn't want to quash the momentum. Bunnie rose from her place to help Reggie with the printer.

On the way back to my seat, I stopped behind everyone, checking that they weren't having problems. Dan worked efficiently, scrolling through the photos. Vee was more perfunctory, tapping the down arrow at a steady clip. I wondered if she thought the search was pointless.

I sat down at my computer and scrolled through more slides. Everyone worked quietly, occasionally stopping to write down the number of an image or print one. My ankle throbbed. I kept working.

Just when I was ready to give up, I saw it. The black rectangle of a vehicle pulling up beside the Claminator. A big pickup truck. I nearly cried out when I recognized the distinctive top Reggie had over his truck's bed. I clamped one hand over my mouth and kept scrolling. Reggie was right in the room! I made myself put my hand back on the desk and tried to look casual or even bored. I didn't dare look over at him. Just a few minutes ago, he'd tried to distract me with a photo of some random tourist on the pier.

In my photos, the shadow of a man got out and went behind the truck. The back of the pickup had almost no light on it, and though I wanted to scroll as quickly as my heart was beating, I made myself slow down, examining each photo. The figure opened the back of the truck and pulled something heavy out. Something I assumed was Stevie. Something wrapped in a dark sleeve that had to be a sleeping bag.

Binder and Flynn had never said anything about a sleeping bag!

The figure pulled the heavy object to the clambake stove. Stevie was a small man, but I thought his dead weight must be difficult to maneuver.

As I watched, the man who had to be Reggie removed a bunch of logs and stuffed Stevie under the Claminator. My hands turned clammy and shook a little. I thought the others must be able to see. Richelle peered around her monitor and arched an eyebrow at me. I gave one small shake of my head, warning her off.

I reminded myself to breathe. I concentrated on the pain in my ankle to take my mind off my fear. What to do? What to do? I scrolled on and watched the figure toss off the pier the logs he'd removed from the fire to make room for Stevie. Then he got in the truck and started to back out of the frame. As I wrote the image numbers on the pad next to me, I became aware of a presence behind me. I moved the image of the front half of the truck off my screen and turned around.

Bunnie. The photo had been very dark, and she was standing a few feet behind me. She hadn't seen the full sequence or the complete truck. Could she even recognize what she'd seen?

"Need something, Bunnie?" I kept my voice steady.

"Just stretching."

She returned to her computer and I looked at the rest of the images in my batch, scrolling to the end. All I saw was the silent pier, apparently empty, with its secret hidden under the metal skirting of the Claminator.

"I'm done!" Dan called out.

"Me, too," Vee said. Richelle nodded she was done also.

"Just a few more," Bunnie said.

I took deep breaths to steady myself. I wasn't going to accuse Reggie here. Too dangerous, even in this room full of people. I had to get the storage device, with this sequence of photos, to Lieutenant Binder right away. "I'm done, too," I said. I waited another agonizing ten minutes for Bud and Bunnie to finish up.

"That was disappointing," Dan said. "Sorry, Julia."

"It's okay. I'm sure what we did find will be very helpful." I made a show of collecting the photos people had printed and the image numbers they'd noted. "Thank you all so much."

"It's what neighbors do," Bunnie said.

* * *

We clustered on the deck, lingering while Bunnie locked the office. The sun was low, but I could tell everyone was reluctant to go. For a couple hours, they'd been part of an exciting drama.

"Can you catch a ride back with Vee?" I whispered to Richelle. "I have an errand to do on the way to town." She started to protest, but I gave another small flick of my head and she understood.

Finally, Dan jumped on his bike and peddled off toward town. Vee, with Richelle in the passenger seat, followed by Bud, waited for a break in the perpetual flow of summer traffic and then pulled their vehicles into the roadway.

Reggie climbed into his battleship of a pickup. Bunnie hoisted herself onto the truck's tall running board and gave him a peck on the cheek through the open window. Poor woman. She had terrible luck with men.

I wanted to be sure Reggie was safely on his way the other direction, back up the peninsula toward Camp Glooscap before I left. But he and Bunnie chatted away, completely oblivious to my hanging around. Bunnie's side of the conversation appeared downright flirty. The image she'd seen on my monitor must have been too dark for her to recognize Reggie's truck. Finally, I gave up waiting. Reggie was so rapt; it seemed the perfect time for me to make a break for it. I pulled past them from my parking spot.

As I waited for an opening in the traffic, Bunnie turned, pointed at me and shouted. She ran around and jumped into the passenger seat beside Reggie as he fired up his truck.

I screeched out of the parking lot, causing a station wagon with a full bike rack attached to slam on its brakes. Were they coming after me? I reached out, angled the side view mirror, and saw the nose of Reggie's truck bulling itself forward, impatient for a break in traffic. He let three cars go by, then rocketed onto the road.

Bunnie must have understood what she'd seen on my monitor and told Reggie! I floored it, using so much body force pain shot up my leg from my throbbing left ankle. In my tote bag was the only piece of evidence that would exonerate Cabe.

I kept the pedal to the metal, but Mom's car barely responded on the uphill grade. Three cars were between us, spread out on the hill, but Reggie was moving fast. The road into Busman's Harbor was a two-lane highway and passing was permitted. Reggie easily overtook the car in front of him. Only two cars between us, and I didn't have the power to pass a go-cart.

Bunnie and Reggie were in it together. Of course, they were. Both hated Stevie. He had stolen all Bunnie's money and caused her husband's suicide. He had given the campsite Reggie felt was his to the Parkers. Reggie loved Bunnie and would do anything for her.

Reggie's truck pulled out to pass again, but was forced back by oncoming traffic. Another coin dropped. Reggie and Bunnie had been together at the clambake. That must have been when they'd planted the camera in the playhouse.

On his next try, Reggie passed the second car. He was speeding, tailgating the remaining car.

I tore my eyes from my side mirror. A turnoff or side road wouldn't help me. I'd be trapped. I beat on my steering wheel, "Go, go, go you lousy piece of crap!" At last, I crested the hill. Not much farther to the harbor and all downhill.

A horn blasted so loud I jerked the wheel. Reggie was coming up right beside me. Headlights flashing, his massive chrome grill loomed in my side view mirror like a monster's maw. Too close! He was going to run me off the road.

Reggie nudged ever closer, honking madly. Bunnie leaned out her window and yelled, gesticulating crazily toward the backseat of my car. *What the hell?*

Something closed around my throat, stifling my scream.

It took me a moment to realize what was happening. Someone in the backseat was trying to strangle me! I scratched wildly at the strong fingers with my right hand as I careened into the oncoming lane, forcing Reggie's truck onto the far shoulder.

The hands squeezed tighter. I clawed behind me, trying to free myself, craning to see who it was, light-headed and desperate for air. Red bolts flashed behind my eyes. I stomped both feet on the brake and the Buick skidded sideways, veering back into the right lane. Reggie pulled beside me again. Through blurring eyes, I saw Bunnie aim a shotgun out her window.

The hands squeezed tighter and tighter. Reggie's truck banged the side of my car, pushing it onto the shoulder. Trying to fight off my attacker with one hand, I jerked my wheel back with the other. But I was no match for Reggie's beast of a vehicle. He slammed me again, harder. The Buick fishtailed wildly, tires shrieking, taking out both the Rotary Club and Kiwanis signs welcoming me to Busman's Harbor. The car was airborne for a second before nose-diving into a culvert with the heavy crunch of metal and a brutal jolt. My door flew open. My body lurched to the left, but I didn't fall out. The hands were still clamped around my throat like a vise. I hit out feebly, desperately trying to hang on to consciousness.

The loudest noise I've ever heard exploded next to me.

"Let her go or my next round won't be in the air." Bunnie aimed the shotgun over my head.

As I slid to the ground, the last thing I saw was Zach from the RV park, raising his hands in the air.

Chapter 41

I woke up in the hospital. My mother slept on the guest chair in my room. The sun was out.

"What time is it?" I croaked, though in truth I wasn't sure what day it was. I hadn't been completely unconscious the whole time. I vaguely remembered Jamie had been the first officer on the scene, and as soon as I recognized him, I knew I'd be all right. I'd tried so hard to find words to tell him what I knew, but couldn't get them out.

My mother opened her deeply circled eyes and looked at the delicate watch on her wrist. "9:00 AM Friday."

So I hadn't lost a day. Everything had happened the previous evening. Mom leaped from the chair and arrived at my bedside in two steps. She kissed my forehead.

It was only then, looking at the love and concern in my mother's eyes, I thought to wiggle my toes. I saw them moving under the lightweight hospital blanket—which meant my eyesight was fine, too.

My fingers and arms also moved to my brain's command. My head wagged from side to side. It was only after I did all these things that I began to feel the ache. My neck hurt. Swallowing made my throat feel like it was embedded with razor blades. My chest hurt, too. And my ankle. Slowly the neurons connected and I remembered my ankle had hurt before the crash.

"Lieutenant Binder?" My voice was a hoarse whisper.

"He's been here, last night and early this morning. You'll need to talk to him, but there'll be time when you feel stronger." She paused. "Christopher was here all night. I sent him back to the *Dark Lady* about an hour ago to get some sleep. He wouldn't leave until he knew you were okay."

Chris. I thought I'd dreamed his face, such a mask of worry and hurt. It brought tears to my eyes that I could cause him so much pain. I'd tried to tell him I was okay, but my voice didn't work.

"Christopher," I repeated. "Why do you call him that?"

"Is that not his name?"

She had me there. "Why don't you like him, Mom? Why do I feel the weight of your judgment whenever his name is mentioned?"

Now I had her. I was her child, lying in a hospital bed, neck still ringed by the damage left by a man who'd tried to kill me. She would have to answer.

But instead she said, "Why do you care what I think?"

The question shocked me. She was my mother. Of course I cared.

She continued. "Do you think when I fell in love with your father, my family, such as it was, supported me?"

Her family, at that point, had been her father. Her mother was long dead and Hugh, the cousin who'd been brought up with her had disappeared. I'd always assumed my grandfather had objected to her romance with and marriage to my dad, though neither of my parents had ever said so to me directly. My father was a high school-educated son of a lobsterman and my mother was the college-educated descendent of a once-wealthy summer family.

"Did you ever regret it?" I asked. "Everything you gave up to marry Dad?"

My mother blinked. "Julia, whatever do you think I gave up?"

I wasn't sure. Life in Boston or New York? A husband who provided a good living without coming to bed smelling, even slightly, of wood smoke and shellfish? My mother loved my father. She loved Livvie and me, and those things added together meant she loved her life. So what did I think she'd given up?

She'd given up belonging—anywhere. That's what I'd always believed in my gut. She wasn't a summer person or a townie. She'd lived two thirds of her life in Busman's Harbor, yet would always be From Away. If she'd married the stockbroker or college professor or physician her father had no doubt imagined, would she have lived a life where she fit in?

I said it to her haltingly, having difficulty finding

the words, and not just because of the pain in my throat. I didn't want to offend or hurt her. But I had to know.

"Is that what you think?" she asked. "Do you think that's why I've led a life without friends?"

I nodded to save my throat. And because I didn't trust myself to speak.

"Your father was my best friend," she said.

I already knew that.

"I was always shy. Always self-sufficient. I spent every summer of my life on an island, after all." She smiled. "I had my books, my life, my wild Maine coast. Honestly, until your dad came along, I didn't think I needed anyone else. I was wrong, of course. I didn't know it, but I'd been waiting for him—and for you and Livvie." She sat on the bed and took my hand. "Julia, I haven't been isolated because I didn't fit in Busman's Harbor. I love this town. I love the Snugg sisters and Gus and the Smalls and all the employees at the clambake. The town has been supportive of me, always, but never more than when your father was ill. Livvie and Sonny did a lot, but they couldn't do it all and run the business, too. People I barely recognized brought us food and took your dad for his treatments. I couldn't have survived without them." She let go of my hand and wiped her eye with a knuckle. "You may think I've been alone in my life, but that hasn't come from the town. That comes from me. It's who I am. Your father was gregarious enough for two people—or for ten. I would hate for you to think I've been lonely. It just hasn't been so."

I thought about the two of us on my first day of kindergarten. Her standing outside the circle of gossiping mothers. Me, standing next to her, staring at the running, screaming children. There was a lot of her in me. She'd found that one person she'd let in. Had I?

"Mom, how did you know Dad was the one?"

"Your dad loved me just as I was. Solitary. Self-sufficient. But he also made me want to be the best person I could be. His love made me reach into myself and find the parts of me that could be generous, caring, thoughtful and bring those forward. Go to those places first. I was certain of his love, but we also craved each other's respect, and worked to earn it every day—or as often as we could."

"Love," I croaked. "Acceptance. Respect."

"Yes," Mom said. "And one more thing. Trust. I trusted your father completely. And it's a good thing I could, because I put my whole life in his hands. Yours and Livvie's, too. I knew everything he did, he did for us. I knew he would never, ever hurt us. Have you found a man you can trust, Julia?"

When I woke up the next time, the sun was low in the sky. I heard murmuring outside my door. One voice, the one asking questions, was indisputably masculine. My hopes rose. *Chris.*

And fell when Lieutenant Binder walked into the room. As he sat in the guest chair, he held up his hand, palm forward. "This isn't an official interview. I come in peace. When you feel better, we'll need you to make a statement about everything that happened last evening. For now, I just want to see how you are."

"I'm fine. A little raspy, as you can hear. No solid food yet. But nothing's broken. They're observing me. Thank-you for asking."

"Glad to hear it."

A silence settled over us. The kind of pregnant pause that comes when both parties to a conversation have a lot to say, but are unsure how to start.

Though I'd seen Binder play the silence game like a master, he spoke first. "You could have been killed."

I was astonished at the anger in his voice.

"You kept information from the police. I could charge you."

"You kept information from me!" I was amazed at how angry I still was. "You never told me Cabe had been accused of murder before, and that's why you locked in on him as a suspect. You didn't tell me Richelle had been Stevie's secretary and had testified against him, even though she was staying in my house. *I* endangered me? *You* endangered me."

"Was Ms. Rose a danger to you? Do you think I would have left her in your house if I thought she was?" Binder paused to catch his breath. "We aren't partners. I don't owe you any explanations. But you shouldn't have kept things from me. Aaron Crane was a danger to you. When did you figure out Zach was Aaron?"

"Not until the moment I looked into his eyes when I was passing out. I should have realized earlier. When he shaved off his beard, he looked so familiar. I thought it was because I'd seen him before, but that wasn't it. He was like a darker version of Cabe. Shorter, but with the same thin build. I also should have figured out he was in the habit of taking Reggie's truck. I think he tried to run me down once. Or he tried to run Cabe down and I was in the way."

"Something else you never told me."

"It happened weeks before all this. Honestly, I thought it was an accident. I didn't make the connection. Cabe made it for me."

"Then there's the matter of the photos you collected from Phillip Johnson. You didn't tell me about those, either. What do you say to that?"

I had nothing to say to that.

"It's a good thing Crane confessed, despite the presence of an expensive lawyer his stepfather sent who all but ordered him not to talk," Binder said.

"Did he say why he did it?"

"You know, to all outward appearances, he had an easy life. His mother remarried when he was two. His stepfather adopted him. He grew up in an affluent suburb. But his mother never recovered from Stevie Noyes' deception and fall. She filled him full of stories about how wealthy he would have been. When she killed herself, Aaron looked for his birth father and eventually found him. But he also saw Cabe skulking around Noyes and got curious. He went through Cabe's things in his boarding house and found Cabe's birth certificate. Cabe was the son of the mistress who'd been part of ruining his mother's life, the mistress who'd testified against

Stevie. He decided to kill their father and frame Cabe."

"He planted the camera in the playhouse."

"It was easy enough to do. That's why he shaved his beard and had his hair cut. He didn't want to attract attention to himself. He paid his sixty bucks and went to the clambake." Binder paused. "Of course, he'd been on the island before. He 'borrowed' boats left on the RV park's waterfront and landed on your beach. That's how he stole Cabe's birth certificate. He had it on him when he was arrested."

"And Cabe's parents' wedding rings and the photo of Cabe with them?"

"In Aaron's pop-up camper. They'll be returned to Cabe in due course."

"I'm glad."

"Aaron was with Reggie Swinburne when Bunnie Getts called to ask Reggie to come to the Tourism Bureau office," Binder continued. "Reggie hung up and told 'Zach' you'd found a big clue about the murderer. Zach snuck over to the Tourism Bureau in the back of Reggie's truck. He was sure you had the clue with you when you left. Of course, you did."

"He hid in the backseat of my car." I'd finally acclimated to being back in Busman's Harbor. I'd left the car doors unlocked.

"He planned to steal the storage device from you, by force if necessary, before you reached the station house parking lot. Once you'd entered the crowded streets of the harbor, there were red lights and stop signs where he might have confronted you. But when he realized when you were still out on the highway and that Bunnie and Reggie had seen him, he struck. He didn't care if killing you meant he would also die. He imagined you, him, and the evidence going up in a blaze of glory, which would still leave Cabe on the hook for Stevie's murder."

"What I don't get is why he hung around after he murdered Stevie. He'd already disappeared once in his life. He was skilled at it."

"The killing wasn't over with Noyes. Part of the reason he stayed was to make sure Cabe got the blame. If you hadn't discovered the camera, I'm sure he would have found a way to call it to our attention. But the other reason was your friend Richelle. Aaron had figured out who she really was and knew she was staying at your house. He planned to kill her next."

I shuddered, remembering the shadowy figure I'd seen in front of the house on the first night Richelle stayed with us. The person I'd thought was Cabe.

"Aaron suffered such terrible losses," I said. "The absence of his father, the suicide of his mother. I'm shocked by what he did, but I'm not surprised he was so angry. To me, Cabe is the remarkable one. His life was such a struggle, yet he remained so optimistic."

"That's one thing you learn for sure in this job," Binder said. "There is absolutely no accounting for human nature."

Bunnie and Reggie came in later in the evening. "You saved my life," I croaked. "Thank you."

"When you pulled out of your parking space, I was up on Reggie's running board. I could see into your backseat. I wouldn't have noticed Zach, except that he moved and I recognized his usual way of dressing exactly like Reggie. When I told Reggie what I'd seen, he put two and two together."

"When Bunnie told me he was hiding in the backseat of your car, the only thing I could think was that he wanted to hurt you. I'm sorry, Julia. I did my best for that boy, but he was a lost soul."

"How could you have known? I'm sorry, too. I thought it was you in the photos. I should have realized Zach was in the habit of borrowing your truck. He tried to run Cabe and me down with it, weeks ago."

"I sleep with earplugs in because of the Parkers, and I always leave my keys in my truck. Everybody in Camp Glooscap does. I can't blame you for thinking I was the killer when you saw my truck in the photos. I'm just glad you're alive."

"Thanks to you and Bunnie."

"She's something, isn't she?"

On their way out, Bunnie came over to the bed and took my hand. "Come visit when you're up and around?"

I promised I would.

Chapter 42

The next morning, I felt better. The doctor came in early and assured me my voice would come back completely once the swelling went down in my throat. She said I could go home in the late afternoon if nothing else turned up.

"You probably don't see that many stranglings in Busman's Harbor," I croaked.

"I wish that were true," she said. "Throttling is the most common form of domestic abuse."

A physical therapist insisted I practice using my crutches. I went up and down the corridor outside my room so many times, I wore myself out. I ate a lunch of soft, unappetizing foods and fell asleep.

I awoke to voices in my room. One, high and feminine, the other low and rumbling. My eyes flew open. Even before I saw him, I knew from the voice it wasn't Chris. But I hoped in spite of my own senses it would be.

Richelle sat in the guest chair. Cabe perched on the arm beside her.

"Cabe."

"They let me go. Thanks to you. They had to. That other guy"—Cabe paused, before he said the rest—"my half-brother, confessed to everything."

"I've told Cabe everything, too," Richelle said.

"We've been talking nonstop since she picked me up at the jail."

Richelle rested her hand on his forearm. He sat back, relaxed. I had never seen either of them looking so unburdened.

Cabe was a good kid. I had said it, Chris had said it, Sonny had insisted on it over and over. He was a good kid despite all that had happened to him. Lilia and Dave Stone had given that boy enough love in his first twelve years to carry him through.

Richelle had done the right thing by giving him up. And she'd done the right thing by finding him again.

When Richelle and Cabe left, I waited, but Chris never came. After my mother's talk about love and trust, about acceptance and support, I spent a lot of time thinking about Chris and me. He had told me he loved me. He'd put his beating heart in my hands. He wanted to know, simply, declaratively, and in the moment, if I loved him, too.

I owed him an answer.

What held me back? Was it my innate snobbishness as Livvie had charged? Did I think I was "too good" for Chris? I couldn't imagine that was true.

Was it my inability to grab hold of my own life, as Vee Snuggs had said? Was I unable to tell Chris I loved him because that caused me to think about the future and where we would live and what I would do? Chris wasn't asking me for a commitment about the future. He was asking me how I felt right now. I understood that.

No, it was the trust part that my mother had talked about. Could I trust Chris?

Where did he go when he disappeared and what was he doing? I didn't think he was off with another woman. Despite his history, I was absolutely secure in his love and—I was surprised to find this as I examined it—his fidelity.

Richelle had fallen in love with a criminal and look what it had done to her life. But she'd known who he was and fallen anyway. Despite my little transgressions of the last few days, I was the straight-and-narrowest person I knew. I had to ask myself, could Chris be doing something terribly wrong? And could I still love him if he was?

Just asking myself the question made me laugh. How absurd I was being! Chris was the most decent person I knew. He, and I was sure of this down to the core of my being, would never, ever do anything that would deliberately harm another human being. And he would never compromise himself, or me. What in the world was I so worried about?

He'd asked me to trust him and I found, when I

poked into the very corners of my soul, that I did. I could always trust Chris to be Chris.

My mother picked me up at the hospital. The attendant wheeled me to the curb, which was ridiculous. I was banged up and sore, but otherwise fine.

When I got home, I unfolded myself from the car and pulled my crutches from the backseat. "I'm going for a walk."

"Dear, do you really think—?"

"You heard the nurse. 'Discharged with no restrictions.'"

My mother sighed. She could see there was no point in arguing. I started down the driveway, using the crutches the way I'd practiced. By the time I reached the street I was exhausted. Vee Snuggs stood on her porch. I imagined her silently cheering me on.

I followed the sidewalk over the hill until it ran out in the back harbor. I hobbled past the shipyard, past Gus's to the marina, rehearsing in my head what I planned to say. "Yes, Chris, I love you. I'm sorry I hurt you by not being able to say it until now. I was worried about too many irrelevant things. I let them get in the way of my feelings."

I climbed onto the dock and walked toward the *Dark Lady's* slip. Painful as it was to move, I sped up. I had to talk to Chris. Now.

The *Dark Lady's* slip was empty.

I collapsed onto a bench, unable to walk another step. "I love you," I said to the square of empty sea. "Come back to me."

Recipes

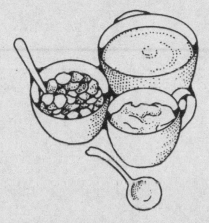

Jacqueline's Lobster Deviled Eggs

Julia's mother Jacqueline is a terrible cook, and like a lot of bad cooks, she's mastered one specialty, which she relies on whenever she's asked to bring something to a party. In her case, it's these scrumptious lobster deviled eggs. (The secret's in the horseradish and smoked paprika.)

8 eggs
3 Tablespoons mayonnaise
1 Tablespoon prepared horseradish, drained
1 teaspoon cider vinegar
1 teaspoon Dijon mustard
8 ounces cooked lobster meat, chopped.
smoked paprika
snipped chives

Place eggs in saucepan covered with water. Bring to boil and remove from heat. Rest in water for 10 minutes. Rinse with cold water. Add ice and allow them to cool. Peel eggs and slice in half lengthwise. Scoop yolks into bowl. Add mayonnaise, horseradish, vinegar, and mustard and mash together. Gently fold in lobster meat. Spoon back into the egg white halves. Garnish with paprika and chives. Chill before serving. Serves 4-6.

Note: These are also excellent without the lobster meat.

Livvie's Lobster Salad

Livvie's the real cook in the Snowden family, and as you might guess, her lobster salad is a specialty. Too bad Julia doesn't accompany her family to the picnic and concert in Waterfront Park, because this salad is terrific. The flavor is tremendous and the scallions and celery add a great crunch.

1 pound lobster meat
juice from ½ lemon
2 stalks celery, diced
2-3 scallions, white parts only, thinly sliced
2-3 Tablespoons mayonnaise
salt and pepper to taste

Chop lobster meat into bite-sized pieces and put in bowl. Toss with lemon juice. Add celery, scallions, and just enough mayonnaise to bind together. Taste, and add seasonings. Serve on plate or in buttered, toasted, top-sliced hot dog rolls.

Livvie's Potato Salad

Livvie made this potato salad for the Snowden family picnic before the fireworks at Waterfront Park. In reality, the recipe comes from one of the author's most precious possessions, a handwritten book of recipes from her grandmother. The vinegar and sugar provide its distinct sweet and sour taste.

4 large potatoes cooked, skins on
2 Tablespoons apple cider vinegar
1 large onion, grated
mayonnaise
sugar
salt
pepper

Boil potatoes until they are easily pierced with a fork. Peel and cut into rounds. Add onion. Stir in mayonnaise (enough to coat). Add vinegar. Add sugar, salt, and pepper to taste. Better if made a day ahead.

Vee's Blueberry Pancakes

At the Rotary breakfasts, Viola Snuggs cooks up blueberry pancakes for a crowd. This delicious recipe has been adapted for home use.

> 2 cups cake flour
> ¼ cup sugar
> 4 teaspoons baking powder
> 2 cups milk
> 1 egg, lightly beaten
> 4 Tablespoons melted butter
> 2 cups Maine wild blueberries, fresh or frozen.
>   If frozen, thaw thoroughly.

Heat oven to 200 degrees.

Stir dry ingredients together. Add wet ingredients and stir. Fold in blueberries.

Melt butter on medium high heat in pan or on griddle. Spoon out pancake mix in ¼ cupfuls.

Flip pancakes when lightly browned on bottom. (Adjust heat, if necessary, to keep from burning.)

Put finished pancakes on ovenproof platter. Top with butter and keep in warm oven.

Serve with real maple syrup, or other syrup of your choice.

Mrs. Gus's Blueberry Pie

Mrs. Gus is renowned for her pies, and rightly so. This is the blueberry.

Pie Crust

3½ cups flour
2 teaspoons kosher salt
1½ cups shortening, lard, or unsalted butter
1 egg, beaten lightly with a fork
1 Tablespoon apple cider vinegar
¼-½ cups ice water, as needed

1 Tablespoon milk (to brush over finished pie
    before baking)

In food processor, using the metal blade, pulse flour and salt to combine. Add shortening and pulse until reaching the consistency of corn meal. Add egg, vinegar, and ¼ cup ice water. Pulse, adding additional ice water, if necessary, until ingredients barely come together in a dough ball. Turn out onto cutting board and pat together evenly into a large oblong. Divide into four pieces. You will need two for the pie. (You can freeze the other two for a later pie.) Refrigerate. Remove from fridge ten minutes before using.

Filling

5 cups Maine wild blueberries, fresh or frozen.
    (If frozen, thaw thoroughly.)

¾ cup sugar
juice of ½ lemon
cinnamon
1 Tablespoon butter

Roll out bottom crust of pie and put in pie plate. Add blueberries. Over the top put sugar, lemon juice, a dash of cinnamon, and add the butter in pats.

Roll out top crust and cover. Slit top. Brush with milk.

Bake at 425 degrees for ten minutes. Then lower oven temperature to 350 and bake 25 to 35 minutes more, until top is brown and fruit is bubbling.

> *Q: I notice there's no tapioca, cornstarch, or other binding agent mentioned. Isn't the pie all runny?*
> *A: Yes, and it is delicious. Even better with ice cream.*

Baked Camp Beans

These beans, made by Phil Johnson's mother, are filling and hearty—perfect after a long day of physical work or play. Common to all the Wabanaki Confederacy tribes of Maine, New Brunswick, and Nova Scotia, soldier beans were originally mixed with bear fat and maple syrup and cooked in clay pots buried with hot coals. They are the progenitors of New England's famous baked beans. This recipe is adapted to make at home (as opposed to at camp).

1 pound soldier beans
1 Tablespoon vegetable oil
3 thick slices slab bacon, chopped
3 thick slices salt pork, chopped
1 onion, chopped
1 large celery stalk, diced, leaves chopped
1 carrot, diced
2 Tablespoons apple cider vinegar
½ teaspoon dried oregano
½ teaspoon dried basil
½ cup tomato sauce
½ cup molasses
1 Tablespoon Dijon mustard
2 quarts water
salt and pepper to taste

Soak beans for one hour. Heat oil in large saucepan. Render bacon and salt pork in oil for about three minutes. Add onion, celery, and carrot and sauté for another three-four minutes. Add remaining ingredients and bring to a boil. Turn down heat and simmer for one hour. Preheat oven to 300 degrees. Put beans in a bean pot or covered casserole and cook in oven for four hours. (Alternative, after simmering, place in a slow cooker on high for four hours.) Check occasionally. Adjust seasonings. If you think it's necessary, remove cover for last hour of cooking to thicken.

Camp-style Ground Beef

This hearty camp meal has the distinctive tarragon and cinnamon flavor common to French-Canadian cooking. Julia is knocked over by how good it tastes. It can be made with either ground beef or ground moose meat.

4 slices slab bacon
2 pounds ground beef
3 onions, chopped
4 large stalks celery including leaves, chopped
8 ounces mushrooms, sliced
3 cloves garlic, chopped
1 teaspoon dried tarragon
½ teaspoon ground cinnamon
1 cup tomato sauce
2 teaspoons apple cider vinegar

Cook bacon until crisp and drain on paper towels. Using 1 Tablespoon bacon drippings, brown beef. Set aside in a bowl. Using another 1 Tablespoon bacon drippings, sauté onions, celery, and mushrooms together for six minutes. Add garlic and cook another minute or two. Add spices, tomato sauce, vinegar, reserved beef, and accumulated juices. Cook together for eight to ten minutes to allow flavors to meld. Either serve alongside baked beans or mix together with beans.

Lu'sknikn

Lu'sknikn is traditional Mi'kmaq bread. It is considered a bannock, *which is a Scottish word that describes a round, flat, quick bread. You can think of it as being in the family of Irish soda bread.*

 4 cups flour
 1 teaspoon kosher salt
 2 Tablespoons baking powder
 ½ cup lard or shortening + additional for pan
 ¾ cup raisins or other dried fruit (optional)
 2½ cups water

Stir together flour, salt, and baking powder in a bowl. Using your hands or a pastry cutter, cut lard into the flour mix. Add dried fruit and stir to coat. Make a hole in center of the flour, add water, and stir. Heat a 10-inch cast iron skillet over medium heat and melt about a tablespoon of lard. Add half the dough to the pan and press out close to the sides of the pan. Using a knife, make a hole in the center to allow steam to escape. Cook for ten minutes, then turn using two spatulas if necessary. Cook for an additional ten minutes being careful not to burn. Check for doneness with a toothpick or a cake tester. Repeat with second half of dough.

Richelle's Tomato Salad

Richelle Rose lives on the road giving tours throughout Maine. When she's home, she craves simple, local food, and in the summer, that means tomato salad. The basic recipe is wonderful. Add in one or more of the options only if you happened to have the ingredient at hand or desire the taste. Because the flavor of this recipe depends so much on the taste and texture of the tomatoes, it should be made only when you have access to really good ones.

4 large tomatoes
1-2 cloves garlic
kosher salt
½ teaspoon dried oregano

Options

red onion, chopped or sliced
cucumber, seeded and diced
oregano, fresh
basil, fresh
8-12 ounces bocconcini (mozzarella bites) or
   other fresh mozzarella

Core tomatoes and slice into bite-sized chunks. Layer tomatoes in serving bowl, salting each layer with kosher salt. Mince garlic and toss with tomatoes. Add any other optional ingredients. Cover bowl and marinate at room temperature for 1-2 hours, stirring occasionally. May be served chilled or at room temperature. Also makes a wonderful fresh sauce for pasta. Serves 4.

Richelle's Tuna and White Bean Salad

This is a light, fresh-tasting salad. When Richelle comes off a long road trip, she can put this dish together from items readily available in her pantry.

2 6-ounce cans light tuna packed in olive oil
½ medium onion, diced
1 clove garlic, minced
1 15-ounce can cannellini beans, drained and
    rinsed
1 tablespoon olive oil
1-2 teaspoons red wine vinegar
salt and pepper to taste

Drain oil from tuna and put in bowl. Flake tuna with a fork. Add onion and garlic and stir with fork. Add beans and gently fold together. Dress with oil, vinegar, salt, and pepper. Allow flavors to marinate at room temperature for thirty minutes to an hour. If refrigerated, best to allow to come to room temperature before serving.

ACKNOWLEDGMENTS

Those who know Maine history will recognize how much Gus's rather eccentric and truncated version owes to *The Lobster Coast: Rebels, Rusticators and the Struggle for a Forgotten Frontier,* by Colin Woodard (Penguin, 2004). If this novel has piqued your interest in Maine or history, or if you just enjoy beautifully written nonfiction, I cannot recommend this book enough.

The story of the Busman was inspired by the life of Reuben Ruby as told in *The Hidden History of Maine,* by Harry Gratwick (The History Press, 2010), the story of Jim Foley as told in *The Lobster Coast* (see above), and a photo of early bus service in Ocean Point found in *The Boothbay Harbor Region, 1906-1960,* by Harold B. Clifford (Wheelwright, 1961).

The line, "As far as he was concerned, terrorists and tourists were in the same boat, and hopefully it was sinking," comes from the self-authored obituary of David McKown, which appeared in the *Boothbay Register* on October 25, 2012. For full-on Maine eccentricity, nothing beats reading the complete article. http://www.boothbayregister.com/article/david-mckown-dies-age-68/4895.

There really is a Wild Blueberry Land in Columbia Falls, Maine and you should go there.

Thanks to Lisa and Chandra Hanscom of Welch Farms in Roque Bluffs, Maine who gave a wonderful tour of their blueberry farm and small processing operation, and who answered my many questions about the blueberry harvest. That's another place you should visit the next time you travel Down East. http://uniquemainefarms.com/uniquemaine-farms.com/Welch_Blueberry_Farm.html.

David Brooks Stess has photographed the blueberry rakers in Maine for over twenty years. His 2013 exhibit at the Portland Museum of Art was the culmination of this work. The photos are hauntingly beautiful. http://blog.voxphotographs.com/2013/04/13/david-brooks-stess-what-23-years-looks-like.

And, as always, if this novel has left you with a craving for a real clambake on a private island in Maine, you should go to the Cabbage Island Clambakes. http://www.cabbageislandclambakes.com.

Thanks to Marilyn Mick and Carolyn Vandam, who explained the tour guide industry to me and made Richelle Rose come alive.

As always thanks to my wonderful agent, John Talbot, and to my editor, John Scognamiglio and the tremendous team at Kensington—so professional and a joy to work with.

My husband, Bill Carito, is the real cook in our family. He developed and tested all the recipes in the book (except the blueberry pie, which is one of my specialties and the potato salad which is a treasured family recipe). I only had to sit at the table with a fork in one hand and a pen in the other, writing down words like, *tangy*!

The Maine Crime Writers accepted me, even though I had only one mystery novel published and was new to Maine. They gave me the courage to write a mystery series set in Maine and I'm so glad they did. Thanks especially to Kate Flora, Lea Wait, Kaitlyn Dunnett and all the crew.

I don't know where I'd be without my first readers, my writers group, Mark Ammons, Katherine Fast, Cheryl Marceau, and Leslie Wheeler. Also, in their guise as the editors at Level Best Books, Kathy, Mark, and Leslie let me out of a whole summer of editing and proofreading. Thank you, thank you. I could never have completed this novel without you.

I can't imagine going on this journey alone, and I've been so lucky to have the support of the Wicked Cozy Authors, Jessie Crockett, Sherry Harris, Julie Hennrikus, Edith Maxwell, and Liz Mugavero. Sherry Harris has done triple duty as valued friend, cheerleader, and editor.

While I was writing *Boiled Over*, my mother faced her final illness and death. This book absolutely could not have been written without the support of my family—Bill Carito, Kate Carito, Rob and Sunny Carito, the fabulous Viola, who kept our spirits up, and most of all, my amazing brother, Rip Ross and his wife, Ann. Steady as a rock.